HOMEC

At the end of the row of fishermen's cottages by the harbour's edge stands an old granite house. First it belonged to Ned's parents; then Ned dropped anchor here after a life at sea and called it home. His nephew Hugo moved in too, swapping London for the small Cornish fishing village where he'd spent so many happy holidays — and now other friends and relations are being drawn to the house. Among them is Dossie, lonely after her parents died and her son remarried. And cousin Jamie, coming home after more than a year, since his career as an RAF pilot was abruptly cut short. Both have to adjust to a new way of life. As newcomers arrive and old friends reunite, secrets are uncovered, relationships are forged and tested, and romance is kindled . . .

SPECIAL MESSAGE TO READERS

HOMECOMINGS

MARCIA WILLETT

ISIS
LARGE
PRINT

First published in Great Britain 2018
by
Bantam Press
an imprint of Transworld Publishers

First Isis Edition
published 2019
by arrangement with
Transworld Publishers

A catalogue record for this book is available
from the British Library.

ISBN 978–1–78541–716–0 (hb)
ISBN 978–1–78541–722–1 (pb)

Published by
F. A. Thorpe (Publishing)
Anstey, Leicestershire

Set by Words & Graphics Ltd.
Anstey, Leicestershire
Printed and bound in Great Britain by
T. J. International Ltd., Padstow, Cornwall

This book is printed on acid-free paper

To Rick

PART ONE

CHAPTER
ONE

Hugo Houghton comes hurrying along the precipitous cobbled street that hurtles down to the harbour; his tweed coat flaps around his long legs and he clutches a bag of shopping in his arms as carefully and firmly as if it were a baby. He pauses to look at the few boats that remain of a once prosperous fishing fleet, which now provide day trips out to sea for the tourists, and then turns along beside the harbour wall towards the tall, old slate and granite house at the end of a row of fishermen's cottages.

Gathering his shopping into one arm, he lets himself in through the massive oak door to a long flagged passage with its series of doorways on either side, which leads through the ground floor into the kitchen at the back of the house. He plunges into the warmth and peace of the big room, dumps his bag on the central table and smiles at the old man — angular, wide shouldered, white haired — who is sitting in a wooden rocking chair by the Aga.

"All well, Uncle Ned?" he asks.

Two dogs scramble up from their shared basket, hurrying to meet Hugo, wagging their tails in that welcoming yet hesitant way that the retriever has,

3

longing to show love but anxious lest it should be rejected. Hugo bends to caress them, sympathizing with how they feel: this has been a problem for him for most of his adult life.

"Good boys," he tells them. "Good fellows."

Hugo begins to unpack his shopping, shrugging off his coat, passing Ned the newspaper, telling him about the friends he has seen in the village shop. He pauses to look out into the small paved area where the early May sunshine is slanting in, lighting slate walls, sliding over wooden tubs of tulips and bluebells. This sunny space is sheltered from the north-westerly wind, and today he might be able to persuade Ned outside for his morning coffee. It's not that his uncle is difficult, rather that he likes to make his presence felt; to show that, despite his vulnerability and physical weaknesses, he is still a force to be reckoned with. After a long and very successful career in the navy — and though he has been retired now for more than twenty years — Ned can still be formidable when he chooses.

To signal his intentions, Hugo opens the door into the little court. At once the dogs make a bid for freedom, jostling to be the first out, and then dashing up the steep flight of stone steps, which leads to the small garden layered into the cliff behind the house. Hugo stands outside for a moment, lifting his face to the warm sunshine, and then goes back inside to find a cloth to wipe the dampness of last night's rain from the wrought-iron table and chairs.

Ned shakes his newspaper as if it is a call to battle as Hugo comes back inside, pushes the kettle on to the hotplate and smiles at the older man.

"Coffee outside?" he suggests tentatively. "It's warm out there."

Ned frowns, considering, then unexpectedly folds *The Times* and stands up. Tall and lean, he picks up his stick and makes his way carefully — and very slightly unsteadily — across the flagged floor towards the doorway. Hugo watches, ready to step forward but pretending that he is unconcerned. Ned hates to be fussed over but since his recent hip replacement operation he has been a little less confident and Hugo has a horror that his uncle might fall.

Ned lowers himself on to one of the chairs and Hugo takes a breath of relief and begins to brew the coffee. He's so happy here, looking after Ned and the various people who come to stay: friends or relations needing a little bit of love and care, of rest and renewal, before returning to the cold world outside these sheltering granite walls. In his mid-fifties, he doesn't regret taking the early retirement package from his job as a producer at the BBC, or leaving London: the BBC was getting busier, open plan, desks with no names. It was good to retreat from schedules and routines and to come here to the place where he's spent so many happy holidays. It's as if he is able to repay some of the kindness his aunt Margaret showed him through his childhood and difficult teenage years. After she died, nearly two years ago, it was clear that Ned wasn't going to be able to manage alone and Hugo knew how much it would break the old fellow's heart to leave the home that had been in the Tremayne family for several generations. There was Rose, of course. Rose Pengelly has been their cleaner since she was a girl, and Hugo has a very special place in his heart for her, but it was too much to ask Rose to take on the extra responsibility. And, anyway, how good it is to be needed: to be able to fulfil the nurturing side of his character.

Hugo piles the coffee things on to a tray and carries it out to the court. The dogs have returned from their foraging and sit either side of Ned, their muzzles pressed against his knees, as if they understand that their presence brings him comfort. Gently he caresses their smooth heads and Hugo sees that he has closed his eyes against the sunshine and is smiling a little in its warmth. He sets the tray down gently on the table and takes up the coffeepot.

Despite his closed eyelids, Ned perceives Hugo clearly. He pictures the strong, broad-shouldered figure, the untidy mass of dark curly hair, liberally streaked with grey, and Hugo's violet-blue eyes. He is very like his aunt Margaret. When her younger sister, Hugo's mother, died of cancer whilst Hugo was still a small child, Margaret took him into her love and care as far as she was able, given that she was a naval wife with a small boy of her own, and Hugo's father was a barrister living in London.

This house, belonging to Ned's parents, was a refuge: a place to which they all travelled to spend leaves, school holidays, to lodge between married quarters. It was home. It was here that he and Margaret had come for extended leave after their son was killed in the Falklands War. Jack was twenty-three.

How odd, thinks Ned, his eyes still closed against the sunshine, that the pain should still be so keen after nearly thirty-five years of loss. So must an amputee continue to feel the ache for a lost limb.

Ned opens his eyes and smiles at Hugo, who is hovering near him. Ned knows why Hugo's relation-ships with women never survive: he is too kind, too generous, too considerate.

Ned counts himself lucky: his marriage was a good one, he has been loved by several women, his son adored him. And now he has Hugo to support him just when he is beginning to feel vulnerable and lonely. He likes Hugo's London friends — members of his camera crew, assistant producers, ex-girlfriends — who come to stay for weekends, between jobs or lovers or marriages, and he likes the occasional lodgers who stay whilst they look for long-term accommodation. Everyone gravitates towards Hugo, as towards warmth and succour, and he helps and heals them where he can. It is good to be a part of that and Ned knows how lucky he is. He drinks his hot, strong coffee, unadulterated by sugar or milk.

"I was thinking that we'd go for a drive," Hugo is saying, "through the woods and up on to the moor. The wild cherry trees are looking wonderful and the bluebells are beginning to flower."

"'And since to look at things in bloom,'" quotes Ned,

Fifty springs are little room,
About the woodlands I will go
To see the cherry hung with snow.

Hugo grins at him. "Strong," he says. "Very strong. We'll have lunch at The Chough and the dogs can have a run on the moor."

Ned grins back at him — Hugo doesn't appreciate poetry but is tolerant of Ned's sudden declamations — dismisses Housman from his mind, and thinks with pleasure of the day ahead. These spring days are a delight to him, filled with promise of the joys to come: of seeing buds opening into a pale tatter of petals; a blackbird sitting on her frail eggs: of the relief to hear the evocative call of the cuckoo and to see the swoop of the first swallow, proving that the Creation is still working.

A bar of music interrupts his reverie and he watches Hugo drag his iPhone from his pocket to read the incoming message.

"It's Prune," he says. "She's been invited out to supper so she says not to wait for her."

"Does she say with whom?" asks Ned.

He feels *in loco parentis* where young Prune is concerned, though at twenty-one she is quite old enough to look after herself. Nevertheless, as their lodger she deserves their protection and he'd promised as much to her parents when they came down from Suffolk to see where their daughter was to be living whilst she works as an assistant gardener at the National Trust property on the edge of the village. The

8

Trust has recently opened a small café and Prune has been taken on to train with the team that has the special responsibility of supplying the vegetables to feed visitors. It was the Trust who recommended the house on the quay as a lodging place for Prune.

"She and the rest of the team are going out with the couple who have been advising on setting up the café," Hugo answers. "It's their last evening so they've invited them all to a fish-and-chip supper at Padstow."

"That sounds like fun," observes Ned. "In which case we'll have a good lunch at the pub and then we won't have to worry too much this evening."

"My name's Prunella," she told them when she came to meet them, sitting at the kitchen table, a dog on each side of her. "But I've always loved gardening since I was small so the nickname was inevitable really."

She was a slender girl, not very tall, with long, fine, fair hair drawn back from a small, pretty, square face, and Hugo smiled at her.

"I hope you won't be daunted by the overwhelming male presence here," he said.

She laughed, patting the dogs. "I've got three older brothers," she answered. "Been there, done that, got the T-shirt. So have I passed?"

Hugo looked at Ned, his eyebrows raised.

"With flying colours," Ned answered.

And now she has become part of the family and none of them has regretted it. As Hugo and Ned sit at ease together, drinking coffee, discussing plans for the garden, enjoying the sunshine, the dogs lie, noses on paws but eyes and ears alert to any suggestion of a walk. So that when Hugo pushes back his chair, stands up and begins to collect the coffee mugs, they are on their feet at once, hurrying ahead of him into the kitchen, ready for action.

They drive up out of the village, skirting high granite walls, and into the woodland at the moor's edge. Ash, hawthorn, alder are beginning to leaf and, beneath their tender buds, the bluebells' haze reflects the cloudless sky.

Ned lowers his window and Hugo slows the car so that they are able to breathe in the fragrance. Amongst mossy boulders, tightly curled fists of bracken push through to stand like question marks above the rocks. Hugo can hear the cuckoo's two notes — C and A flat — and he smiles at Ned in a shared delight.

They pass small fields, hedged about with yellow-flowering gorse, where cows take their ease in companionable groups; tails twitching, chewing things over. The car bumps across the cattle grid and then they are up on the open moor and the dogs begin to jostle and barge each other with excitement. He pulls on to the dry, close-cropped grass, gets out and opens the tailgate so that the dogs are able to leap down and go dashing away, scattering a group of skewbald ponies. The wind is cold. He leans in to reach for his coat, knowing that Ned will stay where he is in the warm shelter of the car, shrugs himself into his windproof jacket and hurries away after the dogs.

Ned watches them go: Brioc ahead as usual, Mortimer following more slowly, showing his age. How many times he and Margaret walked the dogs here; how much she loved this part of the moor: that gleam of a white church tower set all about with rhododendrons down in the valley and, seawards, a rim of gold at the edge of the world. Instinctively Ned folds his arms across himself as if he is holding himself in — or pretending that he is hugging Margaret, being hugged in return. He isn't sure which it is but after a moment he sighs at his foolishness and settles himself more comfortably to wait for Hugo's return.

The small bar of The Chough is busy but the table in the corner by the inglenook fireplace is empty, and the landlord, knowing the treachery of these early May days, has kept the log fire burning. Behind the bar, Ben, a tall, good-looking boy barely out of his teens, sways quietly to the background music: Gregory Porter singing "Hey Laura". His lips soundlessly frame the words and his eyes are full of dreams. A flurry of newcomers jolt him out of his reverie and, as he hurries to serve them, Ned watches him sympathetically, trying to remember what it was like to be that age: untried, hopeful. Not for Ben, yet, the more and more frequent reminders of the past; the mental thumbing of anecdotes as if they are a greasy old pack of cards.

"Which is worse?" Hugo once asked him. "Sins of omission or commission?"

"Omission," Ned answered at once, instinctively. Hugo frowned, thinking about it. "I suppose you're right," he said at last, "but there are an awful lot of things I regret doing. Rushing in where angels fear to tread. Making a fool of myself."

"If those are the worst sins you've committed, be grateful," Ned answered, thinking guiltily of one of his own particular sins of commission with a rather beautiful woman during a short posting to Norfolk, Virginia, when he was helping to run a NATO exercise from the COMSUBLANT bunker.

He glances around the bar. A man has just come in and is being welcomed by another who is standing ordering a drink. They hug each other. Ned is slowly getting used to the sight of men hugging. Everyone hugs these days: rugby players, tennis players, TV presenters. His glance slides past them and he glimpses a young woman at the furthest table, which is littered with coffee cups and plastic mugs. Ned feels a tiny jolt of recognition though he cannot place her. She is talking eagerly to her two companions, also young women, whilst several small children beside them are busy with colouring books. He frowns, trying to place the vivacious face but the memory eludes him.

Hugo is back, carrying two pints of ale, and the two men at the bar are now blocking Ned's view otherwise he might ask Hugo if he recognizes her. Meanwhile, Ben is here with the menus and he is drawing their attention to the specials board.

"Though I expect," he says, smiling at Ned, "that you'll be having your usual?"

Ned smiles back at him, touched by the fact that Ben remembers. How poignant is the genuine kindness of the young as opposed to their thoughtless pity, which is

12

one of the trials of old age. He agrees that he will have the seafood platter, simply because it pleases Ben, who beams at him and then looks at Hugo, who is studying the menu. He orders venison sausages and sits down beside Ned.

"I've been meaning to text Dossie," he says. "We're running low on emergency supplies."

Ned takes a pull at his pint. He approves of Dossie Pardoe, a woman much the same age as Hugo, widowed young, who runs a small business called Fill the Freezer from her home in St Endellion. She supplies home-cooked food to holiday cottages all over the peninsula, as well as catering for dinner parties, children's parties and small special events. They are both very fond of Dossie and are helping her to cope with the recent deaths of her parents. Her widowed son, Clem, has just married again, which is another adjustment, though Ned knows that Dossie is delighted for her son and her grandson, Jakey.

"She's really missing Clem and young Jakey much more than she lets on," Hugo is saying. "I know that she adores Tilly, but it can't be easy to step back after ten years of being there for them and suddenly be a mother-in-law again. They were all such a close unit."

"Invite her to supper this evening," Ned suggests impulsively. He sympathizes with Dossie as she navigates her way through this tough patch and he admires her courage and gallantry. "Then we can talk about topping up supplies."

Hugo raises his eyebrows. "I thought the reason we were having lunch here is because we weren't going to bother about supper?"

"Oh, just do it," says the older man impatiently. "Send her a text."

Hugo shrugs cheerfully, pulls out his phone and Ned sits back in his chair. The group of mothers and children is leaving. They mill about, parents calling instructions, and one small boy shoulders forward ahead of the rest, impatient to be outside. Ned looks at the small determined face, the black hair and dark brown eyes, and is once again pierced by the feeling of recognition. He looks again for the woman he noticed earlier, who is hurrying to catch up with the little boy, calling after him to wait for her.

Ned leans forward to draw Hugo's attention to her but before he can speak the whole party has swept out of The Chough and he's too late.

14

CHAPTER
TWO

Dossie closes the door behind her and stands listening to the sound of silence. No Pa shouting from his den to ask how the day went; no Mo in the kitchen pushing the kettle on to the Aga ready for a welcoming cup of tea or coffee; no Wolfie skittering out into the hall barking a welcome; no Jonno struggling up from his basket, tail wagging. This coming in to the overwhelming sense of absence is the hardest thing: nobody now with whom to share her day, her small successes or frustrations. After Pa's death from his second stroke, and then during the last year of Mo's illness, the bed-and-breakfast business that they'd continued to run so gallantly gradually diminished and, though Dossie's own business continues to flourish, there is a pointlessness to life with which she must wrestle on a daily basis.

It was to Mo and Pa that Dossie returned when her husband, Mike, was killed in a motor-racing accident, leaving her with their small son, Clem. They had looked after him whilst she organized lunches, dinners, cooked special-occasion feasts in other people's kitchens and finally managed to get her business up and running. Mo and Pa had contacts and friends right across the peninsula who were very ready to help the young widowed daughter of their two old friends. And in return, years later, she was able to help them to keep their rather eccentric bed-and-breakfast business running as they grew older and less able. She misses those visitors who, over the years, became friends, bringing their dogs and occasionally, as the years passed, grandchildren. And, on top of all this, Dossie misses the familiar daily contact with Clem and her grandson, Jakey.

She crosses the hall, goes into the kitchen, instinctively glancing away from the dogs' empty baskets. It was almost as if a malign history were repeating itself when Clem's young wife died having their baby. When Jakey was four, Clem decided to return to Cornwall from London and, once again, the family rallied round to support them whilst Clem pursued his vocation, his theological training, and was ordained. Now, six years on, he is chaplain to the Anglican community in the beautiful old retreat house of Chi-Meur, twenty miles away on the coast.

During that time Dossie had grown used to being on call to babysit, to provide food in an emergency, and simply to spend precious time with her son and grandson. She was so happy when Tilly came into their lives: pretty, funny, clever Tilly, who looks after all the IT at Chi-Meur and who has brought a whole new dimension to Clem's life; and to Jakey's, too. They live in the cottage at the end of Chi-Meur's drive and the three of them, plus a retriever called Bells, are a happy little unit. Though they stay closely in touch with her,

Dossie knows she must now step back. She must be tactful and give them space.

It's odd, this sense of desolation each time she returns home. The huge effort required to prepare some food and sit eating it solemnly, all alone. Food is the source of life; it should be shared, be a celebration. Mo and Pa had been the most splendid of hosts, giving to their guests not only good food but an atmosphere of warmth and fun in which to enjoy it whilst making them feel special. After years of travelling the world with Pa's job at Rio Tinto Zinc as a mining engineer, they found it impossible simply to retire to a quiet life and their B and B-ers gave them a purpose. This pretty, gracious Georgian house, with its elegant sash windows and perfect proportions, was an ideal setting for the venture and Dossie can't imagine living anywhere else.

As she opens the fridge and stares disconsolately at its contents, a text message pings in and she shuts the door and takes her phone from her bag. She sees that the text is from Hugo and immediately she is washed through with a sense of warmth, of relief, and even gratitude. She has grown so fond of Hugo and Ned in their big old house down at the harbour's edge in the small fishing village near Polzeath. They have welcomed her into their world, which is almost as eccentric as the world she shared with Mo and Pa. She reads the text and foolishly wants to weep.

Come to supper. We both need you. xx

But she doesn't weep. Instead she laughs and taps out a reply.

You mean that your freezer is empty. I can take a hint. xx

She agrees a time with Hugo and goes back to the fridge. Oddly, this small connection has lifted her spirits and given her the courage to go on again.

"You need another dog," Hugo told her, after Wolfie died. "I know it was difficult when Mo was ill and you were trying to do everything, but it's different now."

She imagined that he was on the edge of saying, "You don't even have to worry about Clem and Jakey now, either," but restrained himself. Or maybe she was just feeling oversensitive. It is hard no longer to be the one Jakey and Clem turn to if there is a problem or something to celebrate.

"Get over it," she mutters, taking the makings of a sandwich from the fridge. "Get a life. Get a dog."

Meanwhile she'll think of some special pudding that she can take to contribute to the supper: she has something to look forward to and the bad moment is past.

Later, as she drives between St Endellion and Polzeath, Dossie thinks about having another dog; of trying to manage a puppy or whether it should be a rescue dog. Either would almost certainly bring problems, yet it would be so good to have a companion again. As she turns westward towards Polzeath, however, a different problem presses in: whether or not she should sell the house. It's not easy when Adam telephones and asks if she's considering putting The Court on the market yet. Her brother, Adam, works for a big London estate agency that specializes in selling country properties.

"Now is the perfect time of year to sell," he said during the last conversation. "It's too big for you on your own, Doss. It'll cost a bomb to keep it up and running."

Since Mo died, Dossie has worked hard to rebuild her relationship with her brother.

"So you scooped the pool, Doss," he said to her bleakly after their father's funeral. "Pa warned me just before he died that he was leaving The Court to you because of all that you'd done for them, but I didn't quite believe he would actually do it. Not that you don't deserve it."

She didn't tell Adam that she'd pleaded with Pa to change his will but their father remained adamant.

"We've helped Adam from time to time," Pa said. "It's not our fault his marriage fell apart and he lost half of everything. You made it possible for Mo and me to stay in our home, Dossie, when we were old, to run our business and to surround ourselves with our friends. We couldn't have done it without you and we had so much fun. This has been your home for most of your life apart from when you were with Mike. Don't forget that."

Once Pa died, Adam changed. Slowly he grew less defensive, easier to be with, as if some challenge, some expectation, had been removed; as if he no longer had anything to prove. Later again, during his visits while Mo was ill, there was a kind of reconciliation, an acceptance at last on each side. Dossie can imagine how hard a blow it was to Adam to be disinherited but she is beginning to hope that she might be able to heal that resentment. She knows, though, that he's right about selling The Court. But how could she bear it and where would she go?

As she drives, surrounded by the cool, blue, infinite sky-spaces that indicate proximity to the sea, she is prey to a sense of panic. She is reminded of the loneliness of those years after Mike was killed. How he'd loved speed! Motorbikes, Formula One, speedboats. He took so many risks that it was hardly surprising that his life ended so tragically. But even back then, desolate though she was, she had small Clem. He was her reason to carry on, to survive, to continue to create a home and a life — and this became a pattern. Until now.

She drives down into the village, past the harbour, and parks her little Golf on the hard area beside Ned's Volvo. As she climbs out her spirits are beginning to rise. Quite apart from the fact that Hugo and Ned have become such good chums, her own sense of pride won't allow her to whinge and whine and pull sad faces in front of them. She opens the hatchback, reaches in for the basket containing the pudding, and takes a deep breath. The massive front door is unlocked as usual and she shouts as she comes into the long hallway. There is a responding shout and the sound of barking, and she smiles with amusement, happiness, and a tinge of sadness at the old familiar response to a homecoming.

20

CHAPTER
THREE

"Bread-and-butter pudding," says Hugo appreciatively. "You know all our weaknesses, Dossie."

Dossie raises her eyebrows. "I seriously doubt that." She rolls her eyes and winks at Hugo. "I bet Ned has all sorts of secrets he's not letting on about."

Ned can't help but smile. He loves the way that Dossie slightly flirts with him and teases him. It makes him feel young again, viable, alive. And he does indeed have secrets that he has no intention of revealing — and the guilt that goes with them.

"And what about me?" demands Hugo, spooning the pudding on to plates. "What about my secrets?"

"I think," says Dossie, finding forks and spoons and then sitting down again at the table, "that your secret is that you're a frustrated concert pianist."

Ned watches Hugo's face with interest as a variety of expressions flit across it: surprise, a little frown, a downward turn of the lips in a tiny facial shrug.

"You might be right," he concedes. "What makes you say so?"

Dossie looks at him thoughtfully. "I think it's the way your face changes when you prepare to play. You become detached. It's as if you are about to enter into another world, which you actually prefer to this one."

Ned is slightly taken aback by Dossie's perspicacity. There was a time when he hoped that Hugo would make his playing his career when he was in his last years at school. It was sad that Hugo's father had never recognized his son's talent or taken it seriously. If his mother had still been alive it might have been different.

"Anyway," Dossie is saying, "payment for the pudding is that you play for us after supper. And don't ask me what. You know how ignorant I am and you only do it to show me up."

Hugo is laughing now. "OK. But you're going to have to start taking it on board and learn. I might play you some Debussy."

"Awesome," says Dossie, who sometimes talks like her grandson, Jakey. "Shall I like it?"

"It'll be joyous," Hugo says solemnly. "Simply joyous."

Ned watches them, amused, as they burst out laughing. They like to do this: to quote lines from TV shows or films that they both seem to know.

How wonderful, he thinks, if they were to fall in love.

They make such an attractive pair: Hugo with his dark curly hair, so kind and warm-hearted, and Dossie, so ashy-fair, so funny, and vital. They are both generous, life enhancing, nurturers.

But this was always my problem, thinks Ned wryly. I was always much too ready to fall in love. Too romantic. Too susceptible. How terrible it is to be so old on the outside and still so young on the inside. He thinks of John Donne's poem:

> I am two fools, I know,
> For loving, and for saying so . . .

But he knows that Hugo is not that kind of fool and Ned senses that although Hugo might be very attracted to Dossie, they are already moving beyond that fragile, magical moment of falling in love. Their friendship is easy, uncomplicated, and Ned is so grateful to be a part of it that he is happy simply to enjoy his pudding and look forward to hearing Hugo play.

Hugo spoons up some cream and mentally reviews what he might play to Dossie. He's rather enjoying his role as entertainer, of musician, though he suspects that she is not quite as ignorant as she claims.

"So what do you like?" he asked her on a previous occasion. "What music do you listen to when you're driving? Or do you listen to the radio?"

She shook her head. "No, I like to listen to music. At the moment I'm really into Jamie Cullum, Nina Simone . . . You know?" She smiles at him. "All that jazz?"

He shakes his head, pretending disapproval. "My cousin Jamie loves that stuff," he told her.

Now, as he finishes the pudding and pushes his plate aside, Hugo remembers that he'd also been rather grateful that Jamie wasn't around to play for Dossie. Jazz piano is Jamie's speciality. It's the story of his life:

his cousin was always ahead; a year older, taller, more glamorous. He was head chorister, when they were both in the choir at Wells Cathedral School, and Jamie was always the one who got the girl when they were teenagers and, as if that weren't enough, he became an RAF pilot. They tease each other, mock each other, exasperate each other, yet between them is an unbreakable bond of love and trust forged long ago as small boys at boarding school.

Hugo frowns. He can still remember the loneliness and the fear of those first awful weeks at school; his mother only recently dead, his barrister father busy and detached. It was Jamie who rescued him; his big, clever, popular cousin who protected him, drew him onwards, encouraged his passion for music. Very few people understood the hard work, the professionalism, the dedication and comradeship required to be a chorister.

Hugo dismisses his memories and reaches for the pad of paper that lives on the kitchen table.

"So," he says, "what wonderful food shall we ask Dossie for this time?"

Ned makes suggestions and watches Dossie, who is stroking Brioc. The dog leans his head against her knees and she bends over him, smoothing his coat and murmuring words of love. Ned can see her longing, her loneliness, and he wishes he could help her. It is clear from the way she makes such a fuss of Mort and Brioc how much she misses having a dog of her own.

"Perhaps," he suggests, "you should take Brioc home with you. On loan, as it were."

She raises her head to smile at him, though it is not one of her usual smiles, and she makes a little face of longing.

"A kind of rent-a-dog, d'you mean? What a fantastic idea. Only he'd miss you all too much. And you'd miss him."

"We'd have Mort," says Ned. "Wouldn't we, Mort?"

Mort, stretched out under the table, beats his tail upon the floor.

"Just don't tempt me," warns Dossie, "or I might take you up on it."

"He'd probably enjoy a break," says Hugo, still compiling his list. "Travelling all over the county. Meeting lots of lovely people. Eating wonderful food. Being top dog with Dossie. What's not to like?"

"Sounds like you might enjoy it yourself," suggests Ned slyly, and they all burst out laughing. "Well, if you won't take me up on that, Dossie, I shall have to start a new campaign. A 'Find a Dog for Dossie' campaign."

"Don't think I haven't thought about it," says Dossie. "It's just not that easy. I'm not sure I could cope with a puppy, and rescue dogs often bring all kinds of problems. And that's apart from the fact of growing to love it and going through all the agonies of losing it again."

Ned can hear the emotion in her voice and Hugo glances up sympathetically. Dossie's head is bent over Brioc's and the two men exchange glances.

"It's time for your recital," Ned says lightly. "Finished the shopping list for Dossie?"

Hugo nods. "All done. Come on, then. I shall play Mozart's D minor Fantasia and if you clap loudly enough you'll be allowed to have coffee afterwards."

As Dossie follows them upstairs to the drawing-room, where the baby grand piano is, she sends up a tiny prayer of thanksgiving for the friendship of these two men. Their affection and kindness, the laughter and sharing, is like a shield and a buckler against her loneliness and sense of loss. She still has good friends, Janna and the Sisters at the Retreat House; she has Clem and Tilly and Jakey, but these two men are very special to her. They have come new to her at a very particular time in her life and she knows that she is just as important to them as they are to her.

The room, which is the whole width of the house, faces west with a view beyond the harbour and seaward to The Mouls. As the sun tips down towards the horizon it is as if the sea catches its light, bursts into flame, and blazes with fire. Dossie stands at the window, arms folded across her breast, watching the sunset as Ned settles into an armchair and Hugo adjusts his position on the piano stool until he is comfortable. As he begins the long slow arpeggios that set the sombre tone of the opening, Dossie is overcome by a stillness of spirit. She doesn't know the piece he is playing, though she recognizes the mournful little tune that follows the introduction, yet the mercurial shifts of mood in the music mirror her own state of mind. Since Mo and Pa died, and Clem married Tilly, she seems to spend her whole time on an emotional roller coaster:

26

tears, joy, grief, laughter, all follow in quick succession. When Hugo launches into the merry little passage at the end, the combined delight of the music and the sunset takes her breath away.

She turns as Hugo plays the last chords with a theatrical flourish, and she and Ned give him enthusiastic applause. He grins at her but remains seated. For a moment he hesitates, eyes turned downward, then lifts his hands to the keys again. He begins to play a slow and steady introduction that leads into a tune so exquisite that to Dossie it is as if a fist squeezes her heart and she can barely breathe. The music is so beautiful it is unbearable. As she watches him she sees the expression she spoke of earlier: of intense concentration, of complete immersion in the music and another world. He repeats the tune with his left hand whilst his right hand creates a shimmering accompaniment. His broad hands move confidently over the keys, his eyes are closed, and there is something so particularly impressive about him, so sexy, that, just for this moment, she thinks that she could almost fall in love with this other, detached, assured Hugo. She turns back to the window, disturbed by her feelings. And now the music changes. The composer is saying something that cannot be defined in words. The tune returns, embellished, intense, reinforced, reaches a climax and then subsides to a sad, resigned little statement that is repeated twice before Hugo brings the piece to a close with a last bright high chord and lifts his fingers from the piano.

There is a silence.

"Was that the '*Widmung*'?" Ned asks at last. He clears his throat to hide the emotion in his voice. "I didn't know you could play the Liszt arrangement. I'm impressed."

Hugo is murmuring deprecatingly that it isn't really up to standard, that he wouldn't want to attempt it in public, and Dossie continues to stare out of the window, trying to control her emotions, her confusion, and to prevent herself from bursting into tears.

Suddenly the front door slams, a voice calls, the dogs bark, and Hugo gets up from the piano. The tension begins to dissolve and at last Dossie turns to look at him.

"That was . . . awesome."

She knows that Hugo is not deceived by this deliberately foolish word, that he sees how much she is moved, and he nods, slightly embarrassed but pleased. Ned looks at her anxiously, aware of her mood. She smiles back at him, nods as if to say: "It's OK. I'm all right," and he gives a little nod in return.

"Let's have that coffee," he says. "Prune's home."

CHAPTER
FOUR

Prune kneels down to embrace Brioc's welcoming and enthusiastic licks whilst Mort butts her with his head and whines joyfully.

"A good day in the greenhouse?" enquires Hugo. "A nice supper in Padstow?" and Prune beams at him.

She feels happy, wanting to laugh and sing: life is good. How much of this is due to Ben turning up unexpectedly at the gardens this afternoon after his lunchtime shift at The Chough, of his coming to find her in the greenhouses and inviting her to a gig at the weekend at a pub in Wadebridge, she doesn't want to analyse too clearly. She really likes him — his readiness to laugh and joke, his directness and quick responsiveness — but she doesn't want to look overkeen: she's known him for only a few weeks and she's made that mistake before.

"We saved some bread-and-butter pudding for you," says Dossie, following Hugo into the kitchen with Ned behind her. "But you probably won't want any if you've been pigging out on fish and chips."

Prune gives her a hug. She has become so fond of Dossie, who seems a part of the set-up here and who has a kind of agelessness about her that makes her feel like a mate. Prune feels really lucky to have got the job with the National Trust, after her two-year course at Bicton College, and to be part of the little team involved in growing the food that will be used in the café. They are all young, excited and enthusiastic about it. But then it's good, too, to come back here and chill with Hugo and Ned — and Dossie when she's around.

"It was really good," she says. "There was live music and the band was amazing. I *am* full up but I don't want anyone pinching my bit of bread-and-butter pudding. I'll save it for tomorrow."

"Take note," Dossie says warningly to Ned and Hugo.

"We wouldn't mess with Prune," says Hugo at once. "She wields a mean pair of secateurs!"

Prune makes a face at him, and she wonders — just very quickly — how it might be to bring Ben here and to introduce him to this odd group of people and whether he'd be intimidated by them, although she doesn't really imagine that Ben is easily intimidated.

"Isn't it a bit like living with your father and your grandfather?" he asked when she described the set-up to him.

She thought about it for a moment then shook her head.

"No, it isn't, actually. They're sort of not like that. Hugo worked as a producer of documentaries at the BBC and he's seriously cool. And Ned's got a really sharp sense of humour. They're just . . . well, people. You know? In the end age doesn't seem to come into it much."

Ben nodded. "Sounds fun," he said.

Even so, Prune can't quite see herself bringing him here, not just yet. She needs to know him better; to feel more confident with him.

Hugo is making coffee but he knows she won't drink any this late in the day. He grins at her.

"Nice brew of dock leaves?" he asks. "Nettles? Root of dandelion?"

It's rather like having her older brothers around, teasing her, and she swings a punch at him.

"At least I shall have a good night's sleep," she retorts as she takes down her box of herbal teas from the cupboard. "What with all this late-night coffee and booze, it's like living with students again."

"Now there's a compliment," comments Ned.

They all settle round the kitchen table and Prune feels Brioc collapse comfortably against her feet. She smiles, sighs with pleasure, and allows herself to feel happy and on the edge of falling in love. Hugo's phone pings and he takes it out of his pocket.

"Jamie," he says, "asking if he can come and stay. Hoping to get down quite soon."

"Of course he can come and stay," says Ned impatiently. "He knows he's always welcome here. This is his home. How is he?"

Prune watches the two men as Hugo taps out a reply. She hasn't yet met Jamie, though Hugo has talked about him: how they were at school and uni together, how Jamie married soon after he arrived at RAF Lyneham, after he'd got his Wings, but that the marriage broke up a few years later. It's clear from the way Hugo talks that Jamie is a bit of a hero to him, which she thinks is rather sweet. She's looking forward to meeting him and seeing how he and Hugo act together. She can imagine that, despite the fact that Hugo and Jamie are in their fifties, it'll be rather the way her brothers behave: joshing, insulting each other, sharing the in-jokes and phrases that go way back to childhood.

"Not great," Hugo is saying, answering Ned's question. "No change, apparently."

"Isn't he well?" Dossie asks, concerned.

Prune knows that Dossie hasn't met Jamie either but that she understands that he is important to Hugo and Ned. Hugo hesitates, as if he is deciding how much or little he should say.

"He's had these vertigo attacks," he says at last. "It started with a cold, then terrible dizziness. Actually falling over. Said he thought he was having a stroke. He had three in that first week. He was grounded, of course. Pilots are susceptible to colds, inner-ear infections, but nobody can pin this thing down. He hasn't flown for more than a year."

"How terrible," says Dossie, shocked. "Quite awful for him."

"It's utterly bloody," says Ned, quite violently. "One minute you're a pilot. Next minute you've made your last flight without even knowing it. Utterly bloody."

He shakes his head almost as if he were in pain, as if he can't believe the cruelties of life and, watching him, Prune remembers that Jamie is Ned's late brother's son and that Ned's own son was killed on RFA *Sir Galahad* in the Falklands War. Jamie must be very special to him. Her eyes meet Dossie's, and they exchange a glance that shares the concern they feel, and the helplessness. Neither of them knows what to say.

"Anyway," says Hugo, trying for a more upbeat note, "he's coming down to see us before too long. So that's all good."

"In which case," says Dossie, quickly picking up on the positive tone in Hugo's voice, "I'd better get the freezer filled. Give me that list, Hugo, and I'll see what I can do. Does Jamie have any favourite puddings?"

"Sticky toffee," Ned answers at once, and Prune is oddly touched that Ned should remember such a thing.

She sips her peppermint tea whilst Dossie peers over Hugo's shoulder, studying the list. Ned suggests additions, and Hugo writes them down. Prune's attention drifts: she wonders what she might wear to go to the pub with Ben. Imperceptibly her spirits rise.

CHAPTER
FIVE

Hugo goes out with Dossie to her car, followed by the dogs, who are about to have their last walk. As Hugo stands beside the car, one eye on the dogs, talking in a general way, he wishes he could summon up the courage to invite her out, to a film, to supper, to the pub, but at the same time feels an odd constraint. Dossie has become a chum so quickly, so unexpectedly, that it almost feels inappropriate to suggest it. He wishes — not for the first time — that he had Jamie's style, his ease with women, but meanwhile he remains tongue-tied and when she says, "Isn't that sunset amazing?" he answers, "Joyous. Just joyous." Then they burst out laughing together.

They both loved the TV comedy *W1A,* about the BBC, which Hugo promised her was so true to life he'd had to watch it from behind the sofa, and now the catchphrases have become part of their conversation.

We can laugh together, thinks Hugo, watching her drive away. And that is very special.

He calls to the dogs and climbs the track that leads up from the harbour to the cliffs, still thinking about Dossie. He knows that Uncle Ned considers him a wimp.

"Ask her out," the older man cries impatiently. "Get tickets for something. She's a damned attractive woman. What are you pussyfooting about for? She's missing her parents and that boy of hers. Her whole life has changed round and she's feeling rootless and lonely. She needs someone to anchor her, to get her focused. She should get married again."

Hugo's tried to explain that though Dossie might be feeling these things she is nevertheless independent, has her work, her house, and she isn't some princess in a fairy tale who needs rescuing by a prince so that they can get married and live happily ever after.

"Well, I suppose it doesn't have to be marriage," Uncle Ned observed thoughtfully, rather mischievously, and then he saw Hugo's shocked expression and he began to laugh. "Yours is such a serious generation. Ah, well. Never mind."

Hugo pauses on the cliff path to look back to the west. The sun has set now but the low-flying tatters of clouds are streaked through with scarlet and gold and crimson, and the lights of a ship gleam far away on the horizon. The wind has dropped and he hears the sea's unceasing swell and sigh as it pours itself against the black granite cliffs, running into the deep underground chambers far below his feet, and he can smell the faint nutty smell of the gorse that grows in tall banks beside the path. Mort barks and there is a flurry of paws on sandy earth as the dogs dash away after a rabbit.

As he follows the dogs along the path, his thoughts run forward to the prospect of Jamie's visit. Not long after his cousin had begun to have these terrible vertigo attacks he was given two weeks' leave.

"I'd drive down," he said to Hugo, "but to be honest I'm a bit worried about the driving with this condition, and the train makes it even worse."

"I'll come to you," Hugo said at once. "How would that be? Just for a couple of nights."

Now, he stands quite still, hands in his pockets, remembering his shock at the sight of his tall, charismatic cousin coming out of his cottage in Witney to meet him, walking with a stick. The truth of his illness was far worse than he'd let on over the phone.

"I know," said Jamie with a wry smile, seeing his expression. "I can't walk straight and people laugh because they think I'm drunk. I wish! Can't drive, though that may pass. Can't ride a bike. Can't fly."

The bitterness in his voice was unmistakable and Hugo did not know how to comfort him.

There were more investigations during the next few months but there was no external evidence to go on, no effective tests available, no meaningful results. Meanwhile the weeks passed and all the while Jamie's future prospects, his hopes to avoid retirement and continue in service, were vanishing. He had devoted his whole working life to his aircraft, to the Hercules; to understanding every aspect, every foible. He is — or rather he was — a valuable asset, worth keeping in harness past the normal retirement age. The possibility that he might never fly a Herc again is unthinkable.

"And you know what's worse than that?" he said to Hugo, one evening later during that stay. "Because

36

there are no answers it makes you begin to think it's all in your own mind. OK, yes, I know it isn't. I know these symptoms are real enough but that's what it *feels* like sometimes. And that's a very black and dangerous path to go down."

As Hugo stands watching the stars pricking out in the eastern sky, his heart is wrenched with pain for his cousin. It will be so good to see him. At least there will be an opportunity to nourish him, to try to help him: he'll be coming home to them after more than a year.

Homecomings. Hugo thinks of Dossie going back to her empty, silent house and instinctively he pulls out his phone and texts her. Then he calls to the dogs and turns back along the path.

As Dossie drives home, travelling eastwards towards St Endellion, she too can see the glimmer of stars above the distant bony scrawl of Rough Tor. Thoughts blunder in her head like moths around a candle: Hugo's magical playing, Prune's instinctive hug, Ned's outburst against the random cruelties of life. She wonders if she will be invited to meet Jamie. She knows that she will feel a little bit hurt if she isn't, though she knows, too, that there is no requirement on Ned and Hugo's part to make the gesture. But she's looking forward to meeting Jamie. A few things that Hugo told her about him have already aroused her interest.

"He has the need for speed," he told her. "That's one of his expressions. 'I feel the need. The need for speed.'"

"*Top Gun*," she says at once. "Mike loved that film."

She and Hugo began to sing "Take My Breath Away" and then burst out laughing together.

"He mocks our ancient Volvo," Hugo said ruefully. "He's got a classic MGB roadster and he really canes it. God, he loves that car. He's even fitted it with a CD player."

It was then she told Hugo about Mike and his passion for racing — cars, boats, motorbikes — and how he'd died. Hugo looked shocked. He hadn't known the details of Mike's death.

"I'm so sorry," he said gently. "It sounds as if he and Jamie would have had a lot in common."

He sounded almost wistful and she guessed that he was remembering times when this glamorous cousin had been something of a threat, though Hugo is a very attractive man and must have made quite a few conquests of his own. She thinks about Jamie, and the cruel stroke of fate that is threatening his career, and Ned's outburst.

Dossie's never been invited to supper before — many coffee or tea moments, but not supper — and she suspects that the invitation came from Ned.

"We must do this more often," he said as he gave her a farewell hug. "It's been a lovely evening."

She held his tall, bony frame tightly for a moment and then began to laugh. "It's only my bread-and-butter pudding you're after," she said. "Don't think I'm deceived."

"Not a bit of it," he said at once, releasing her, looking down at her. "There's your banoffee pie. That amazing trifle you make . . ."

38

Dossie smiles to herself, remembering. It's odd that it should be so good to be with the two of them; not as wife or mother, nor as sister or daughter, but simply as herself. There is no commitment here, no responsibility, except that of a friend, an equal. Because there is no shared past there is all the novelty of learning about these two, of discovering new things. Soon she will invite them to The Court, cook a meal for them, move the relationship forward a little.

She is well aware of Hugo's dilemma: that he cannot decide whether or not to invite her out. Part of her hopes he won't. Despite that odd moment of attraction she felt when he was playing, she fears it might spoil things — change the dynamic of the relationship between the three of them — and she has no wish to hurt him. She suspects that deep down he feels the same: that vital spark is absent.

As she puts the car away, then lets herself into the house bracing herself against the silence and the emptiness, a message pings in and she opens her phone to look at it. It's from Hugo:

It was a great evening. Thanks for being a part of it. Let's all do lunch at the pub soon. x

Dossie stands in the hall, staring at the message, knowing that he'd been thinking of her coming into the house alone and she marvels at the love that comes from unexpected quarters. She goes into the warm kitchen, switches on the lights, dumps her bag on the long, ancient oak table, and looks around at the familiar references of her life: Mo's much-beloved hand-painted tea plates ranged along the dresser shelf, Pa's set of four sketches of sailing boats on the wall beside the Aga, on the windowsill a blue pottery vase that Clem made at school, a photograph on the bookshelf of a much younger Jakey holding Wolfie in his arms.

Dossie pours a glass of water and stands drinking at the sink, staring out into the darkness. She puts down the glass, takes her phone and taps out a text:

It was great. Yes please. I'd love to. x

She finishes her water, picks up her bag, turns out the light and goes upstairs to bed.

CHAPTER
SIX

Rose Pengelly lets herself into the house, calls out her usual "H'ya" and hangs her jacket on a peg. The dogs come skittering down the stairs and she pats them, then drives them before her along the passage.

"Only me," she calls up the stairs, and hears Ned's shout in response.

She's guessed Hugo's out — no car outside — and often these days he goes shopping alone. Ned's not too nifty since he had his hip done. Rose goes into the kitchen and looks round her, deciding what to do; where to start. Definitely the kitchen first, she decides: it's in a right old muddle. The bathrooms next; then a quick vacuum round. Rose shoos the dogs to their baskets, then collects cloths and cleaning fluid, the dustpan and brush, and beeswax polish from the cupboard under the sink. It's a big house, there's plenty to do, but she's still managing to keep up with it. Not much has changed in this kitchen since she started work here more than forty years ago, after Admiral Sir Matthew retired and he and Lady Tremayne moved to Cornwall.

Hardly more than a tacker she'd been in those days, helping her mum, earning a bit of pocket money. A few years later, when her mum was ill, she'd taken over some of her work. They'd been very kind to her, Lady T and the Admiral. Way back then she'd called Jack's parents Commander and Mrs Tremayne, and it wasn't until after Jack died that the formality was dropped. A kind of friendship was forged between the two younger women during those weeks that Margaret spent here alone with Lady T and the Admiral whilst Ned was at sea, and later at the MOD in London.

Rose remembers those earlier days: Ned and Margaret coming for a week's leave, bringing Jack. Jamie and Hugo travelling by train from their posh school upcountry. As she scrubs and cleans, Rose smiles as she thinks about Jack: only a few months younger than she was but years older in worldly experience and confidence. Jack-the-Lad, she called him. Oh, how she'd loved him; how she'd wept for him, privately, when he was killed out there in the Falklands. She missed him, missed his laughter and his teasing, and his hands and his lips. She still relives those evenings, long past, down on the beach in the shadow of the rocks and up on the cliffs in the shelter of an ancient quarry.

"Your mum and dad'd kill us if they knew," she'd say, clinging to him.

"My mum and dad'll never find out," he'd answer. "And, anyway, Dad . . ." and then he'd fallen silent, kissing her into willing compliance.

She knew what he meant, though. Jack's father was always polite and kind to her, but she could tell that he was the kind of man who loved women. She saw it

42

when the Tremaynes had their friends visiting: that sparkle, the temptation to flirt just a little bit. That's where Jack got it from, she reckoned. He was so easy in his skin; ready for a joke and a laugh.

His cousins were like him, Hugo and Jamie, but they were several years younger and Jack was their hero. They followed his lead, calling her "Petal", "Blossom", "Flower". "Oh, watch out! Our Rose is in a thorny mood today," they'd cry. It's good to have Hugo back — so much shared past; so many memories — though it took a while for Jack's charisma to lose some of its power before she could really appreciate Hugo's qualities.

Rose takes down the pretty plates from the dresser shelves, the mugs from the hooks, preparing to dust and polish. Presently she'll make coffee and take some up to Ned. She knows how much he mourns Margaret and how much he still misses Jack. They came on leave here after Jack was killed, and Margaret stayed on when Ned went back to sea. Lady T and the Admiral took it all so bravely.

"You'd never believe they were grieving," Rose said to her old dad, who was a fisherman.

"That's the stiff upper lip we keep hearing about, maid," he told her. "But they're a family of sailors and they know, just like the rest of us, that the sea don't have no favourites."

Ned grieved, though. She'd see the tears start up in his eyes when Jack's name was mentioned, see him standing at the open door of his son's bedroom, and she wished she could give him a hug and tell him how much she missed Jack, too, but she knew that, for all Ned's friendliness and kindness towards her, he would think it inappropriate. Apart from the generational difference, and his military background, she was Rose Pengelly: fisherman's daughter, cleaner. She understood that. Her old dad had the same kind of pride.

Back then, Rose remembers, after their son's death, Margaret remained strong and withdrawn and, watching Ned's pain, Rose wondered how he assuaged his grief, though she could make a good guess. And now he's going through it all again since Margaret died. Unexpectedly Rose thinks of the words of the old Burial service: "Thou knowest, Lord, the secrets of our hearts . . ."

But Rose knows the secrets of this household, secrets nobody else knows, and she smiles to herself.

"Never trust nobody," she tells the dogs, and goes to fetch the vacuum cleaner.

The shopping is done and packed away into the car, and Hugo glances at his watch. Plenty of time for coffee and a moment to regroup in Relish. He strides away into the town, across Foundry Court towards the café. Already, though it is still early in the year, people are sitting at the tables outside, the cherry trees are blossoming, the sun is shining.

With a sense of well-being he goes inside, waving to the girls at the counter, pausing to check out the deli, before ordering a flat white and sitting at one of the round, wooden-slatted tables. He thinks about his morning, about the rest of the day, but his attention is taken by a group of young women who sweep in, pushing buggies, toddlers at heel, laughing together. Hugo smiles at their liveliness, their energy, and one small boy particularly engages his attention. He has soft, very dark hair and dark brown eyes, and he glances at Hugo with a bright, intelligent look, which Hugo seems in some strange way to recognize. Even as he tries to define his reaction, one of the young women looks around, calls to the child, and smiles at Hugo almost apologetically.

This time the shock is much greater. Hugo's expression is so unguarded that she looks surprised, raises her eyebrows questioningly as if she is wondering if she has met him but can't remember him.

"I'm so sorry," Hugo says at once. "Just for a moment I thought you were someone I knew. Forgive me for staring at you."

She laughs and he thinks how pretty she is with her long red-brown hair, and how strong the resemblance to the girl he remembers so clearly.

"Emilia," he says, unable to help himself. "She was called Emilia with an E. Sorry. This is crazy. You must think I'm out of my mind." He laughs too. "Honestly. This is not a pick-up line."

"But that's seriously weird," she says, sobering a little. "My mum's called Emilia with an E. We're supposed to be very alike."

He shakes his head in disbelief at this coincidence. "I knew an Emilia when I was at university," he says. His heart is beating fast now. "In Bristol. Her mother was performing in a Shakespearean season at the Old Vic and Emilia was with her."

"Really?" The girl looks surprised and pleased. "Wow. That's so amazing. They often travelled together when Granny was doing rep. What's your name?"

Hugo feels anxious; there are so many complications here.

"I'm Hugo," he says lightly. It seems natural to stand up, to hold out his hand and she takes it quickly, firmly, and shakes it.

"I must tell her," she says. "I'm Lucy Weston." The small boy rushes up again, stares curiously at Hugo, studying him with his head on one side, then dashes away again. "And that's Daniel," she says.

"Are you on holiday?" Hugo asks, not wanting the conversation to finish just yet.

"I am at the moment but soon we shall be locals. Tom — that's my husband — Tom and I have bought a cottage in Rock." She rolls her eyes. "I know. Isn't it just the most amazing thing? A holiday cottage in Rock? I still can't believe it. We're over from Geneva getting stuff moved in." She laughs and shakes her head. "I'm sorry if I seem a bit hyper. It must sound as if I'm crazy or something but it's just so exciting I keep telling everyone I meet."

Hugo smiles at her, touched by her enthusiasm, reminded of Emilia's natural open friendliness with complete strangers.

"That's wonderful," he says.

"And what about you?" Lucy asks.

46

"Oh, I'm a local," he answers. "We're practically neighbours. Well, sort of. Across the cliffs in Port Quin Bay."

At this moment a member of her party calls to her, a child falls over and begins to cry, and she makes a face at Hugo, waves her hand.

"I'll tell Mum. Maybe see you around?" And she hurries back to her friends.

He sits down, staring after her whilst other images jostle in his memory: Emilia, with her laughter, her passion for music — all music, any music — her love of dance. How she bewitched him. She was always surrounded by men but she liked to be with him. His knowledge and love of classical music impressed her. He took her to concerts at Colston Hall: to lunchtime recitals given by some of the university students. It was at one of these that she heard Schumann's "*Widmung*" played as an encore.

"What was that?" she whispered, deeply moved, leaning close to him under the cover of the applause. Her hair brushed his cheek and he longed to put an arm around her; to hold her close.

"It's the '*Widmung*'," he answered. "Robert Schumann. Liszt's arrangement."

"Can you play it?"

"I'm probably not up to the Liszt. I can play Clara Schumann's arrangement."

"It's wonderful. Could you learn it? Just for me?"

He laughed, then. "That's a very big ask."

"But you could try?" she insisted.

"I could try."

She slipped an arm around his neck and lightly kissed his cheek, and he had to shut his eyes and clench his fists to prevent himself from touching her. He prayed that the "*Widmung*" might be the magic that would bring them closer together. He found a recording of it and invited Emilia to come to his room to hear it. He set the scene: opened a bottle of white wine, arranged a plate of smoked salmon sandwiches. Knowing Emilia's predilection for sitting on the floor, he put some cushions beside the bookcase. As usual she seemed pleased to see him, giving him a hug, accepting a glass of wine and subsiding to sit cross-legged on the cushions. He put the record on, picked up his own glass. Her face changed as the "*Widmung*" began — she seemed transfixed by it — and he watched her, holding his breath. And then the door opened and his cousin Jamie walked in.

Even now, thirty-five years later, Hugo can remember the expression of ludicrous dismay on Jamie's face as he took in the intimate scene, and the way that Emilia got to her feet in one smooth, quick movement as she stared at the newcomer. There was a moment of utter silence and at that precise moment Hugo knew, quite surely, that all his hopes were vanquished.

The atmosphere changed, re-formed, introductions were made and Jamie took a glass of wine.

"I'm really sorry, mate," he said regretfully afterwards to Hugo. "I should have just walked straight out again."

Hugo remembers how he gave an angry, resigned snort of laughter.

"It wouldn't have made any difference," he said bitterly.

But, oh, how hard it was to watch Jamie and Emilia falling in love. They were both so beautiful, so charismatic, so perfectly matched. How hard to hear about the parties and the summer balls and the fun they shared whilst Jamie was first at Cranwell and then at RAF Church Fenton. To everyone's surprise he failed his Fast Jet course, but he did the Truckie course, graduated to RAF Finningley and got his Wings. He and Emilia got married the year after Jack was killed in the Falklands and it was whilst Jamie was a Hercules captain at RAF Lyneham, six years later, that Emilia left him.

Hugo sits staring at nothing in particular, remembering his jealousy and anger during those early months of their courtship and how he felt slightly vindicated when the relationship broke up: they'd both lost her. Fragments of conversation with Jamie occur to him: "She was bored stiff most of the time." "She didn't really connect with the other wives." "She should have found a job but she spent too much time going back to see her actor friends in London." And, tellingly, bitterly: "Emilia never wanted children."

Hugo frowns, thinking of Lucy, and her small dark-haired son. Abruptly he swallows the last of his coffee, gets to his feet and goes out. Lucy is sitting at one of the tables with her friends, Daniel asleep in a buggy beside her, and she lifts a hand to him. He smiles at her and walks quickly away, back to the car.

Lucy watches him go, then turns to smile at one of the other mothers.

"Who's that?" her friend asks. "Rather dishy."

Lucy shrugs. "Apparently he met my mum when he was at uni. Weird or what? Seemed rather nice, actually. Thought I looked just like her."

But the friend, distracted by her baby, who begins to cry, is not particularly interested in Lucy's mum, and Lucy relaxes and thinks how odd it was that the man — Hugo, wasn't it? — should see the likeness. Soon, though, her thoughts drift back to the tile-hung cottage with pointed eaves on the village street in Rock, looking across the estuary to Padstow. The cottage is small and the pretty garden is tiny but, hey, who cares with all this — the moors, the beaches, the cliffs — on its doorstep? The mortgage is huge, of course, but Tom's bonus, combined with Mum's generous contribution when she sold the house and moved back into Granny's flat, was enough for the deposit. And, after all, thinks Lucy, Mum can use the cottage whenever she likes while we're in Geneva. She can bring her chums down once it's all been done up.

The owner was a tough cookie; not prepared to negotiate. The cottage had been in her family for years, apparently, but she was taking up a job in an investment bank in New York and just wanted to be rid of it — but at a top price — and since there was plenty of competition they didn't dare to dither. Getting a cottage in Rock is the most amazing thing ever, and they've reconnected with some friends whose parents live in Polzeath.

Lucy sighs with contentment. She's having the best time: making plans, choosing furniture.

"Just don't go mad," warns Tom.

The crucial thing is the new kitchen, which she is arranging to be fitted. She has to go back to Geneva soon but Mum will be coming down to supervise, bless her. On an impulse, Lucy takes out her phone and rings her.

"Hi, Mum," she says. "Just sitting in the sun here, outside a café in Wadebridge. You OK?"

They chat for a while, make plans, and it's only after the call that Lucy remembers that she's forgotten to tell her mother about her old friend Hugo. Dan wakes, struggles to sit up, and she rummages in her bag for juice and forgets about the encounter.

CHAPTER
SEVEN

"So I thought I'd come down for the weekend," Adam is saying. "Have you got a problem with that, Doss? It would be good to have a catch-up. Perhaps see Clem and Jakey and Tilly. I know weekends aren't necessarily a good time for Clem with Sunday services and all that, and you're probably rushed off your feet with work and social engagements . . ."

Briefly, Dossie wonders if her instinctive wary reaction to his familiar, slightly negative approach is more her problem than his. Perhaps her brother genuinely feels, even now, that he might not be welcome here: that those past arguments and rows have not been forgotten — or forgiven.

"It would be great," she answers, unable to thrust away the guilt she feels that she owns The Court whilst he got nothing. "Will you drive down or come by train?"

"Are you kidding?" he asks. "You mean, seriously, I might use public transport?"

"It's not that bad," she answers, amused.

"As long as it's not high tide at Dawlish," he answers, "or there are the wrong sort of leaves on the track."

She gives an involuntary choke of laughter. He can often make her laugh, more so, in fact, in these last few months since Mo and Pa died. He's becoming a tad less stressed, more open. As they fix the time that he'll arrive, say their goodbyes, Dossie wonders how tough it must have been for him: sent back to England to prep school at eight years old, coming home at regular intervals to a different house in a new country, whilst his parents travelled with Pa's job. Adam lives with his life in his pockets. He wears jackets with a multitude of them so the things most important to him can be zipped safely away, so that he can't lose them, a habit acquired from travelling as a boy with British Airways aunties. Pa used to say that the relationship with his son went wrong when they came home and he was no longer someone Adam could brag about; that he preferred his parents living in exciting foreign countries than having them in Cornwall running a bed-and-breakfast establishment. But Dossie can quite understand that it wouldn't have been easy for Adam to invite teenage public school boys, who were used to being taken to Gstaad or the Caribbean for their holidays, to come to stay at a B and B in Cornwall. She knows that Adam was not happy at boarding school. He was neither academic nor good at sports. He was a cool, quiet boy. They were never particularly close, even in those early years of her marriage with Mike. Adam was still at university then and the six years between them no longer seemed to matter, but to her surprise Mike understood Adam.

"The poor old fellow's in a bit of a mess," he said. "He hasn't found out where he fits in yet. He's a very private kind of guy. Life's not going to be easy for him, Doss, so cut him some slack."

Mike took Adam motor-racing, out in his speedboat, introduced him to his friends. It was through one of these friends that Adam was offered his job at the big London country property agency. Clients liked him; he learned fast about properties and estates — and then he met Maryanne.

How happy they all were when he told them that he was marrying this bubbly, extrovert girl. How they hoped that she would unlock this self-contained, unemotional man, warm him into life. It seemed, instead, that Adam's inability to connect chilled even Maryanne's vitality. The marriage didn't last and he never remarried, despite several relationships.

Dossie wanders into the kitchen, stares at her notice board, but she isn't really seeing her work schedule. She's thinking of the weekend ahead and how she can continue to forge a positive relationship with her brother. Perhaps, after all, it might be simplest to sell the house, split the proceeds between them, and hope that they might start again. She wishes she had someone to talk to — Hugo, perhaps — but it seems disloyal to discuss her brother and her family with someone she hardly knows. Maybe she could invite Hugo and Ned and Prune to lunch, or supper whilst Adam is with her; surely there could be no harm in that? That way they would come to know her brother and then, at some later date, it might be possible to talk her anxieties through with them.

54

How seductive it is, thinks Dossie, to imagine sharing with someone; to open one's heart, to ask for advice. Where does that come from, that need to be known, to be understood, to be loved?

She remembers her last disastrous love affair and snorts derisively. It's always been a weakness with her since Mike died: the longing to fall in love again.

"You have the worst instincts with men I've ever known," a friend once said to her. "You're so gullible. Why do you infallibly pick bastards?"

"They're always the best looking," she joked, but the remark hurt her, probably because it's all true. She *is* gullible, she *is* optimistic and they *are* good-looking. Life seems rather pointless unless you're sharing it with someone you love.

Dossie looks around the kitchen. Is she imagining that by selling her home and sharing the proceeds with Adam he might become closer to her? Or would he just take the money and run? But, anyway, he's right. She can't really afford to stay here, to manage the upkeep of this house, so at least with his contacts he might get a good price for it.

Suddenly she is weighted with depression, with loneliness. Her usual mantra, "Get a grip. Get a life. Get a dog", doesn't work for her at the moment. Battling with misery and tears, she drags out her phone and texts Hugo.

Could you Ned and Prune manage lunch here to meet Adam at the weekend? x

To her huge relief, he answers promptly.

Prune is working this weekend but otherwise that's great. Saturday or Sunday?

Dossie thinks about it and decides on Saturday. Adam will be down on Friday evening and she doesn't know when he means to leave on Sunday. She replies to Hugo and at once she feels more cheerful. Later she'll FaceTime Jakey and see how they all are. Meanwhile she'll get on with some work.

Hugo puts his phone down, writes the lunch date on the wall calendar and goes back to the kitchen table. It is covered with photographs. He's been promising Ned that he'll sort them out, put them into an album, but as usual he has become distracted by them. He picks up one and then another. Here he is, best man at Jamie's wedding. Jamie, handsome in his uniform, smiling into the camera with Hugo beside him. "He's my wing man," Jamie always says when he introduces Hugo to his mates. And here they are again at school, Jamie playing bass guitar with Hugo on the keyboard in the background. They'd both played the piano, both played in the school orchestra. Hugo picks up another photograph and stares at Emilia, laughing out at him with Jamie beside her. He experiences a similar shock to the reaction he had earlier at the Relish café: how alike they are, Emilia and her daughter, Lucy. He looks closely at the photograph and puts it down again. He

56

still can't quite see how Jamie's marriage broke apart: they were so much in love.

Hugo bends to stroke Brioc, who presses against his leg. Then Hugo turns away from the table, remembering Emilia. She was so vivid, so alive. Her father was a musician, a flautist with one of the symphony orchestras, her mother was an actress. Emilia's life was unsettled, bohemian, but she loved it, loved her artistic, unpredictable parents. Perhaps Jamie was right and it was this that had been the root of the trouble, after all. Perhaps those early years on a married patch with the rules and regs of military life, the separation, had contributed to Emilia's sudden decision to leave Jamie. That it should have been for a man more than ten years her senior was an extra blow to his cousin's pride. She'd met Nigel at her mother's London flat; an amusing, handsome, Hugh Grant-type of actor, who was having great success in a TV sitcom.

"The humiliation's bad enough," Jamie said, "without seeing the bastard grinning out at me from the television every time I turn it on."

Later, Nigel made a couple of films and then faded out of the public eye. Emilia had faded out of Jamie's sight with him. There was no reason to remain in touch. Hugo looks at the photograph again — at the happy smiles, the hopefulness in their faces — and seems to feel the past all around him. Hugo picks up another photograph: he and Jamie amongst a group of choristers in blue cassocks and white frilled ruffs, holding candles, the Christmas tree behind them. Stanford in C, John Ireland's "Greater love hath no man": was it the sense of duty, of dedication, of professionalism instilled by the music that bound them together as boys and still holds them close? The Christmas Celebration, an event always held in the last week of the Michaelmas term, certainly contributed to his love of performance, his sense of theatre, that delicate balance between the religious and secular. He grew up determined to find a way to work in an artistic environment with like-minded people. Despite his musical ability, his love for the piano, he knew that he hadn't the temperament to be a public performer and so, encouraged by the school motto, "*Esto quod es*" — "Be who you are" — he decided to join the new intake of interns at the BBC. Jamie chose service to his country and joined the RAF, becoming a Hercules captain, a "Truckie" pilot, flying on operations in the Gulf, Bosnia and Afghanistan. Very different worlds.

And now here are photographs of Jack as a boy, as a young naval officer, of Ned and Margaret, holding glasses of champagne, laughing together, after Jack's Passing Out Parade at Dartmouth. Hugo gazes at these pictures of his beloved aunt, of his cousin, so happy, so alive. It's still almost impossible to believe that Jack, so vital, so full of humour and determination, should have died. Hugo remembers what fun they shared, though he had such admiration for his older cousin. Even Jamie was in awe of Jack; both of them devastated by his death.

On a sudden impulse Hugo gathers the photographs together and bundles them back into the big envelope. He doesn't want Ned to come in from his bridge group and see them. There's too much bereavement and sadness, too many failures and disappointments. He glances at his watch: just time to take the dogs for a walk before Ned comes home wanting supper. The exercise will raise his spirits, put him back on an even keel. Who was it, he wonders, who said that life has to be lived forwards but can only be understood backwards? Just at the moment he can't understand anything. And if he's feeling like this, how about poor Dossie, battling with loneliness, and Jamie, struggling with this terrible threat to his career?

Hugo groans, shoves the envelope to the back of a shelf in the dresser, and calls to the dogs.

CHAPTER
EIGHT

Adam drives into the empty, open-fronted barn, sits for a minute, still listening to the end of an interview on Radio 4, and then switches off the engine. He's not surprised that Dossie's car isn't here. He left London earlier than he planned but, knowing that she's taking a supply of food to a holiday complex in St Ives, he decided not to text her. He's quite pleased to be here on his own: to give himself some time to adjust to the rural silence, to look at the gracious, pretty house with its freight of memories.

He stands in the warm May sunshine, hands in his jeans pockets, and stares around him. He can see signs of neglect in the garden that Mo loved so much; the window frames need touching up. His thoughts dart back to the time when Pa's mother lived here: an indomitable, tough old lady with a will of iron. He and Dossie stayed with her during exeats and half terms, and once for the whole of an Easter holiday whilst Mo and Pa were between continents, moving from South Africa to Western Australia. Dossie, in her teens, seemed to take everything in her stride. She was allowed to have her friends from Truro School to tea or to spend the day. His school friend,

Christopher, lived too far away to come to St Endellion. It seemed so unfair that Dossie was allowed to go to Truro School whilst he was sent upcountry to prep school.

Adam wanders round the outside of the house, aware of birdsong, of the scent of lilac, of the patchwork of fields all about him. There should be a dog somewhere around; there have always been dogs. Mo should be on her knees, weeding a border, and Pa shouting from somewhere, asking where the garden string has got to, or the secateurs, or that coffee was ready. Yet, somehow — and he's not proud of this — it's a relief that they're not here to question him, ask how the job's going or if he's got a new girlfriend.

It was always like that: a sense of expectation, never to be fulfilled. He remembers overhearing a couple of B and B-ers talking; old friends of Mo and Pa.

"A miracle that they had a son at last," he said to his wife. "After all those miscarriages, Pa was off his head with joy."

"Especially when that last miscarriage was a boy," she replied. "D'you remember? They were distraught. They wanted one so badly. My goodness, he'll have a lot to live up to, poor boy."

Adam balls up his fists and crosses his arms, staring up at the back of the house, remembering the succession of disappointments over the years, in his indifferent school reports, in his lack of physical prowess; in his failure to get to a top university: Pa's raised eyebrows when Adam told him he was joining the agency in London. He'd hoped his only son would be an engineer, join the army.

"Mike set it up," Adam said quickly, defensively. Mike could do no wrong in Pa's eyes. "I'm going to be training with one of his friends."

"I suppose if that's what you really want," Pa answered.

On an impulse, Adam walks back to the front of the house, down the drive and out into the lane. He strides quickly, hardly noticing the white hawthorn blossom in the hedges, the red campion in the ditches. He strides across the road and into the churchyard, around the west end of the little collegiate church to where Mo and Pa are buried beside Granny and Grandpa. He stands looking down at the graves. There are wild flowers in containers — Dossie, he thinks — and the grass is newly cut.

He is filled with emotion: grief, anger, love, despair.

"I'm sorry," he says silently, bitterly, to them. "Sorry that I could never be the son you wanted. Maybe that other son, the one that came before me, might have been more the sort of son you wanted. You'll never know how much I tried but it was never good enough. And the really terrible thing is that all I feel now is a sense of relief because I haven't got to keep pretending that I don't mind that I wasn't what you hoped I'd be. That I was useless at school, that my marriage fell apart, that I didn't give you any grandchildren, that I always seemed to get it wrong. And the fact that I feel relief makes me feel a complete shit, too."

He turns away from the graves to stare beyond the churchyard, across the further wall, to the distant shine and shimmer of the sea. In the surrounding fields tall, feathery grasses and bright yellow buttercups ripple in the south-westerly breeze. The sun is warm on his shoulders and, as he breathes in the scent of hawthorn and new-mown grass, he allows some of his tension to flow out from him. As his fists unclench and his arms fall to his sides, just for a moment he feels so free; free from the bitterness of being sent away from home when he was barely eight years old to a cold, bleak boarding school, a small lonely boy who found it so difficult to join in, and was punished for it. For this moment it seems that all the pain, all his anger, is being carried away on that clean, salt-scented wind.

Although he knows that it is an illusion, he wants to weep, but instead he turns back, passing under the great yew, out through the gate and into the lane — and then pauses in surprise. Because there is Dossie, at the end of the lane, waiting for him.

"Hi," she says, as he crosses the road. "I thought you might be here," and she puts out her arms and hugs him. After a second, he responds, and it is as if, for the first time for many, many years, he really has come home.

Dossie holds him tightly before letting him go. She is surprised by that sudden, instinctive response. Adam isn't given to demonstrations of affection, he finds it difficult to show his emotions, and as they turn for home she is confused by her own reactions. For so long now it seems that they have been on opposite sides. She knows it was because she agreed to support it, to help them with it, that Mo and Pa were able to continue with their B and B-ers once they were too old to manage alone. Adam thought it was time they retired, sold The Court and downsized. They argued bitterly about it. At the time, she and Adam were both in difficult relationships and now Dossie regrets the angry words they exchanged. She longs to reconnect with him; to make their relationship work.

"This is the bit I hate most," she says to him, unlocking the door. "Coming into a silent, empty house. There always used to be something going on and dogs rushing out to meet me."

Adam doesn't dismiss what she says with a shrug or a half-smile, as she fears he might, but stands still as if he, too, is listening to the silence.

"You should leave a radio on," he says. "That way there would always be music or someone talking when you come in. It wouldn't feel so bleak."

She stares at him, seeing bleakness in his own face, and she hurries ahead of him into the kitchen so that he doesn't see that she is near to tears, touched by the fact that he's taken her seriously and not made light of her feelings.

"That's a good idea," she says, pushing the kettle on to the Aga. "I hadn't thought of it. Mo always had Radio 3 going. Or I could get a dog, of course. What d'you think?"

She waits: this is the test question. This is the moment when he will talk about her selling The Court, about not being able to manage it on her own, but Adam says neither of these things. He stands with his hands in his pockets, staring at the dogs' beds.

"What breed would you get?" he asks at last. "Which was your favourite of all the dogs?"

She's taken off guard and fiddles about with mugs and coffee — Adam never drinks tea — whilst she thinks about it.

"It's difficult," she answers at last. "I loved old Jonno, of course, and his inability to keep away from water. And Jess. Gosh, I don't know. What about you? Which was your favourite?"

"Molly," he answers at once. "I loved Molly. I was gutted when she died."

In that moment Dossie has a mental picture of Adam as a small boy of eight or nine, sitting cross-legged where the dogs' beds are, their grandmother's beautiful field spaniel lying across his bare knees, his blond head bent over her and his hands gently caressing her smooth brown coat. For the second time in a few minutes Dossie wants to cry. She turns to look at him and is shocked by the same bleak look on his face. She guesses that he is remembering those exeats from school; the half-term holidays they spent here at The Court.

"Were you very unhappy at school?" she asks involuntarily.

"Yes," he answers immediately, not moving, still with that grim expression. "I hated it. I hated it so much I thought I might die of it."

She can think of nothing to say that does not sound trite.

"I suppose," she says, at last, "if you are abroad and moving around all the time with your work, it's difficult to give your children a proper home life and a decent, uninterrupted education."

"In which case," he answers swiftly, "don't have children. I shall never have children. I'd be too afraid I might get it wrong for them."

Dossie is taken aback by his response, at the pain that emanates from his tense figure.

"I had no idea it was so bad for you," she says gently.

"Why would you?" he asks, almost indifferently, as though he wouldn't expect any attention to be paid to his suffering.

"Were you bullied?" she asks tentatively.

"Yes," he says. "Yes, I was bullied because I was so homesick. I had my head forced down the loo, I was mocked because I called my parents Mo and Pa, and I was caned for not joining in."

She takes a breath but, before she can speak, Adam rushes on as if he needs to say it all; to say the words at last.

"I didn't bring friends home but Mo and Pa never asked why or seemed to wonder about it. I hated school because I wasn't very bright and because I was useless at Games." He shrugs. "And nobody seemed to care much about that either."

She is silent, not knowing what to say or how to help him.

66

He looks at her at last and then half smiles. "Sorry, Doss. Forget it. Long time ago."

"Clearly not," she answers. "I had no idea it was that bad, Adam. I should have noticed."

He shakes his head dismissively. "You were already in your middle teens, thinking about boys and pop stars when I came back to England to school. A few years later you were married to Mike."

"That's not the point. You're my little brother. I should have picked up on it. You were always . . ." She hesitates, not wanting to sound as if she is criticizing him. "You were a funny little boy. Kind of distant. Even in the holidays when Mo and Pa came home and were living here you seemed not to want to be a part of it."

He looks at her, as if puzzled by her lack of understanding. "Can you begin to imagine what it was like, Doss? After twelve weeks of a prison-like existence, coming back to a houseful of B and B-ers? No time just to be with Mo and Pa. Always someone else around. Pa telling me to turn the telly off, go outside, to remember that breakfast was between eight and ten. Can you imagine what it was really like for someone like me? To be asked by well-meaning people a dozen times a day whether I enjoyed school and which subject I liked best?"

Dossie tries to remember those latter years of Adam's school life. She was doing her Cordon Bleu course, living with friends in London.

"I'm sorry," she says inadequately.

Adam shrugs. "Well, let's face it, it hasn't been a walk in the park for you either, has it?"

"Well, you know what they say?" She tries to sound upbeat. "Life's shit and then you die."

His face lightens. "I'm not arguing with that."

The kettle boils and she makes tea for her and coffee for Adam; strong, no milk, no sugar. Just like Ned has it.

"I hope you won't mind," she begins hesitantly, thinking it's time to change the subject, "but I've invited a couple of friends to lunch tomorrow. They started out as clients but have kind of morphed into chums. I think you'll like them. They live down on the coast near Polzeath. Ned and Hugo."

She explains their backgrounds, how kind they've been to her, and tries to ignore his speculative, teasing half-smile and raised eyebrows.

"They sound nice," he agrees, grinning provocatively at her across the table, as she puts the mugs down with a plate of lemon drizzle cake. "And both of them unattached, you said?"

"If I were you," she advises him, "I'd shut up. Or you might not get any cake."

Adam laughs. "I'll take the hint and look forward to meeting them."

Dossie sits opposite him, delighted by this new sense of comradeship between them, bemused and grateful for this moment.

"But you still haven't answered my question," he says, cutting two slices of cake and pushing her plate towards her.

"What question?"

68

"If you were to have another dog, which breed would you choose?"

Adam watches Dossie trying to decide. He knows that he's wrong-footed her, though not deliberately, by his reactions. She was expecting him to be antagonistic, prickly, defensive. After all, it's been his modus vivendi for most of his life: his protective armour to cover his sense of insecurity; his sense of aloneness. He can't quite get to grips with this new feeling of freedom, of the beginnings of a release from the persona that has been so much a part of him. It's strange to sit here in the kitchen alone with Dossie, without the old familiar tension gripping him whilst he waits for some kind of interrogation from his father. "Your maths report is very poor." "Pity you didn't make the first fifteen." "You won't get to a good university with those grades." The only time he really pleased them was when he married Maryanne — he'd been so proud of her, confident of their approval — only for him to have it all fall around his feet. "Divorce? But why? She's such a lovely girl . . ." As usual, it was all his fault. He never told them that though she was a delightful, bubbly extrovert she was also extremely high maintenance and rather spoiled, and that when he tried to curb the spending there would be rows. It would have felt disloyal, as if he were making excuses, and so naturally he was the scapegoat when the marriage fell apart. Yet everyone loved Mo and Pa; everyone said what wonderful people they were.

Echoes of the past are all around him, anxiety clutches at his gut, but then Dossie asks, "I can't decide on the breed but do you think I could manage a puppy?" and the memories fade as he stares at her across the table, wrenching himself back to the present, focusing on her again.

"I can't see why not," he says. He wonders, now that his sense of rejection, of failure, has receded a little, just how hard would it be for Dossie to leave The Court, to start again somewhere new.

"The question really is," he goes on, "whether or not you can afford to stay on here. Whether you'd like a smaller modern place that is easy and cheap to run or to stay here and sink slowly into decaying grandeur."

"Oh, definitely decaying grandeur. That's a no-brainer," she answers promptly, and they both laugh.

He raises his coffee cup to her. "Decaying grandeur it is."

She watches him curiously. "You know, I really thought I was going to have a fight on my hands."

He quirks his eyebrows, makes a face. "Your decision, Doss. The Court's yours to do as you please with, keep or sell."

"I know that. Even so." She pauses. "Look, it wasn't anything to do with me, you know, Mo's and Pa's decision. They thought it was a way of paying me back for making it possible for them to stay on long after they'd have had to give up."

He knows that she's trying to make him feel better about it, to show him a reason for disinheriting him

70

that will be palatable to him. He is seized with all the old antagonism, the helplessness and futility of his attempts to please his parents, the bitterness and insecurity — and yet perhaps the grip is now not quite so strong. He's been the outsider for so long that it's almost impossible to imagine that he might belong again and be part of what's left of his family.

"Look," he says quite gently. "I was never a part of the life that went on here. Nobody asked my opinion about anything. I never really fitted in anywhere." He searches for some kind of way forward and suddenly, instinctively, he knows what it might be.

"Let's forget all that, Doss," he says. "It is what it is. Tell me about Jakey. I can hardly believe he'll be going to big school in the autumn. How's he doing?"

He watches as her anxious expression fades and changes into pleasure, pride in her grandson.

"He's doing well," she says. "He'll be going on with a lot of his friends from his primary school so that's all good. He won nearly all the prizes at the last Sports Day, which he's really thrilled about. And he's very good at maths."

Adam's demons jostle at his lips. He wants to say, "He'll be OK then. Pa would approve," but he swallows the bitter words, and drinks some coffee, disappointed by his swift negative reaction. This is going to be much harder than he hoped.

"Clem asked if we could go over for tea tomorrow," Dossie's saying. "He's got the afternoon off and he says they'd love to see you."

If Adam's smile is wry he can't help it. He doubts very much that Clem said anything of the kind but he nods and finishes his cake.

"Sounds good to me."

He sees her relief and is heartened.

Dossie feels quite weak with relief. She can't quite believe what is happening. It's as if some kind of transformation has taken place, though she can't think how or why. Were things really so bad between Adam and Pa? Of course Pa could be a very tough cookie, and relationships between fathers and sons are often difficult, but it shocks her to think of the bitterness that has pursued Adam down through the years.

Looking back, it was as if Adam always arrived at The Court armed ready for battle, and so it became a self-fulfilling prophecy. Dossie is filled with sadness, anxiety, but also with a new hope that some miracle might occur. She knows how quickly Adam can swing into defensive anger but wonders if he can be led, somehow, into a new sense of self-security and slowly regain confidence. She believes that the little family at the Retreat House might be a part of that healing — and maybe Ned and Hugo and Prune, too.

"How about a walk before supper?" she asks. "Or was getting down to the church and back enough for an old townie like you?"

He smiles lazily at her banter but doesn't rise to it.

"Sounds OK to me. I'll get my stuff in from the car."

She watches him go out, takes a huge gasping breath of relief and begins to clear the table.

72

CHAPTER
NINE

Prune steps out of the greenhouse and stands in the cool air of the early evening. She's been succession sowing: carrots, endives, purple sprouting broccoli, French beans and salad crops. It's good to come out from the warm, damp atmosphere, from the vegetative scents of earth and growing things, and breathe the heavenly perfume of the *luteum* that grows just here. How magical the gardens look with their flowing patterns and shapes and colours. Azaleas and rhododendrons, as tall as trees, follow the curve of the paths that vanish amongst the bushes; red and white magnolia blossom lies thickly scattered on the bare earth around their roots as though an exotic rug has been flung down. A blackbird hops along the top of the yew hedge, trimmed as flat as a shelf, and cocks a yellow-rimmed eye at her. Prune suspects that his nest is somewhere near and stands, unmoving, until he gives a sudden warning cry and swoops into cover. Buckets stand and a big stiff-bristle broom leans against a stone bench, and two of the gardeners appear and pick them up. They wave to Prune and she waves back. She's beginning to feel a sense of comradeship, of being part of a team, which is important to her, but she also needs these moments of separateness. It is necessary to her to be able to allow her thoughts to flow freely, to be a part of this: the peace of the gardens, the quality of absolute availability to her deeper inner world.

Prune sits for a moment on the edge of the stone bench, watching a squirrel darting amongst the delicate wood anemones and knobbly roots, and listening to the yaffle laughing up in the woods behind her. Suddenly she glimpses the flash of his green wing, his swooping flight, and she smiles with delight. She stands up and stretches, and makes ready to go home. It's lucky that it's a short enough distance for her to be able to cycle to work from the house on the quay. And tonight Hugo and Ned have invited her to go with them to The Chough for supper. It means that she'll see Ben, although he'll be working, and there will be a walk for the dogs along the way. Life is good.

Later, when she walks into the pub with Hugo and Ned, she feels a frisson of pleasure to see the way Ben's eyes widen when he sees her; the way he smiles. She deliberately hasn't texted him so as to surprise him, and she's glad now. It boosts her confidence to see his delighted reaction. Hugo is already at the bar ordering pints for himself and Ned. Before he can ask what Prune would like, Ben has produced a bottle of apple and pear juice, which is her favourite just at the moment. She smiles at him, acknowledging the fact that he's remembered, and they share a brief, private moment before she sits down with Ned.

The look the older man gives her, however, makes her suspect that perhaps it wasn't such a private moment after all, and she knows that she's blushing a bit but she can't seem to help it. Luckily a couple come to sit at the next table, which involves a slight reordering of the chairs. Hugo arrives with the drinks and the moment passes.

Prune settles herself more comfortably, Ben brings them each a menu.

"The pie of the day is steak and ale," he tells them, "and the soup is spicy tomato and lentil."

He's trying to catch her eye but she stares at the menu, not wanting to give herself away again. The two men order the pie, Prune orders gnocchi, and Ben goes back to the bar. She takes a deep breath and smiles at Hugo and Ned almost defensively but they are talking about having lunch with Dossie the next day and she relaxes.

"It's a shame that you're working and that you can't come," Hugo says to her. "I'm looking forward to seeing The Court. It sounds rather a nice old place. Of course, the church is famous for its summer music festival. The programme arrived this morning, actually. They're doing Berlioz' *L'enfance du Christ*. Martyn Brabbins is conducting . . . Mark Padmore . . . Susan Bullock . . ."

Prune's eyes drift back to Ben behind the bar as Ned and Hugo discuss the festival. Ben winks at her and she gives a little grin of pure happiness.

Ned watches these exchanges out of the corner of his eye and is filled with so many different emotions:

pleasure, amusement, sentimentality and envy. How good to be young again, and in love: to have it all before you. He leans back in his chair as fragments of conversation drift around him.

"I told him, you should see the other guy." . . . "The service was appalling. A very tiresome waitress. I said to her, 'What would be "fantastic", dear, would be if you stopped saying "fantastic".' " . . . "We've been married for forty years and I haven't found the off switch yet." . . .

Sometimes he can hardly remember his own recent past. It's odd that the later years of retirement should fade whilst a memorable run ashore in Naples, a "show-the-flag visit" to Piraeus, the two-year posting to New London, Connecticut on the Staff USN Submarine Development Squadron, should now be so vivid to him. He finds that he's thinking about Jamie. He's decided to retire from the RAF; to make the move. "Better to jump than be pushed," he said to Hugo.

Ned is seized with impotent rage on Jamie's behalf. If he does decide to cut the mooring rope, he'll be adrift for the first time in thirty years, and he'll still have his debilitating health problem to deal with, as well as huge new adjustments. Jamie has told him of how the dizziness can disturb his equilibrium; about the migraines, the occasion when he was buying a birthday card, lost his balance and fell over, crashing into a window display, and the looks of disgust and suspicion from the staff and other shoppers.

76

"They thought I was drunk," he said. "The trouble is you never know when it might creep up on you. I was going to buy a little light plane when I retired. Keep it at St Mawgan. Maybe give private flying lessons. But not now."

Ned drinks some of his local ale and wonders what Margaret would be saying now; what advice she might give. He winces at the all-too-familiar twinge of guilt that accompanies his memories of their relationship. Thank goodness she never knew about his indiscretions; his infidelity. He couldn't have had a more perfect wife: pragmatic, capable, loyal. Even when Jack was killed in the Falklands she outwardly maintained her self-control though there was a sea change, something within her radically altered. He often wondered how she managed when he was back at sea and she was alone. How strong and brave she was. He was the one who privately raged and wept at the death of his son. Ned gives a silent snort of self-disgust: he'd always been too emotional, too romantic. He controlled it, of course, stiff upper lip and all of that.

Ned takes another sip of his ale and he wonders how much Jamie is really suffering.

Hugo is thinking of Jamie, too. Ben, behind the bar, has put on some music and is miming the words to Billy Joel's "Piano Man", one of Jamie's favourites.

"You should have been a concert pianist," Jamie still tells Hugo. "You had the talent, you lucky bastard, those big hands that can stretch more than an octave."

"You know I couldn't," is his reply. "I don't have the temperament. The preparation, the expectation, would have killed me. I hate people looking at me. I prefer to be behind the camera. I'm a team player, not a soloist."

He knows that in some strange way, despite Jamie's impressive profession, his glamorous cousin slightly envied his bohemian life in London; the BBC in-jokes, and what Jamie calls his "luvvie-lefty" friends. He got on very well in that circle, and they, in turn, always loved to see him and to hear about his other world. They pulled his leg, sang "Take My Breath Away", but treated him with great respect, especially during and after the two Gulf Wars. It was good for Jamie to come to London back then, to unwind with Hugo, with these media people; chatterers who loved to be in the swim. The parties would often end up with Jamie playing jazz piano in someone's flat. Unattached women — and sometimes attached ones — fawned on him, but Jamie seemed impervious, though he often spent the night with one or other of them. "Your serious cousin," they called him because he would never drink if he were driving, or flying the next day.

"You're a risk analysis freak," Hugo would say. "You don't just have a Plan B. You have a C, D and an E . . ."

His cousin would laugh at the exaggeration. "You have to if you're a pilot," he would reply.

It puzzles Hugo that Jamie never married again — he must have had so many opportunities — and he wonders again quite what went wrong between his cousin and Emilia. He finds himself thinking about Lucy, and small Dan, and tries to imagine the scenario should she come face to face with Jamie. She is so like Emilia that it would be a shock to him. He wonders why the thought of warning Jamie that Lucy's around fills him with a kind of dread, especially just at this time when Jamie is vulnerable. Hugo reaches into his pocket for his phone to send his cousin a text, but just then the food arrives. Hugo sits back in his chair and decides to wait until after supper.

It's still light when they come out of the pub, and Hugo drives by twisting, secret lanes to the clifftop where the dogs are released and run free. Prune runs with them, laughing, leaping, encouraging them.

"How nice to be young," says Hugo, watching her whilst keeping pace with Ned's slower steps.

"And in love," adds Ned, smiling at Prune's antics, knowing how it feels to be in love: exuberant, fizzing with excitement, slightly crazy. Her mood is all because of that tall, good-looking young fellow in The Chough. Ned understands exactly what Ben and Prune are experiencing and, just at this moment, with the sun drowning in the sea and the moon rising, sharply curved as a scimitar, he would give everything he has to be young again and feel as they do.

Glancing at Hugo he sees that, though his nephew is clearly sympathetic to Prune's behaviour, there is no reminiscent stirring in his blood, no sense of envy or longing to be in love.

Perhaps, thinks Ned, it is because he's still young enough to be considered viable; to be taken seriously.

He walks slowly, leaning on his stick, and thinks of times past; of women he has known and loved who added colour and glamour and fun to his life, especially when Margaret grew distant after Jack's death. Their physical relationship had slowly dwindled into a quick hug, a comforting pat, but all her early passion seemed to die out of her. It was surprisingly lonely. He was a tactile man, an affectionate man, and to be gently, politely, but firmly repulsed was very hard. He was not proud that he continued to seek solace elsewhere, and he wonders if Hugo is doing the same when he makes those dashes away to London to see his friends.

Prune is running back to them, the dogs in close pursuit. The dusk is falling and it's cold. Ned stops walking and, taking the hint, Hugo waves to Prune, gestures back the way they have come, and they turn for home.

CHAPTER
TEN

As lunchtime approaches, Adam is surprised at how nervous he feels at the prospect of meeting Dossie's friends. He still can't quite get used to The Court without Mo and Pa: at how laid-back it feels. Nor was he prepared to find how easy it is to be with Dossie. The age gap between them seems to have vanished, she asks his opinions, his advice, and he senses her vulnerability. This especially weakens his veneer of indifference, his unapproachability. He allows his guard to drop a little, although instinctively he's waiting for criticism or rejection. Instead she makes him laugh, involves him, until he's behaving as if he has every right to be here, making decisions, helping her to organize the lunch.

Deep down, though, he's wondering about Ned and Hugo, about how to play it. He can tell that Dossie is very fond of them and he's interested to see if she's even more keen on Hugo than she's letting on. Oddly, he feels quite protective about her; he doesn't want her to get hurt.

Then Ned and Hugo arrive and it all kicks off. Adam's taken aback by Hugo's warmth and natural-ness, though when he meets Ned the old wariness returns. The older man's military bearing, the straight keen gaze and firm handshake, and Adam's a boy again, waiting to be asked how he's doing, what he's achieved, what his prospects are. But then Ned smiles at him and makes some friendly, joking remark about Dossie's cooking and the moment passes.

And now Adam sits at the end of the long table, furthest from the Aga, where Pa used to sit, and raises his glass to them and Dossie beams at him as they tuck into her delicious fish pie. Adam takes a sip of the sauvignon blanc and marvels at this extraordinary weekend that he's having. His life has turned on its head; he feels as if he's stepped through the looking-glass and everything is a different way round. Yet he can't get over the truth that it's because his parents have died that he's feeling this new affirmation, of being slowly and painfully unfrozen, and his guilt threatens his resurrection.

He smiles quickly at Ned, who is watching him with a quizzical gaze, and concentrates on the conversation between Hugo and Dossie.

"Ah," Hugo is saying, "but you've forgotten WRM."

Dossie frowns, puzzled. "WRM?"

Hugo sighs, shakes his head. "What Really Matters. Do keep up, darling," he says, and they both burst out laughing.

Ned grins at Adam. "Take no notice of them," he says. "It's rather like being a member of the Secret Seven. You have to know the codes and the passwords."

Adam laughs, too, and his pleasure expands, filling him with warmth. He can see why Dossie likes these two, though he can also see that her affection for Hugo is merely friendship, on her side at least. He's not quite so sure about Hugo. He takes a deep breath, stretches out his legs cautiously and then realizes that he's acting out of habit, back in the past, afraid of kicking one of the dogs. He is struck anew by the awareness of how hard this must be for Dossie: Pa and Mo gone, Clem remarried, no dogs. He looks at her as she stands to serve more of the fish pie, smiling at something Ned is saying, and he experiences this new and unsettling feeling of compassion. He'd had no idea that coming back to life was so confusing; so exhilarating.

From time to time Dossie glances at Adam, fearful that he will feel ill at ease, become withdrawn, but miraculously he appears perfectly relaxed. He's refilling Ned's wine glass, listening to a story Ned is telling him about a naval incident, and as he catches her eye Adam sends her a tiny wink of reassurance as if he's guessed that she might be worrying about him.

This change in her brother is nothing short of miraculous to Dossie, though she is sad that it has taken so much pain for him to reveal himself to her. They talked again last night about school, about his fear of rejection and disapproval, his resentment at what he saw as rejection by his parents. She listened to him, trying for the first time to put herself in his place, remembering that both Mo and Pa were tough, critical, products of an earlier age when self-control was absolute and you played up and played the game, even if you didn't quite know what the game was or the rules involved. Because she showed all these qualities when Mike died, because she grafted, Mo and Pa supported her, approved of her, and it's difficult for her to forget all that or that she was angry with Adam herself on quite a few occasions when he seemed selfish and uncaring.

"We're all of us damaged in one way or another," she said last night, "and none of us knows which way it might take us. We have to cope the best we can."

She was afraid to say too much, nervous about getting it wrong and spoiling this new rapport between them. Now, she wants nothing more than that Adam should feel at home here, as he never could when their parents were alive, and what could be better than this: to see him sitting there at the table, playing host to her friends? And how well he is doing it, listening to Ned, joshing with Hugo, as if he's known them for ever.

Dossie is beginning to believe, to hope, that there will be few difficulties later with Clem and Tilly and Jakey. She guesses that Adam needs to feel a member of their small family unit and will make every effort to play his part. But can it last or will some unguarded remark, some memory, throw him back into his old self?

She finishes piling more fish pie on to Ned's plate and sits down again. A thought crosses her mind.

"Where are the dogs?" she asks Hugo.

"We left them at home," he answers. "They're fine."

"You should have brought them," she says sadly. "I wasn't thinking."

"Next time." He smiles at her. "Assuming there will be one?"

"I hope there will be," says Ned promptly. "The trouble is I can't make the excuse that we never have food like this at home now that Dossie fills the freezer for us."

"So if you do a return match and ask us back," says Adam, smiling at the older man, pretending dismay, "does it mean that we still get Dossie's cooking?"

And everyone laughs.

Ned is aware of currents ebbing and flowing around him. He feels Dossie's tension and he was aware of that brief but unmistakable flinch when he shook Adam's hand. He wonders what the younger man was seeing in that moment. A greater authority, a reminder of a discipline he resented? Ned is very used to such reactions after thirty years at sea, and he also noticed the flash of hostility in Adam's eyes, as if he were preparing himself for battle, though it was over in a moment. Nevertheless, Ned wonders what was at the root of it.

He finishes his pie, raises his glass to Dossie in appreciation, and sees the resemblance to her brother as she smiles back at him. When Adam and Hugo begin to talk about London — recent exhibitions, films, concerts — Ned notices, too, that Dossie is clearly unaware of her brother's interests in the arts. She listens, watching Adam's face, as if she is searching for something she has been missing and is only just beginning to learn and understand.

"Of course you must come to us for lunch or for supper," Hugo is saying. "When do you go back to London, Adam?"

"Tomorrow afternoon," Adam answers, rather regretfully.

"But you were saying that you have some leave due?" Dossie reminds him, almost eagerly.

Adam raises his eyebrows, as if he is surprised and touched that she should remember it.

"Yes." He hesitates. "Well, yes I have."

It's not as if he is unwilling to commit himself, thinks Ned, watching him, but rather as if he can't quite believe that he'll be welcome here. But even on his short acquaintance with Dossie this is almost too bizarre for Ned to contemplate and once again he wonders what has gone before.

"Excellent," says Hugo. "We can make a date. You can meet Prune."

"And the dogs," adds Dossie. "You'll love the dogs, Adam."

"Oh, no." Adam pretends to groan. "Don't get started on dogs."

And the conversation immediately turns on whether Dossie should have a dog and, if so, which breed, puppy or rescue, and finishes with the delightful suggestion that they should all meet at The Chough next day for Sunday lunch before Adam heads back to London.

Ned finishes his wine with satisfaction. It's being a very good day, and lunch at The Chough tomorrow will round the weekend off perfectly.

Lucy, sitting in the corner with her friends, sees Hugo come into the pub and wonders whether to speak to him. She hesitates. It's just a tad embarrassing that she's forgotten to mention him to Mum, and anyway, he seems to be with quite a group of people so perhaps it's best just to keep quiet.

She sits back a little, so that she is half hidden by one of her companions, and gets on with her lunch. It's becoming a bit of a habit, eating out while the kitchen at the cottage is being disassembled, and she's enjoying herself. It'll be good, though, to get home to Geneva and to be with Tom again. For the last few weeks it's been a bit like being a kid, moving round with Dad on different film locations, or staying in Granny's flat in London, where there were always random people dropping by, sleeping on cushions or in a sleeping bag on the floor if she had friends stopping over. There was always something going on, a bit of a party.

It's like that at the cottage at the moment, but Dan is loving every moment of it and luckily the beds have arrived at last, so Mum will have somewhere to sleep when she comes down next week. Instinctively Lucy glances across to the table by the inglenook but Hugo is sitting with his back to her, talking to a woman with silvery blonde hair and a man who looks as if he might be her brother. There's a much younger girl with them, and an older man.

Lucy settles back again. She won't disturb Hugo but she will definitely tell Mum about him. After all, she'll be here on Tuesday and they might want to get together. It'll be nice for her to meet an old friend, not that she's short of friends, but even so . . .

It can't always have been easy for Mum at the end, once Dad stopped getting so many good parts and started drinking too much. She never had any kind of career herself, always occupied with Dad, and then with Granny, who worked until she died.

And, of course, thinks Lucy, looking after me. Amongst all that boho chaos Mum was always there for me.

She glances rather guiltily at Dan. The nanny is already all lined up for when Lucy starts work full time in the autumn. There will be no Mummy to meet Dan from school, no Granny to be dropped off with in an emergency, but that's the way life is now. It is what it is. Danny will be fine; just fine. And meanwhile there's the cottage in Rock for wonderful holidays. He'll learn to surf and walk the cliffs, and the memories will stay with him all his life; just like hers are of theatres and film studios and Granny's flat off the King's Road.

Her group are getting ready to leave. She glances again at Hugo but he and his friends are all tucking into the roast beef, talking and laughing together, so that Lucy and Dan are able to slip by unnoticed. Outside, however, Lucy takes out her phone and sends a text:

Hi Mum. Just met an old friend of yours called Hugo. Says you knew each other in Bristol back in the day. All great here. See you soon. Love from us both. xx

There. That's done and everything is fine. Just fine.

The Chough is very busy and Hugo is enjoying himself talking to Adam, discovering all sorts of things about this man who is Dossie's brother. Hugo wasn't prepared for Adam's passion for film, for art, and his questions about Hugo's work are intelligent. He's seen some of Hugo's documentaries and is fascinated by the people he has interviewed and worked with. His reading is extensive, to the extent that Hugo suspects that Adam has never really fulfilled his ambitions. He suggests this gently, almost jokingly, but Adam agrees very readily.

"I have to say," he answers, "that this isn't quite where I saw myself at this age, but to be honest, back then, I was just really grateful to get into a top London agency. I didn't do that well at school and I wouldn't have got to a first-rate university. I couldn't cope with my father going on about it. You know? Those conversational pin-pricks? 'Well, we can't all go to Cambridge.' Or, 'So remind me. Where's Reading again?' Not really meaning it, of course, but that, 'Oh, come on. Can't you take a joke?' thing that makes you feel that not only are you a failure but that you haven't got a sense of humour either."

Adam speaks lightly, almost dismissively, about the past, but Hugo can see that there is real, hidden damage here. He is aware that Ned, Prune and Dossie are deep in conversation and he wonders how to react to this unexpected confidence. He wants to show sympathy, to draw parallels with his own aloof, successful barrister father, who regarded the BBC as some kind of left-wing kindergarten for underachieving adults and hoped that Hugo would go into the Foreign Office.

All the while, however, he is aware of Dossie and wondering at what point she might suddenly take part in the conversation. Hugo knows how fond she was of her father and he fears this could be embarrassing and awkward.

"Next time I'm in London," he says to Adam, "I'll take you in and introduce you around," and Adam looks pleased.

Then Ben arrives to take their order for pudding, and the difficult moment passes.

CHAPTER
ELEVEN

Emilia turns, struggles into consciousness, disturbed by loud harsh cries. She raises herself and then falls back on her pillow with a smile: it's the gulls wheeling over the estuary, screaming to each other as they swoop above the cottage. She lies still, readjusting to her surroundings, remembering that she's here in Rock, in Lucy's spare bedroom. She raises her arm so as to peer at her watch and groans: twenty past five. Not even Danny will be awake at twenty past five, but she knows that she won't be able to go back to sleep now, not even if she begins silently to recite one of the longer speeches from her mother's Shakespearean repertoire, which has always been a good method for inducing sleep. She was invaluable when it came to listening to Mama's lines: prompting her when necessary, which wasn't often, or simply reading the other part, quietly, expressionlessly, so that Mama knew her cues.

Well, there's no Mama now, no Papa off to rehearsals or to a concert; no Nigel dashing away to Elstree or a film location. She's alone in London, whilst Lucy and Tom and darling Danny are living in Geneva. Emilia shifts, rolls on to her side. She misses them all and especially she misses the magical world of the theatre;

the emotional backstage scenes, the rows and the bitching, the extravagant making up afterwards, and the general madness of it all. Dear old Mama had kept going until she'd dropped down quite suddenly between Acts One and Two of *The Importance of Being Earnest*, and now it is as if life has been put on hold. It's rather colourless and dreary, and it's a relief to come down here, to be with Lucy and Danny before they go back to Geneva and she stays on to oversee the installation of the new kitchen.

She feels restless, something nagging slightly at the back of her mind, and she sits up, swings her legs out of bed and looks around. The room is not yet fully furnished. There's not too much spare cash and, for the moment, Emilia is making do with the bed, which is very comfortable, a small, upright, rush-seated chair and a rather nice, if battered, old pine chest that Lucy found in a second-hand shop, which has a mirror propped on top of it.

Emilia hesitates, sitting on the edge of the bed. She can't risk waking Lucy and Danny by having a shower but she feels a desire to be outside, to be walking. Quickly she stands up and drags on the clothes she discarded yesterday, peers into the mirror and brushes her tangled hair, and then, very cautiously, she opens her bedroom door and stands listening. There is no sound. Quietly, oh so quietly, she crosses the landing and creeps down the stairs, praying that no boards will creak.

She longs for coffee but the requirement to be outside is more imperative than her need for caffeine, so she takes Lucy's fleecy jacket from its hook, lets herself out of the front door and closes it gently behind her. There is no anxiety in her mind about leaving it unlocked. This is Rock; it is half past five in the morning and there is nobody around. Emilia walks down to the beach, her hands in the pockets of the jacket. She feels dissatisfied, restless. It's odd how rootless she feels since Mama died. Even after Nigel died there was still Mama's work, her friends, her routines. There remained that aura that surrounded her mother, which always included Emilia: the recognition wherever Mama went, that touch of glamour, the excited whispers, of having attention focused on her, which spilled out and included whomever was with her. Her mother had the talent to make people believe that she cared about them. She remembered the faces of those who had worked for her, the names of their children and their dogs.

"Hardly rocket science for an actress, darling, is it?" she'd murmur *sotto voce* to Emilia after some flattered, delighted fan or stagehand remarked on her wonderful memory, and Emilia would want to choke on her suppressed laughter. It was the same with Nigel in the glory days. How good he was at it: the deprecating smile in a restaurant when there was a little fluttering sound of applause as they were shown to their table; the little wave of the hand to some adoring fan smiling hopefully at him in the street.

Emilia stands looking across the estuary at the boats at their moorings, keel to keel with their reflections.

The trouble is, she thinks, it's like a drug. This need to be the centre of attention, not caring what people think whilst pretending that you love them. What shall I do without it?

There's another thought at the back of her mind, which she doesn't want to acknowledge: a sense of guilt and uneasiness that has begun to surface recently, ever since she got Lucy's text saying that she'd met Hugo. It knocked her off balance, flung her back to a past she didn't want to think about. She digs her hands more deeply into her pockets whilst memories nibble at her reluctant consciousness: Hugo in Bristol, taking her to concerts, to parties, to the zoo up on the Downs.

Mama was playing in a Shakespeare season at the Old Vic; Gertrude, Lady Macbeth. Hugo came regularly to the performances and Emilia first met him backstage with a friend who knew one of the young actors in the company. They all went out for coffee and it was rather sweet to see how stage-struck, how star-struck Hugo was. He was so simple, so open and thoroughly nice — and very attractive. He thought her mother was wonderful, and impressed that her father was principal flautist in the Bournemouth Symphony Orchestra.

"I think he's in love with all of us at once," Mama said, when she met him after a matinee. "Do be kind to him, darling Milly." And she *was* kind to him, enjoyed his company, made him happy, and, just occasionally, wondered if they might have a future together — until Jamie came on the scene.

Emilia gives a little shiver, wraps her arms across her breast, and then turns with a start as someone shouts her name. Dan is running across the sand with Lucy following a short way behind him.

"Granny," he shouts. "We couldn't find you." He flings himself at her knees and she bends to pick him up and swing him round. He laughs down at her, his dark brown eyes merry, and her heart is constricted with love and anxiety — and something else that she doesn't quite recognize yet.

"We thought you'd run away," laughs Lucy, panting up behind him, "but you didn't leave a note so we decided to try the beach. Are you OK?"

"Absolutely fine," declares Emilia. "Couldn't resist coming out to smell the ozone, but I'm dying for coffee. Didn't want to wake you up earlier."

"Dan hasn't had anything yet either," says Lucy. "Come on. Let's go home and have some breakfast."

She glances sideways at her mother as they cross the lane and go back into the cottage. Mum's been just a tad odd since she arrived in Cornwall: kind of distracted, preoccupied. She's been a bit like it since Granny died, selling the house and moving back to the flat off the King's Road, almost as if she's hoping to resurrect old times. Of course she's missing all of them: Dad, Granny and Gramps, but Mum seems quite capable of containing grief or sadness. Dad's death hadn't come as a shock. He'd been drinking heavily and his liver was shot to pieces. Lucy's really sad that he never met Tom, or saw Dan. He was a loving, neglectful, fun kind of father and she still misses his silly jokes, his childlike love of attention, of admiration. Yet both her parents sometimes seemed like strangers: disorganized, hedonistic, devil-may-care. For herself, she likes order, continuity, security. Perhaps it is the result of her chaotic upbringing.

"Your mum's an odd one," Tom once said. "It's as if she's acting a part. She knows how a bereaved person ought to behave and that's how she does it, but I'm not sure she really feels anything. She should have been an actress like her mother."

Lucy remembers how she protested, shocked by his observation, yet at the same time she recognized that there was a spark of truth in what he was saying. Just lately her mother behaves as if she's not quite sure what her role is any more. For so long she was a part of the crazy media circus that surrounded Granny, Dad and, at one remove, Gramps, but now she seems slightly lost. Lucy believes that she's moved back into Granny's flat in the hope that it will restore her sense of belonging: to keep her connected to the world she knows and loves best.

Of course it was rather a pity that Tom was offered the job in Geneva, which took them away from London just after Granny died. Though, as Lucy points out, it really isn't that far — only a quick hop on to a plane — but she knows it's not the same as Mum being closer at hand, being more involved in what Dan is doing. Deep down, however, Lucy knows that her mother is more interested in going to first nights and end-of-run parties than being maternal. Sometimes she feels resentful and hurt about this but most of the time she accepts it. It is as it is. Her own upbringing was bohemian, but full of love from different quarters, and her own career in marketing is important to her, so she can't really sit in judgement.

Even so, she can sense this slight change in her mother's behaviour and she hopes that these next few weeks here at the cottage might settle her down a bit.

"You're sure you'll be all right, Mum?" she asks, as she swings Dan into his high chair and goes to the fridge to get him some milk. "You really don't mind being here on your own?"

"Of course not. But you must leave proper instructions about everything. I'm not taking any responsibility if the cooker's not the one you ordered or the units are the wrong colour."

"Don't worry. Everyone's been briefed and I shall be in touch with them all the time. I'm sorry to leave you with the chaos but I have to go back for this meeting and to check things at home. We'll be here again soon and if there's a real emergency one of us will come straight over."

"It's not a problem," her mother says placidly. "It'll be a wonderful excuse for eating out all the time."

Lucy laughs. "I believe you. I bet the minute we're gone you'll invite all your mates down from London and have barbecues and picnics. You'd like that, wouldn't you, Danny? Perhaps I ought to leave you with Granny."

"Yes," says Dan, beaming at them, banging his cup on the tray. "Stay with Granny."

"What d'you say to that then, Mum?"

"Not on your life," comes the prompt answer. "Not without a working kitchen. Actually, not even with a working kitchen. No, no. I'm a hedonist. I shall eat out and thoroughly enjoy myself."

"And maybe," Lucy says teasingly, "you'll meet up with that guy you knew. Hugo, isn't it? You obviously made an impression on him, back in the day."

And there again is that odd, fleeting expression on her mother's face: wariness, speculation. Then Dan drops his cup on the floor and screams, and Lucy is distracted.

CHAPTER
TWELVE

Dossie drives across New Bridge, glancing down at the River Camel where little boats swing at their moorings as the tide makes, on past Wadebridge and then she heads out on the road to Padstow. She's looking forward to seeing Janna, her old friend and ally, to talk over Adam's visit. Janna cares for the few remaining elderly Sisters at Chi-Meur, and her take on life is always direct and often amusing.

Dossie drives through the lanes that lead to Peneglos, turns in past the Lodge House where Clem, Tilly and Jakey live, and slows down. They'll all be at work or at school at this time of the day but it's worth a quick knock on the door. There's no answer so she gets back into the car and sets off again along the drive. She passes in front of the old house with its stone-mullioned windows and stout oaken door, and round to the Coach House, which was converted for the use of the Sisters when the convent became a retreat house. Janna has her own quarters at the end of the Coach House, with its own entrance through a little courtyard. This way she is able to retain her independence and privacy, which are very important to her. Despite her devotion to the Sisters, Dossie knows that Janna still likes popping over to Padstow to see her old mates, to have a beer with them. She is a wild, free spirit and six years at Chi-Meur hasn't changed that.

Janna is in the courtyard, watering the pots and tubs that are filled with flowers and herbs: tall red and yellow tulips, gold-brown wallflowers, silken-faced pansies, chives, thyme. She waves as Dossie climbs out of the car.

"How gorgeous," cries Dossie. "It's looking so pretty. We can have our coffee out here. I've brought cakes."

She hugs Janna, who is dressed in layered Indian cotton garments of scarlet and indigo, curly hair tied up with a scarf, and still looks like the traveller who arrived, walking along the cliffs and into Chi-Meur, all those years ago.

"Blown in on a westerly," said Sister Emily, smiling with delight, "and what a wonderful day for us it was."

Dossie follows Janna inside. The room is not large but it has a kitchen corner with a breakfast bar, a small wood-burning stove and a comfortable sofa covered with a piece of plum-coloured velvet. A door gives access into the rest of the Coach House. Dossie knows that Janna likes this compact space; she is happy here. The little courtyard is her special joy. This, plus the view from her bedroom window, which looks beyond the cliffs to the sea, gives her a necessary sense of freedom.

"So how was Adam?" asks Janna, going straight to the point as she makes coffee. "Did he persuade you to sell up and split the proceeds?"

"No," answers Dossie slowly. "It was really odd. Nothing like I was expecting. We had several long talks about how it was for him as a child, how unhappy he was at school and how bitterly hurt he was that Mo and Pa didn't seem to notice or care."

She reaches for one of Janna's pretty hand-painted plates and sets out the little cakes. She still can't quite come to terms with Adam's volte-face: this unexpected Adam, who is amusing, thoughtful, even kind. Janna is watching her curiously and Dossie shakes her head, shrugs.

"I know. It's weird. I was utterly dreading it. Well, I told you that. And then he was different. He said it was because there was no expectation any more. Nobody questioning him about why he wasn't achieving more, doing better. I had no idea that it was so awful for him. I mean, I know Pa could be difficult and tough, but I just didn't realize what a negative effect it had on Adam, or that he was so miserable at school. Pa didn't have much time for people who whined about life being tough. He'd say that it was character building. I think the six years between me and Adam probably didn't help back then. I was a teenager by the time he was beginning prep school so I was probably totally self-absorbed. It's just so tragic because I know they loved him so much. I mean, how can that happen? I remember talking about it to Mo once and saying it must be to do with genetics, and that Adam was just completely different from the rest of us, but now I'm beginning to wonder . . . God, it would break my heart if Clem didn't know how much I love him. Or Jakey."

"No fear of that, my lover," says Janna, picking up the tray and carrying it out into the courtyard. "Jakey was over here yesterday with that old dog of theirs and telling me about the tea party you all had together. Seems to me like he definitely reckons Adam. They played football out in the lane."

Dossie follows her and sits at the wooden table. She smiles at the thought of Jakey and his black Labrador, Bells, visiting Janna. Jakey has loved Janna since he was a little boy of four. Back then Dossie wished that Clem and Janna would fall in love but now she knows it would never have worked. They remain very good friends, though, and Tilly has been welcomed into that relationship. Dossie is always very glad to know that Clem's marriage has had no negative effect on his earlier friendship with Janna.

"We were lucky to find Bells," Dossie says. "Yes, it was a great tea party. Tilly was brilliant. How I love that girl."

She sips her coffee and looks around at the pretty courtyard, breathing in the heavenly scent of the wallflowers. She loves it here. Janna, the wanderer, the traveller, has been able to create a place of peace and security, to make her visitors feel special, and Dossie is grateful for her friendship.

Janna watches her; sees her relax. She knows how hard Dossie is working to create this new relationship with her son and grandson, to make Tilly feel welcomed and loved, and to allow them the space they need to grow

102

together. It must be difficult not to drive over to the Lodge on an impulse with some special treat, not to look after Jakey while Clem works, not to organize birthdays and be available; to step back from that central space in their lives, which has been hers for the last ten years. Especially now that her parents have died and she is alone.

It would be good, Janna thinks, if Adam were able to fill some of the emptiness that Dossie is now finding in her life.

"So when's he coming back again, then?" she asks. "I've never met this brother of yours. You must bring him over."

She can see that Dossie is thinking about it, with pleasure and surprise that this might now be a possibility.

"I'd like to," she says. "I'll bring him over for coffee and we'll have a moment."

Janna smiles: Dossie and her moments. Coffee moments, cake moments, moments of love and laughter.

"The amazing thing," Dossie says, "is that he's got some leave due and he says he'll come down for it. I could hardly believe it. I actually think he wouldn't have asked but it got mentioned when we were having lunch with Hugo and Ned."

"Aha," says Janna. "Hugo and Ned. Thought they'd be cropping up before too long."

"Oh, shut up," says Dossie, laughing. "I told you. They're just mates."

Janna thinks back to Dossie's last disastrous love affair with a man who allowed her to believe his wife was dead. The discovery of the truth was a terrible shock and Janna was full of rage on Dossie's behalf. Dossie was devastated. At least there is no sign of that madness — the joy and irrepressible happiness that falling in love brings — when she talks about Ned and Hugo.

"You could bring them to tea, too," offers Janna slyly. "Just so I could give them the once-over."

"I might just do that," says Dossie. She glances around her. "They have a courtyard rather like this but they haven't got your green fingers." She pushes the plate of cakes towards Janna. "So how are the Sisters? Are they behaving themselves?"

Janna chuckles. "Do they ever? It's a terrible hard thing to keep them on the straight and narrow. Especially Sister Emily."

"No change there then," says Dossie.

She stretches and leans back in her chair, closing her eyes in the sunshine. Janna sees that she looks peaceful, that some of the strain of the last year has left her face. As she watches her, Janna really hopes that things might just stay quietly like this for a while, with no alarms, no changes, no expectations: just this peaceful moment in the sun extending out calmly into their lives. Dossie stretches again, sits up, reaches for another cake, turns and grins at her.

"Do you ever get the feeling," she asks happily, hopefully, biting into her cake with relish, "that something really good is about to happen?"

104

Janna's heart quails a little. Her hopes begin to vanish. She recognizes that look and generally it means trouble.

Prune stands up and glances around her. She senses some kind of change: a shiver of wind, a cloud hiding the sun. She's just finished planting out beans brought on in the glasshouse. The soil has warmed up during these last few weeks and it's ideal now for outdoor sowing. It's also the right time for the Chelsea Crop — named for the Chelsea Flower Show — for chopping back half of certain perennials to prolong flower. So far she's only attempted some goldenrod but she's pleased with the day's work.

Prune gazes over the gardens, inhaling the scent of the yellow *luteum,* instinctively huddling against a gust of wind that stirs the rhododendron leaves, so that they clap together, and whirls the blossom to the ground. In the west, clouds are beginning to stack, giant pillows of grey and white. She thinks about Ben, wishing they had more independence. Ben lives in at the pub, and she knows that he's still very slightly shy at the thought of meeting Ned and Hugo on their home ground. Slowly, satisfactorily, their relationship is developing and somehow she must persuade him, try to break the ice, so that he can come back to hers and they can spend time together.

Prune closes up the glasshouses, walks through the gardens, and collects her bicycle from the estate office. She cycles away, down the drive and along the lane that runs beneath the high granite walls of the estate. The wind is rising, buffeting her as she pedals, and she feels the first few drops of rain. It's chill now, but she pauses for a moment on the quay to watch the cloud towers forming and toppling along the horizon. She still feels that sense of change in the air: it's unsettling, challenging. The tide is out and the boats lie stranded on the mud, no life beneath their hulls, mooring ropes slack. Another flurry of rain, a stronger blast of wind, and she hurries to put her bicycle into the little shed and let herself into the house.

She calls out, "I'm back." Mort barks and she hears Hugo's voice reassuring him. It's good to be home.

PART TWO

PART TWO

CHAPTER
THIRTEEN

Jamie drives his MGB out of RAF Brize Norton and heads south for the A361. He has planned this moment: his last Dining-In in the Mess, his last Happy Hour to say farewell to his friends, his last meeting with his squadron commander. He's closed up his cottage and packed his bag, and now he's driving south-west to Cornwall.

Until this moment he's always had a sense of purpose. His life was organized, planned, controlled, certain. Now the only true security left to him is Ned and Hugo. His instinct is to go home to them. He's measured out his life in homecomings. A successful career is one, with the same number of take-offs as landings. Well, he's certainly achieved that. He can still remember his first flights in the Bulldog at Bristol University Air Squadron and the calm voice of his instructor saying, "You see those trees, Tremayne? The runway's on the other side of them so be a good chap and put the power on." He recalls the exhilaration of his first solo, his instructor saying, as they rolled down the taxiway, "Stop here, Jamie. I'm hopping out. Go and do a circuit on your own," and that terrifying, glorious feeling of setting off into the sky with nobody sitting there beside him. Back then, each time he had a good day it was such an extraordinary feeling that he could believe he was invincible, a living embodiment of pure joy.

He passes through Broughton Poggs, heading south towards Swindon, and by the time he joins the M4 at Junction 15 he's listening to Dire Straits, eleven minutes into "Telegraph Road", and he's ready to motor. As he accelerates on to the motorway he reflects that at least he is still able to drive, though it is hedged about with fear. He is always aware, ready for the hint of giddiness that foreshadows a vertigo attack, and he's learned to recognize the first signs in good time. He needs to watch his speed. It's so easy to find he's doing eighty without realizing it, and especially to this particular track. He's chosen it to give him a boost. "Telegraph Road" was a favourite of his and Hugo's in the eighties and it reminds him of those days when they were young, and full of hope and confidence.

Perhaps it is because of their shared past that he and Hugo remain close. They share so many memories: jokes, school, the loss of parents, the break-up of relationships. He envied Hugo his bohemian life in London. His cousin has so many friends; people gravitate towards Hugo, love him, pour out their troubles, make him godfather to their children.

Jamie glances at the clock and decides that he'll stop at the Gordano services for a snack and a breather. He intended to text Hugo with a rough ETA but he was too anxious to get going, to be on his way, to remember

110

to do it. Not that it really matters. He'll let Hugo and Ned know as he nears Cornwall. They are aware that these days he makes regular stops, doesn't push himself. He made it sound quite casual.

"I'll see the boss mid-morning," he told Hugo, "and then be on my way."

"Be careful," admonished his cousin. "Don't let that crazy car get away with you. You still drive far too fast. No rolls at zero feet."

"Don't worry," Jamie answered. "I'm not planning on it."

"That's what worries me," said Hugo.

Jamie smiles, remembering Hugo as a small boy at school with his unruly mop of hair and wide eyes: angelic in his blue cassock and white ruff, devastated by the death of his mother. His own parents were abroad — British Council — and he and Hugo often travelled together to the house on the quay for half terms or to meet up with his family for holidays. The house was a constant, a point of reference in their lives, and he rather envied Hugo for being able to retire there, looking after Uncle Ned, taking the dogs for walks up on the cliffs.

But then again, he thought, look at me. Squadron Leader James Tremayne Retired: emphasis on the "Retired". He buries the thought at once, not wishing to let the resentment rise again.

Jamie wonders how much Hugo misses his life in London, how easy it's been for him to move on. It will be good to have a catch-up.

★ ★ ★

Back on the road, after half an hour's stop at Gordano, he switches the CD to Jacques Loussier's *Play Bach* and heads south. He's slowing down for some roadworks on the hard shoulder when he notices the brown tourist sign indicating left to Wells Cathedral, Glastonbury Abbey and Tor at Junction 23. On a sudden impulse, as he reaches the junction, he checks his mirror and swings on to the slip road, then turns left towards Wells. He's surprised at himself — he's not given to unconsidered actions — but he surrenders himself to it, driving roads he hasn't travelled for forty years, until at last he arrives in the town.

He parks on Cathedral Green, climbs out and stands looking at the cathedral, remembering how he always thought that the two towers look unfinished, as if their steeples have been whipped away. A small boy whizzes past on a little scooter and young mothers stroll with buggies. He leans into the car for his stick, and locks the door. As he crosses the grass he can hear the faint sound of music and he sees that there is a new public entrance, very smart in wood and glass. He follows the corridor in, drops a five-pound note into the begging box and now he is in the West Cloister, the big door is open, and he can hear the organ: Bach's Prelude and Fugue No. 2 in C minor, which he's been listening to in the car but in a very different form. It is quiet in here but not still. People are moving around, some with guidebooks in their hands, some going about their church business, and a group of singers are arriving,

112

mustering round their conductor, discussing their programme.

Jamie stands, leaning on his stick, gazing up at the magnificent scissor beams supporting the pillars of the crossing tower. He's forgotten how spectacular, how unique, it all is. And it's odd that everything should appear bigger than he remembers. Usually it's the other way about: places seem so much smaller after years of absence. It's as if it's all been waiting for him, unchanged, unmoving, for the last forty years. Then quite unexpectedly his memory plays a trick and he sees the nave full of parents: mothers in smart outfits, heels clicking on the flags, fathers with city suits bundled under warm overcoats. The choirboys, jostling, whispering as they wait, and the choirmaster muttering, "Settle down, boys, settle down." The dying away of chatter, complete silence, and then "Once in royal David's city" . . . That lone, pure voice. The year he was Head Chorister it was Hugo's voice . . .

Suddenly the clock strikes the quarter-hour, jolting him back from the past. He remembers the clock — another old friend — the jousting knights that herald each fifteen minutes of the day, rushing round the clock face whilst the Quarter Jack bangs out each quarter with his heels. Tourists stop to listen, whilst the members of the choral society have now assembled themselves into a group in the choir stalls.

He hoped, way back, that his own children might come here to school; that he and Emilia would come to hear them perform. Perhaps they would have played the piano, as he did, sung in the choir, and his heart aches with a sense of emptiness, of loss. The young organist, with his co-opted page turner — both, no doubt, from the school — has finished his Bach and is quietly playing the hymn "Dear Lord and Father of mankind". To Jamie's surprise he is able to remember the words to the first verse ". . . forgive our foolish ways, re-clothe us in our rightful mind, in purer lives thy service find, in deeper reverence, praise . . ." but now the group is ready to rehearse. The conductor raises his hands. The voices rise: "My soul, my soul, there is a country . . ." Hubert Parry's *Songs of Farewell*.

Jamie stands, listening. How is it that music can throw you back to the past like this, reminding you of lost hopes, failed dreams? He sees again the bleak, utilitarian office and the sombre face of the senior medical officer as he delivered his verdict.

"I think it's time to face facts, Jamie. We've done everything we can; you've taken every test available. I don't know how long it will take for these symptoms to subside — if they ever do. I can't even say for sure what it is that's wrong. I can't pass you fit for duty, let alone flying duty. Realistically, I think it's time for you to think about what you're going to do next."

The rest of the interview was just noise as far as Jamie was concerned.

". . . be sure to support you . . . access to medical care . . . write to your Squadron Commander . . ."

He became aware that the doc had finished speaking. There was nothing left to add.

"Thank you, sir."

114

He stood, put on his cap and, as he prepared to salute, realized that the Wing Commander was already up and out of his seat, his hand extended in friendship. They shook hands.

"I'm sorry, Jamie. You will let me know if you need anything."

He nodded, turned and walked out through the medical centre into the car park. It was raining . . .

The voices of the choir rise: ". . . Thy God, Thy life, Thy cure" — and the anthem ends. Jamie wheels abruptly, goes out and across the Green to the car. He gets in, makes a three-point turn, and drives back out of the town towards Glastonbury. Before he reaches the M5 he pulls into the side of the road and takes out his phone.

Got delayed. ETA 18.00. En route.

He waits for a moment, guessing that Hugo will be on the alert for messages, and almost instantly a text pings in:

Three green lights. Cleared for landing.

Jamie smiles — Hugo always gets RAF jargon wrong — puts his phone away, and heads for Cornwall.

By the time he arrives, nearly three hours later, he is exhausted; near the limits of what his disability will permit. He pulls in beside the Volvo and sits for a moment, with the engine switched off, before he climbs

115

out of the car and stands still, head bowed, steadying himself. He breathes in the fresh salty air, listening to the gulls, but before he can set off towards the front door it opens and Hugo is there, coming out, hugging him.

"What kept you?" asks Jamie, disguising his uprush of affection at the sight of his cousin, pretending casualness.

"You can hear your car coming a mile off," answers Hugo. "Took your time, didn't you?"

Jamie struggles between truth or a bluff and decides on the truth.

"I stopped off at Wells," he says. "Made a detour and went to see the cathedral."

Hugo is staring at him in pleased amazement. "Really? What a fantastic thing to do. It's weird, isn't it, going back? I've done it once or twice. Went in for choral evensong a couple of times."

"I was too early for that," says Jamie. "But the members of a choral society were practising. They were good. It was very . . . moving. They sang Parry's *Songs of Farewell*."

Hugo smiles at him, his eyes full of understanding. Very quietly he begins to sing: " 'My soul, my soul . . .' "

"Shut up," says Jamie, thumping him on the arm. "I've had enough nostalgia for one day."

He opens the passenger door, heaves out his bags, and together they carry them into the house.

Ned stands up as Jamie comes into the kitchen and stretches out his hand. Since Jamie was a small boy

116

they have shaken hands at meetings and departures, and even now Ned cannot quite bring himself to hug these boys of his, much though he loves them. His generation was not brought up to hug and he feels uncomfortable with it. He grips Jamie's hand, pats his shoulder, noticing that his nephew still has that tough youthful look that is part of his genetic inheritance. He feels a mix of pride, affection and a huge sympathy, though he shows none of these things but merely makes enquiries about the journey whilst Hugo holds up a bottle of gin with an expectant look on his face.

"A small one," answers Jamie in response. "I'm still not good with alcohol but a small one would be great. After all, I shan't be going anywhere."

Ned thinks of, and dismisses, several questions that seem banal in the light of Jamie's health problems and is relieved when Jamie crouches to make a fuss of the dogs, allowing himself to be licked and welcomed by Mort and especially Brioc. From a puppy upwards, Brioc has always had a very special affection for Jamie. Out of all the family he is Brioc's favourite. Nobody quite understands why, but it is necessary for Jamie to make a special fuss of him before standing up to take his glass.

"He stopped off at Wells," Hugo is saying. "Went to have a look at the old place. Pity he didn't catch a choral evensong. I must admit it made me quite weepy when I did that."

As the cousins begin to reminisce, to banter and joke, Ned watches them with love, and a terrible sadness, as he tries to imagine Jack being here with them; his own boy, the victim of war at so young an age. He is glad that Hugo and Jamie are not noticing his pain, which strikes so fresh, so sharp, despite the passing of the years. These two boys — he still thinks of them as boys — are a comfort to him but his own son is irreplaceable. The ghost boy has grown with him through the years. He's imagined him as a married man, a father, at moments like this with Hugo and Jamie.

Hugo is handing him a glass and he takes it and raises it to Jamie.

"It's good to have you home again," he says — and he sees, just for a moment, an odd expression on Jamie's face: a mix of surprise, pleasure, and finally acknowledgement that, yes, this old house on the quay, with its warren of rooms, is his home.

"Thanks," Jamie says. "To be completely honest I couldn't think of anywhere else to go. Handing in my ID card and then going back to the cottage seemed a tad tame. Anticlimactic, if you see what I mean. Coming down here just felt the right thing to do."

"I'm glad to hear it," answers Ned. "And I hope you'll make it a long stay. We've got a lot of catching up to do." He sees the flash of bleakness in Jamie's eyes, glimpses the younger man's suffering, and swiftly attempts to deflect it. "For instance," he says, sitting down again, "I've always wondered how you managed to remain being called Jamie throughout your career. I always understood that the RAF could only manage words of one syllable."

He sees the smile that begins in the corners of Jamie's eyes, his amusement and acknowledgement of the old inter-services raillery.

"I won't disillusion you," he answers. " 'Never let the truth get in the way of a good dit.' Isn't that what you say in the navy?"

"Oh, stop it, both of you," groans Hugo. "You've only been here five minutes, and don't say, 'He started it,' either. Perhaps I should have joined the army and kept you both in your place."

"The army!" Jamie begins to laugh. "You know what they say in the army? 'Mind over matter. We don't mind and you don't matter.' No, I should think the BBC was quite cut-throat enough, from what you've told us over the years. Are you missing it much?"

"He doesn't have a chance to miss it," Ned answers, before Hugo can speak. "Most of its employees seem to spend half their time down here."

"Once a meejia man, always a meejia man, darling," agrees Hugo. "I need my fix."

Jamie begins to laugh and Ned sees that he is back on firmer ground, the bad moment has passed. He relaxes more comfortably in his chair and sips appreciatively at his gin and tonic.

The front door opens, a voice shouts, "Hi, only me," the dogs rush out, and Hugo says: "Oh, good. Now you'll meet our Prune."

Ned watches Jamie's face as Prune comes into the kitchen escorted by Mort and Brioc. That look — assessing, slightly wary — is typical of a man who is slow to give his trust. Prune is looking similarly

119

cautious. They shake hands and Hugo hurries to smooth over the awkward moment by asking Prune if she's had a good day, if she'd like a drink.

"Not that sort," she answers, glancing at their glasses, rolling her eyes. She looks at Jamie and ventures a joke. "It's rather like being a student again, living here. But you knew that already."

His eyes narrow with amusement and he holds up his glass. "Why else would I be here? The question is, how long will the gin hold out?"

She shakes her head reproachfully. "That is such a First World problem."

There is a little surprised silence, then Jamie roars with laughter, and Ned realizes that he's been holding his breath, hoping so much that Jamie and Prune will hit it off together.

"Our Prune is very fierce," Hugo is telling Jamie. "Very sensible about what she drinks and eats."

Jamie raises his eyebrows. "Knitted cabbage?" he asks her sympathetically — and she bursts out laughing.

"I can see I shall get no help from you," she says. "It's like being back at home with my brothers. Thank goodness for Dossie."

"Dossie?" Jamie looks enquiringly.

"Dossie is the most amazing cook," Hugo tells him — and Ned detects the least hint of embarrassment in his voice. "She runs a business called Fill the Freezer and keeps us supplied with delicious food."

"But not knitted cabbage, so don't worry," says Prune. "Lots of pies and puddings and cake. And she's gorgeous, too."

"I like the sound of Dossie," says Jamie, with a grin. "When do I get to meet her?"

Ned sees the fleeting expression on Hugo's face — anxiety? resignation? — and guesses what he must be feeling. If only Hugo had been more proactive, grabbed his opportunities, he might be in a much stronger position now with Dossie. As it is . . .

"Any time you like," Hugo is answering nonchalantly. "I'll send her a text and ask when she's got some spare time."

"And," adds Prune, with a rather touching indifference that fools nobody, "I was wondering if I'd invite Ben over some time, if that's OK? I know you already know him but I'd like to show him where I live."

"And knit him some cabbage?" enquires Jamie teasingly. "Who's Ben?"

"Shut up about the knitted cabbage," answers Prune without rancour. "He works at The Chough. I suppose you know The Chough?"

"Yes, I know The Chough," agrees Jamie.

"Of course you can invite him," says Hugo. "We all like Ben."

"And Dossie," Jamie jokes. "Don't forget Dossie."

They begin to laugh, to make plans. Hugo starts to text, whilst Ned listens and watches with the now familiar mix of pleasure, pain, joy and sadness. Already he is beginning to wonder how Dossie and Jamie will react to one another.

CHAPTER
FOURTEEN

Jamie turns in his sleep and startles into wakefulness as something wet and warm lathers his face enthusiastically. "Christ!" he mutters, hauling himself up, and then falls back again with his eyes closed as Brioc watches him, panting in expectation. This has been the routine since Brioc was a puppy: when Jamie is home Brioc is allowed to sleep in his bedroom.

Now, Jamie wipes his face with the back of his hand, opens an eye to look at the hopeful Brioc and then glances at his watch and groans.

"Seriously?" he asks. "You are seriously suggesting you want to go out at half past five in the morning? What is it with you, you crazy dog?"

Brioc's tail switches to and fro across the floor, and with another groan Jamie pushes back the duvet and sits up. The room spins, rolls, twists, and he grips the edge of the mattress in frustration. Without light his eyes cannot help him to find stability, and the only alternative is to wait until his inner ear calms and his brain takes control again. At these moments he might as well be at sea and he knows if he stands he will fall.

"Shit," he mutters.

Brioc stands and moves to put his head on Jamie's thigh as if to provide reassurance, and his presence is welcome in this fluid world. Still sitting on the edge of the bed, he drags on his clothes. Then he reaches out for Brioc, who waits obediently beside him whilst Jamie stands, balancing by gripping the dog's big furry ruff and leaning against the side of the bed. Still holding Brioc's collar he makes his way across the room, picks up his old leather jacket and opens the door. Mercifully it is lighter on the landing. Glancing down he gives a jerk of his head to Brioc, who slips noiselessly out and down the stairs, to stand hopefully at the front door, watching Jamie, who follows him slowly, holding the banisters. In the hall Jamie steps into his boots, picks up his hiker's stick and then lets them both out into the half-light of early morning. He knows that old Mort won't want to be disturbed yet and that Brioc will enjoy this moment alone in his company. He can't understand why Brioc has singled him out for this special affection but he values it.

Together they skirt the little harbour and climb the track to the cliff. Looking out to sea, then inland across the fields, Jamie feels an overwhelming sense of gratitude that he has this to come home to, especially now when his career, his life, his health, are all in transition. The deep rural silence, the over-arching sky, the sense of infinity, comfort him. Cushions of pink thrift and purple mallow edge the stony path, and he can hear the strange, eerie cries of the baby gulls, which are packed on rocky shelves, out of sight on the cliff side below him, whilst their parents circle and scream above his head.

He walks quickly, wielding his stick expertly, whilst Brioc races ahead and then turns and runs back as if to encourage Jamie onwards. Just for this moment he feels free, enabled; that he can look forward hopefully. His bitterness and anxiety dissolve in this wild, rocky landscape, and for the first time since he was disabled by this illness, grounded, frustrated, his spirits are lifted. It will be life-changing to have no structure to his life: no routine, no responsibilities. He still wonders how he will manage to feel viable, to make something worthwhile of his future, but he feels just a little more positive about it now.

Brioc is back with a stone, which he lays at Jamie's feet. Jamie picks it up and hurls it as far as he can, laughing to see Brioc racing away after it. The exertion causes a wave of dizziness, and he has to pause, leaning on his stick, until his balance realigns. He walks on slowly; the instability recedes as the world brightens and the horizon becomes more distinct. As he walks, the sun rises to the east above the stony skyline and washes the world in its light. All is well again.

By the time he and Brioc arrive back at the house on the quay Prune is up, sitting at the kitchen table with Mort at her feet and eating some kind of health-giving cereal. She's wearing pyjamas covered by an old, loose-fitting cardigan, and sheepskin slippers. With her hair pulled back and her smooth skin she looks about twelve.

124

Jamie thinks: I might have had a daughter like this — and his heart twists in an odd sense of painful longing.

"Looks tasty." He nods towards the cereal. "What is it? Chicken food?"

She grins back at him. "Granola. It's very good. I suppose you'll be going for the full English?"

"If I'm lucky." He pushes the kettle on to the hotplate. "No point offering you coffee, I suppose?"

"None at all." Prune shakes her head. She raises her mug. "I'm having redbush."

He rolls his eyes, reaches down a mug from the dresser, peers into the cupboard. Brioc has finished drinking and now pushes his cold wet muzzle into Prune's lap.

"Aaargh!" she exclaims. "Awful dog. That's cold. Where did you go? Along the cliff?"

Jamie nods. "It's a bit of a hike up through the village and out on to the moor so we took the easy option."

He makes coffee and sits down at the table. It's good to do this: to sit here with Prune, at ease, refreshed by his walk with Brioc, and to feel no stress.

"So tell me about Ben," he says casually. "He must have come to The Chough since I was there last."

He sees the flush of colour run up under her cheeks and is amused and touched all at once. How exciting to be so young, and in love.

"He's the bar manager," she says, proudly. "He lives in. You have to if you're the bar manager. He really wants to go into IT. You know? Websites and stuff? But he needs to earn some money first."

Jamie drinks his coffee, listening to her, caressing Brioc's head, which now rests against his knee.

"It's the place to be," he agrees. "IT is where it's at. Go for it, Ben."

Prune beams at him. "He's going on a course in Newquay in September."

"That's good," he says. "Newquay's not too far away," and he smiles a little as he watches her look rather shy again.

The door opens and Hugo comes in wearing an ancient dressing gown. Jamie begins to laugh.

"Good grief," he says. "Don't I recognize that old thing? Weren't you wearing it at school?"

"Do you have a problem with that?" demands Hugo. "I found it when I moved down and it's come in jolly useful."

"I told you," says Prune. "It's like a student's grot here. My dear old APs would be horrified. And they think you're so respectable."

Jamie winces. It occurs to him that Prune's "Aged Parents" are probably the same age as he is.

"Nonsense," says Hugo. "They know perfectly well that we're nothing of the sort. I shall make Uncle Ned's coffee and take it up to him and then we'll have breakfast." He raises his eyebrows at Jamie. "I suppose you want the full works?"

Jamie sees Prune's eyes expectantly upon him and he knows that he cannot disappoint her.

"Of course," he says — and she snorts and rolls her eyes.

"Told you so," she says. "You are just so predictable."

126

"So are you," he counters. "Granola. Redbush. Knitted cabbage. What does Ben think about it?"

Prune purses her lips. "I'm working on him," she says.

"I bet you are, the poor bugger," says Jamie with so much feeling that Prune begins to laugh.

"It's difficult," she admits, "with him working in a pub, to keep him on the straight and narrow. But at least he's given up smoking."

"Well, that *is* an achievement," agrees Jamie. "I'm looking forward to meeting him."

Prune gives him a candid look. "It'll be a bit daunting to meet all three of you properly so you must be nice."

Jamie raises his eyebrows. "Nice? Nice? Oh, yes. I think I remember nice. I'll give it my best shot."

Prune sighs, gets up. "I can see I'm wasting my breath."

"We shall be good practice for him," Jamie says encouragingly. "After all, it might come to a point where he has to meet your parents and your three brothers. If he can get past us it'll be a walk in the park for him."

"What'll be a walk in the park?" asks Hugo, coming back in.

"Nothing," answers Prune quickly. "I'm going to have a shower."

She puts her bowl and mug into the dishwasher, gives Mort and Brioc valedictory pats and goes out.

"So what do you think of our Prune?" Hugo goes to the fridge and begins to assemble the makings of breakfast. "We count her a definite asset to the household."

"I agree," says Jamie, "and I can't wait to meet Ben. I think poor Prune is nervous at the prospect."

"Daniel in the lions' den?" suggests Hugo. "But he knows me and Ned from The Chough."

"Not quite the same, though, is it? Meeting you socially in your own home. Three against one."

"I think it's a good idea to invite Dossie. Rather as though we're having a little party and it's not just all about Ben. Perhaps Adam might be down and he could come as well."

"Hang on," says Jamie. "Who's Adam?"

"Dossie's brother. I think you'll like him. Yes, that's what we'll do. We'll have a little party."

"Sounds like fun." Jamie stands up and makes his way carefully across the kitchen, one hand always in contact with a surface, to pour himself more coffee. These days his efforts to retain equilibrium are on the verge of becoming subconscious, unnoticeable. His homecoming has been one of warmth, of reassurance, and rather than the bleakness of an ending there seems to be the promise of a new beginning.

Breakfast is over by the time Rose arrives, but only just. To mask her pleasure at the sight of Jamie after such a long time, she rolls her eyes, sighs as if in disbelief to see them all still sitting round the table.

"Lucky for some people," she says, resigned, "hanging about all morning with nothing to do. Some of us have to work."

128

Hugo laughs but Jamie pushes back his chair and stands up, holding his arms out to her.

"Morning, Rose," he says. "Prickly as ever, are we?"

She returns his hug, gives him a quick peck on the cheek, hiding her delight at his greeting, not quite knowing what to say. Hugo has warned her about what's happened and she guesses that the last thing Jamie will want is a long face and sympathy.

"And I expect you're as untidy as ever," she counters. "Well, you know the rules. Anything left on the bedroom floor goes in the rubbish."

"Rose doesn't take prisoners," Ned reminds him, smiling.

"Don't worry, Rose," Hugo says. "We're going out so you'll have a bit of peace and quiet. We were just arguing for and against the merits of Padstow or Polzeath. I want to go to Padstow and Jamie is for Polzeath."

"No change there then," she answers briskly. "Can't remember a time when you two weren't arguing about something."

"Now I know I'm home," remarks Jamie to no one in particular.

There is a tiny silence and then the sudden pushing back of chairs, of bustle and movement. Rose meets Jamie's eyes and feels that tiny jolt of recognition; as if she is looking at Jack thirty-five years on. She nods at Jamie, as if to show that she knows all that has happened to him, and he smiles back at her, acknowledging everything she has not said to him.

Once they've all gone, she puts the necessary cleaning materials into a bucket and carries them all upstairs. It was Margaret who bought a second vacuum cleaner to be kept on the first floor, to save Rose carrying it up two flights of stairs. It was the kind of thing Margaret thought about. It wouldn't have occurred to Lady T in a thousand years.

Ned's room is the tidiest, probably because of all those years away at sea on a submarine. Rose begins the usual routine of dusting, polishing. She pauses to look at the photographs he keeps on the mahogany chest: of Jack as a child with Margaret, and as a young man in naval uniform, proud parents on either side. Rose picks up a photograph of Margaret and looks closely at it. Margaret is dressed quite formally, dark hair tidy; she looks smart, attractive, just as Ned liked to see her. Rose recognizes the scarf that is tied around Margaret's throat. It's a silk scarf that Ned brought back after six weeks away at sea. They had a run ashore at Naples and he bought the scarf there. It's a pale green silk, covered with splashy red flowers, and Margaret was wearing it the day Rose overheard her talking to Toby McIntyre in the kitchen. Even now she can remember the words Margaret used, and the way her fingers twisted the ends of the scarf tied around her neck.

"I can't believe that you knew and you never told me, Toby. You just let me go on as usual and all the while everyone knew that he's been unfaithful to me. Pitying me. Smiling behind their hands."

130

"Not everyone. Be fair, Mags. It's not that simple . . ." Toby was mumbling, both elbows on the table, his fair curly head in his hands.

Rose could just glimpse him through the half-open door. She'd seen him before, at drinks parties or a dinner party, when she'd been called in to help Lady T and the Admiral.

Margaret closed her eyes, screwing them up as if she were in pain. Her hands twisted and twisted the scarf. It was odd, thought Rose, that she should look so different, much more attractive, with her face so alive with anger and hurt, and her hair all anyhow where she'd dragged her hands through it.

"I know he's a flirt but I never thought he would actually do anything. I trusted him," she said. "God, what a fool I've been."

"It doesn't mean anything," Toby was insisting. "I keep telling you, Mags. It's not important to him. It's . . . *une bagatelle.*"

Margaret opened her eyes, lifted her chin and stared at him. "Because saying it in French makes it more civilized? More acceptable?"

"No," he cried. "No, Mags. I'm just saying these things mean nothing to Ned."

"And you can't see that that makes it even worse?"

"Oh God."

Toby buried his face in his hands again and she stretched her own hand across the table to him.

"Sorry, Tobes," she said. "This isn't your problem and I've no right to shout at you. It's just that this letter from this *bloody* woman . . ."

Rose stepped back then, warily, silently, shocked by Margaret's language, her passion. It was so unlike her that Rose didn't know what to do, where to go. Hesitating, she could still hear their voices.

"Will you confront him?"

"No. No, I shan't. He'll never know that I know. Oh, I know he's silly with women, that flirtatious kind of thing, but I didn't believe he'd do more than that."

"I'm sorry . . ."

"What for? I shouldn't have asked you to come over but it was a shock. I just needed to know the truth from someone I could trust. After all, we've been friends even before either of us knew Ned."

"You know I'll do anything I can."

"I know. Look, you'd better go. Ned's parents will be back soon. I'm going home next week. Jack's got some leave."

"I'm going back, too. Look, why don't we have lunch . . .?"

Rose could hear chairs being pushed back and she made a swift, silent retreat up the stairs. But, later, when she went down again, the scarf was lying on the kitchen table. Margaret never wore it again. Rose found it shoved to the back of a drawer in the bedroom upstairs. A year later, Jack was killed.

Now, as she stares at the photograph she remembers how, when Ned asked if she'd like anything of Margaret's to remember her by, Rose asked for the scarf.

"The one you bought her in Naples," she reminded him, and watched as a variety of expressions flitted over his face: surprise, confusion, shame.

"Of course," he muttered, discomfited. "I'm not sure where it might be. I haven't seen it for years."

"I know where it is," she assured him. "She kept it here."

He nodded, frowning, slightly put out, but Rose didn't mind. She took the scarf from where she'd laid it, wrapped in tissue paper in a drawer, many years ago and showed it to him. Ned stared at it.

"I'm sure she'd like you to have it," he said at last.

Rose puts the photograph back on the mahogany chest. She likes to wear the scarf from time to time to remember how things were: the scene in the kitchen with Toby. It was then that Margaret began to change. Not because Jack died. Death is one thing, betrayal quite another.

CHAPTER
FIFTEEN

Emilia drives in the narrow lanes, amused as she always is by the odd names on the fingerposts: Pityme, Splatt, Stoptide. She has driven Lucy and Dan to Newquay airport and now she is alone again. In London this would be no problem — there's always someone to meet up with — but here in north Cornwall she wonders how she will manage.

"I'll be back next week, Mum," Lucy said. "Once I've sorted these few things out I'll dash over for a couple of days. You'll be OK, won't you?"

"Of course I will. Stop fussing." Emilia shook her head at Lucy's anxiety. "What could go wrong?"

"I know. I'm being silly. But let me know if you have a problem."

With promises and reassurances Emilia saw them off and now here she is driving into Rock, parking against the seawall opposite the cottage, and climbing out of the car. She lets herself in and stands in the tiny hall. When she first saw the cottage, Lucy showing her round full of pride and excitement, Emilia was aware of an atmosphere, a miasma that seemed to cling about the sitting-room, drifting on the stairs: a negative vibe of discontent, resentment, old grievances.

Despite telling herself that this was nonsense the sensation remained, although Lucy and Tom seemed to be unaware of it. The next time she visited Rock it was as if the presence of the little family had vanquished it: Lucy's delight at owning this little cottage, Tom's pragmatic confidence, Danny's enthusiasm and vitality, had somehow expunged the atmosphere. Just now and again Emilia caught a whiff of it, of bitterness and anger, but it was fleeting and she wondered who had been the previous occupant.

"It was owned by several generations, the agent said," Lucy told her. "Grandmother, then daughter, then granddaughter. The granddaughter was offered a job in New York — I think he said that she was an investment banker — and she decided to sell. It's so rare for any properties to come on the market here. We're just so lucky."

In the sitting-room is a little drop-leaf table by the window where Emilia can eat while the kitchen is being dismantled. She puts her bag on it and gazes out of the window across the estuary to Padstow. Perhaps she'll catch the ferry and go across for lunch — or maybe she'll drive to Wadebridge and go to the café where Lucy says she met Hugo. Slowly, now that she is alone, Emilia allows herself to think about Hugo. Unexpectedly, as she calls up the past, she seems to hear again the "*Widmung*" and her heart beats a little faster. She remembers hearing it for the first time at a lunchtime piano recital given by one of the university students, and even now she can remember how much she was moved by it. Hugo was so sweet, finding a recording of it, playing it to her in his room — and then Jamie came walking in. She was sitting on the floor, amongst a pile of cushions, and she rose to her feet as if she were drawn up by strings. She sees again the brown eyes and black hair, and his expression of dawning dismay that he'd interrupted what might have become an intimate scene. She was aware of Hugo's disappointment, and felt a fleeting sympathy, but it was as nothing compared to the first shock of seeing Jamie.

So this is it, she thought. This is what they all write about and sing about. This sense of recognition, lust, helplessness, longing.

Then Hugo was introducing them, persuading Jamie to stay and have some wine, and as she shook hands with him, looking into those brown eyes, she knew that he was feeling exactly the same way. Poor Hugo didn't stand a chance. There was a glamour about Jamie, not only because of his good looks and charisma, but also because he was going to join the RAF, to become a pilot; a glamour that she was used to in her mother's company: that head-turning sense of being special, different.

Emilia hugs herself tight, remembering. Her mother fell in love with Jamie at once — "Gorgeous, darling" — but her father was more cautious: "How will you manage as a service wife, sweetie? He'll be away a lot. Please do think carefully." But Emilia could see and hear only Jamie.

As she stares unseeingly at the ferry plying across the river, she tries to pinpoint a moment, find a reason for abandoning him. Of course, it's not so simple: it's

136

rarely one obvious thing. After those two years of balls and parties, of weekends and fun, after the excitement of the courtship and the wedding, with the guard of honour drawn up outside the church door, then real life began on the RAF base at Lyneham. It hadn't occurred to her that she would simply become one of the many pilots' wives, living in dreary married quarters. Here she was neither special nor glamorous. She didn't fit with these other women, who were either training to be nurses or were career wives, thinking only of their husbands' promotions, who disapproved of her wearing jeans. When Jamie came home from missions he didn't want to make decisions — he spent his whole life making split-second decisions — or to be worried about the dreariness of the furniture and curtains. This was her responsibility. That's when she should have started to look for a little house off the base where they could make a home and start a family — Jamie so wanted children. Instead she fled to London at every opportunity, to the flat on the King's Road.

If only . . . If only he'd been home a bit more. If only the other wives had been more fun. If only she hadn't been so young — only twenty when she met Jamie, twenty-four when she married him — and had been ready for the responsibility of parenthood. And it was then, when the glamour was rubbed thin and loneliness was pressing in, that she met Nigel. Fifteen years older, experienced, amusing, hedonistic, and popular. The sitcom he was appearing in was a huge success; everyone adored him. She simply couldn't resist him.

137

I was still so naïve, Emilia reminds herself defensively, and Jamie was away so much.

She can still remember the shock on Jamie's face when she told him. They'd been making love — for how could she refuse him when he was just back from his Falklands detachment? — and then as she poured him a glass of wine she began to explain, in halting, hesitating, anxious phrases, how she thought that their marriage wasn't going anywhere; that it had been a mistake. He listened to her with a mounting disbelief, told her that she was just having a funny five minutes and that she'd get over it. She was unable to make her case and when he asked her if she'd met someone else she instinctively denied it. They made love again; he was passionate, loving, possessive, as if by this intense physical activity he could bring her back to her senses, and as soon as he left the next morning she ran away to London; to Nigel.

Emilia turns back into the room. She feels confused, remorseful, emotional. Suddenly she longs to see Hugo again. What must he have thought of her? She wonders if she might be able to make him understand — and give her news of Jamie. She feels quite sure that Hugo would have married and had children, though Lucy told her that he was alone when she saw him in the Relish café.

"He was with a group of people in The Chough," she said, "but not with anyone special as far as I could see. I hope you meet up with him, Mum. He seems really nice."

138

On an impulse, Emilia picks up her bag and hurries out. She gets into the car, reverses out of the space, and heads towards Wadebridge.

It is only when she is sitting at a table beneath the flowering cherry trees, with a pot of tea in front of her, that it occurs to Emilia that she might not recognize Hugo even if she were to see him. She recalls him in her mind's eye: tall, broad-shouldered, a mass of dark curly hair and very blue eyes. It is indeed amazing that he has seen the resemblance to her own young self in Lucy, but would he recognize this older Emilia? After Lucy told her how they'd met she peered into the mirror, trying to trace that young girl's lineaments in this middle-aged face. She doesn't look too bad, she tells herself, though her red-brown hair began to grey quite early and she decided to colour it. Nigel didn't like the thought of her being grey-haired, he enjoyed having a young and attractive wife, and he encouraged her to dye it. Poor darling Nigel never quite recovered from his inability to replicate his early success on television and in the end became rather needy; anxious to be recognized, remembered by the public.

Sitting in the dappling sun, Emilia watches two women with a boy of about ten laughing together at another table and wonders what Hugo is doing now. She knows that he joined the BBC but she lost touch with him once she and Jamie were divorced, though she followed his career with interest. She wonders what he looks like — how foolish of her not to ask Lucy — and how she would react if he were to come walking in now.

139

She knows that this new strange neediness to see Hugo, to reconnect with him, is a longing to revisit the past and in some strange way to receive absolution from him for preferring Jamie — for abandoning both of them. She let them both down. She wants to tell him her own side of things and to make him understand. How easy it is to mistake that terrible, urgent need, that overwhelming lust and longing, for the real thing. How good it would be to talk to him now, to have his approval, now that they are all older and wiser.

Emilia sips her tea and wonders if she is, actually, all that much wiser. Might not the much-vaunted wisdom of old people be simply the loss of passion? She did love darling Nigel, of course she did, but wasn't it that same treacherous glamour, that seductive scattering of gold dust, that made her believe that she was in love with him? And wasn't it that within a few weeks of leaving Jamie — oh, the difficulty of writing that letter! — she discovered that she was pregnant? What choice did she have? Nigel was utterly delighted. They'd been lovers for a while and this confirmed to him the rightness of their liaison. He felt as if in some way they were being blessed; absolved. And how he loved Lucy; how proud that she looked just like her beautiful mother.

Emilia sits quite still. She thinks back to those days, the shock when she began to miss her periods — the pill made her ill and she wouldn't use it so sometimes precautions were a bit sketchy — and how she wondered if the baby might have brown eyes and black hair. Oh, the relief when they presented her with this pretty little daughter with a fuzz of reddish-dark hair

140

and blue eyes. She burst into tears and Nigel was rushed in to share her joy. He ordered champagne.

The two women, one with silvery blonde hair, the other dark-haired with gypsy-looking clothes, are getting up from their table. The boy has gone ahead with a black Labrador that must have been lying under the table. He calls back to them.

"Dossie," he shouts. "Dossie. Can you bring my jacket?" and the blonde woman picks up the coat and waves it to show that she's heard him, and they all go off together.

Emilia watches them leave. A breeze stirs the blossom and she shivers. She hasn't noticed that the sun has vanished behind a veil of thin high cloud and that there is a chill in the air. She longs now for Hugo to appear, and she invents the scenario, rehearsing the words she will use in her head, imagining his response.

Down on the coast the tide turns. Out in the Western Approaches storm clouds begin to mass. The wind is rising and Emilia pulls her jacket more closely around her, but still Hugo does not come.

CHAPTER
SIXTEEN

Dossie drops Jakey, Janna and Bells off at the Lodge and drives away. She has several orders to deliver and then she is going to see Hugo and Ned. Hugo sent a text saying that Jamie was down and that she must come in to meet him. She is delighted to be included, to feel that she is a friend, though she is apprehensive. It is clear that Hugo slightly hero worships Jamie, that he is a more serious man than Hugo and, of course, his career as a pilot has been impressive. Dossie wonders if the usually relaxed, easy atmosphere might be dispelled, if Hugo might be different in the presence of this charismatic cousin, and she is determined not to be impressed.

She makes her deliveries and drives on to the house on the quay. Jamie's MGB has been parked as far forward as possible beside the Volvo and she is able to pull in close behind it. She looks at the roadster for a while, then reaches to pick up a tin containing a variety of small cakes and gets out. Outside the door she hesitates and then opens it and calls, just as Prune does, "Hi, it's me." The dogs begin to bark and Hugo comes out of the kitchen behind them as they race down the long passage to meet her.

"Dossie," he cries, and she hears just the tiniest tension in his voice.

"I've brought cakes," she answers cheerfully, and he beams at her as the dogs jump around them.

"Joyous," he says. "Just joyous," and they both burst out laughing at this silly, familiar joke. So their entrance into the kitchen is a confusion of dogs, and Hugo leading her in, saying, "Dossie has brought cakes." The man sitting at the table looks up from writing in a card — a slightly quizzical, assessing look — and begins to get to his feet.

And she is shaking his hand — a strong, quick grasp — before turning to Ned who, not to be outdone by the younger man, is also getting up and demonstrating his privilege of established friendship by giving her a hug. She returns his embrace, indicating the tin.

"I hope it's not too late for tea," she says. "I took Jakey and Janna to Relish but that doesn't mean I can't have another."

"If we can hold Jamie off the gin and tonic for another ten minutes it will be a very good thing," says Hugo. "Tea it is."

Dossie looks at Jamie and sees how his smile creases the corners of his eyes before it reaches his mouth.

"I hope you like cake?" she asks, and opens the tin and holds it towards him.

He bends to look into it. He is taller than Hugo, his black hair only slightly touched with grey. He looks tough, fit, slightly formidable.

"Of course he likes cake," says Ned impatiently, and Jamie looks at her and she sees that little smile again.

"Does he take sugar?" she asks of no one in particular, and they all burst out laughing and the tension evaporates.

"I shall be delighted to have tea and cake," he assures her, and she smiles at him and begins to take the cakes out of the tin to cover a sudden and very foolish attack of shyness.

"How is Jakey?" Ned is asking. "And Janna? We hear a great deal about Janna. You must invite her to meet us."

"Well, she said almost the same thing to me," Dossie answers, taking a plate from Hugo and arranging the cakes. "But I don't think I shall get her here. She'd be too intimidated."

"Intimidated? By us?" Hugo stops in the middle of his tea-making to stare at her in surprise. "Seriously?"

"Janna's a very odd person." Dossie is aware that Jamie is sitting down again, watching her, listening with interest, and she stops fiddling with the cakes and sits down at the table, turning towards Hugo. "She had rather a damaged childhood. Her parents were travellers and her mother died from drink and drugs when Janna was small. She's still a gypsy at heart and I always half expect to find that she's up and gone."

"Who is Janna?" asks Jamie. "What does she do?"

Dossie turns back to look at him. She sees that he is really interested, not just being polite, and she warms to him.

"Janna has had lots of jobs in pubs and restaurants on the north coast," she tells him. "Then one day she turned up at the convent, Chi-Meur, and they offered

144

her a job, working in the kitchen, cleaning, anything that she felt happy with. My son, Clem, and my grandson, Jakey, were living there, too, back then. Clem was wondering whether to continue with his theological training after his wife died having Jakey. We all became very close friends. Janna lived in the caravan in the grounds, which suited her really well."

She pauses, takes a breath, and glances at Jamie again to see if he is still really interested. He is watching her intently and raises his eyebrows as if inviting her to continue.

"So when the convent became a retreat house, and the four remaining Sisters moved into the Coach House, they persuaded Janna to stay on to look after them. Much against her will."

"Why much against her will?" asks Jamie.

"It meant her moving in with them because one elderly Sister needed special care and so Janna would lose the independence and freedom of the caravan. Clem saw that two rooms at the end of the Coach House could be made into special quarters for her, with her own entrance and a little courtyard, as well as an adjoining door to the Coach House."

Dossie stops again and glances round anxiously. Can they really be interested in all this?

"And so she did," she finishes rather lamely. "It's worked so far but Janna is slightly like a moorland pony that might kick up its heels, toss its head, and gallop away if it's confronted by the unexpected or feels too confined. Sorry." She shakes her head. "I'm making her sound . . . well, inadequate. Which she really isn't. She's very strong and brave and nice. But I still think she'd feel intimidated coming here to meet you all."

She looks again at Jamie, now feeling a complete fool, but he is frowning, as if he is thinking about what she's saying.

"In that case then surely the best thing is for her to meet anyone new on her own territory," he suggests. "And probably one at a time."

"Me first," says Hugo at once. "I like the sound of Janna."

"Yes," says Dossie with relief. "That's exactly right."

"Me next," says Ned, coming to sit at the table. "I want to meet her, too."

Jamie meets Dossie's eyes and gives a little grimace; a little shrug. He sighs.

"Typical," he says sadly. "Littlest, least and last. Story of my life."

In the uproar that follows Dossie sits back and lets out a breath of relief and happiness. She's having the best time.

Ned reaches for a cake. Occasionally, when they are all sitting round the table like this, he feels like an elderly grandfather at a children's party. He can see that Hugo is watching the interplay between Jamie and Dossie, aware that they find each other interesting, wanting Jamie to shine, though not so much that Dossie is completely dazzled.

Ned saw that brief expression of approval on Dossie's face as Jamie got to his feet, the flicker in Jamie's wary eyes, and he suspects that Hugo doesn't stand a chance. He had his opportunities and he missed them, thinks Ned impatiently, yet he knows in his heart that the mysterious magic of attraction can't be manufactured. Though it must have been hard for Hugo, sometimes, to live in the shadow of Jamie. Littlest, least and last!

Ned gives an almost silent snort at Jamie's misrepresentation of the facts and Dossie looks at him enquiringly.

"I was wondering," he says blandly, "when Adam will be down again. Is he here for the Bank Holiday?"

"Yes, he is." Dossie looks pleased; surprised. "It's great that he wants to come down again so soon."

"Well, we all had lunch at yours last time so it's our call this time," Hugo says.

"Perhaps he should come to the party," suggests Ned. "He's already met Prune, and he knows Ben because of his being at The Chough. Do you think he'd like that, Dossie?"

"I think he'd love it," she answers at once. "I didn't know you were giving a party."

"It was just an idea so that Jamie could meet people," says Hugo. "You were on the list, of course, but we've pre-empted that now . . ."

"So if there's anyone else you think I should know," says Jamie to Dossie, "don't hold back, now that you know I'm Billy No-Mates."

She laughs at him. "I'll give it my best shot. Perhaps you'd like to meet Sister Emily and Mother Magda? It depends how many people you're planning to invite."

"Since you'll be the one catering for it," says Ned drily, "perhaps you should be the one to answer that."

"Hang on," protests Jamie. "That's a bit tough on Dossie, isn't it? If we're giving a party I'll do the catering."

There's a moment's silence and Ned smiles to himself as he sees that Hugo is taken aback and that Dossie is gratified: she's not used to people offering to cook for her.

"It'll have to be good," says Hugo, pulling himself together. "Dossie's an expert."

"Then I'll have to try to impress her," answers Jamie matter-of-factly, looking at Dossie. "Won't I?"

And Dossie seems at a complete loss for words. She begins to get up, saying something about going home, whilst Hugo suggests she should stay for supper and Jamie continues to watch her with that slightly quizzical expression that says nothing and everything. Ned can see that she'd like to stay but won't allow herself to accept.

"No, no," Dossie is saying. "I've got stuff to do and . . . but thanks. Maybe another time. And you must bring Jamie over to see The Court, Hugo. Bring the dogs this time . . ." She goes out with Hugo hurrying after her, the dogs at his heels.

Jamie sits staring at his plate, with an odd inward look.

Love, thinks Ned with sudden exasperation. Wonderful, terrible old love. Damn it. I hope this doesn't ruin everything.

There is a moment's silence after Dossie and Hugo go out. Jamie sits still, unwilling to meet Ned's eyes. He hadn't expected such an attractive, amusing woman to be a close part of the household.

"Fun, isn't she?" asks Ned casually, reaching for his stick and standing up.

"She's left her cake tin behind," says Jamie, pushing back his chair. He has no intention of allowing Ned to trick him into any admissions. "And the cakes."

He begins to clear the table, putting the cakes back into the tin.

"Not a problem," answers Ned comfortably. "She'll be back."

Hugo comes in. "It's raining quite hard and it's cold. I wish she'd stayed to supper."

Jamie wishes she had, too. He'd seen the momentary hesitation and thinks about it.

"So when is this party going to be happening?" he asks. "If I'm going to be catering for it I shall need notice. Our lovely Rose will help me."

"You won some brownie points there," observes Ned. "Dossie isn't used to being catered for."

"It looks like we shall have to wait for Adam now," says Hugo. "The more the merrier. Maybe by that time we shall have met Janna and she'll be persuaded to come. That will even out the numbers a bit. I'll text Dossie and tell her to get it organized."

He picks up his phone and Jamie watches him, slightly surprised that he should text her so soon after seeing her. It hasn't occurred to him that Hugo might be interested in Dossie other than as a friend. Hugo has never been particularly romantic. At the parties in London Hugo was always the brotherly figure and, apart from that time with Ems . . . Jamie frowns at the remembrance.

"I'm sorry about barging in like that, mate," he said to Hugo afterwards. "I had no idea. I should have walked straight out again . . ."

And Hugo said something like, "Well, it wouldn't have mattered." There was a bleakness, a bitterness, but he'd made no fight of it. And I'd never have pushed it, thinks Jamie, if I'd believed he was really in love with her.

"The thing is," Hugo's saying, as he taps out his message, "she hates going into the empty house so I often send her a text when she goes home."

And that just about sums Hugo up, thinks Jamie: the kind, thoughtful, caring brother. He feels a huge relief that his cousin and Dossie are in no way an item; that there is nothing between them except a really close friendship. No way could he have poached . . . He gives a little inward laugh at the way his thoughts are hurrying ahead.

"Time for a drink," he says. "Anyone feel like joining me?"

It's raining as Dossie drives back towards St Endellion. As the windscreen wipers swipe to and fro she mutters to herself.

"Stop being such an idiot. Get a grip."

150

She's hoping that she didn't let it show how much she'd have liked to stay on, sitting at the table with Hugo and Ned and Jamie, talking, sharing, feeling so relaxed. She really hopes that Jamie didn't see that moment of hesitation that betrayed her neediness when Hugo invited her to stay to supper; that he had no idea of the confusion of her emotions. She's wondering now if she imagined that little flash of interest in his eyes when he first glanced up at her; the way he watched her with that inscrutable yet slightly amused expression.

Perhaps she's been a fool not to stay, but some small vestige of pride, of independence, got her to her feet and out of the kitchen. She'll be sorry when she gets home to the empty house, knowing that she could have stayed there with them all. And part of her guesses that she won't have fooled Jamie for a single moment.

She thinks about him, so unlike Hugo in almost every way: wary where Hugo is enthusiastic, assessing where Hugo is open, confident and cool where Hugo is anxious and eager to please. Hugo's warmth and generosity of spirit makes him lovable and attractive but Jamie is altogether a tougher proposition. Dossie shivers a little at the prospect of getting to know him and gives herself a mental shake.

"Get a grip. Get a life. Get a dog," she mutters. But somehow the familiar mantra doesn't bring her any comfort.

As she drives out of the village, past the old church that crouches like an ancient grey dog, hunkered down against the Atlantic storms, she sees a woman in the churchyard. Dossie recognizes Rose Pengelly, the

151

Tremaynes' cleaner, and slows down to hoot and wave to her. She's liked Rose the few times she's met her at the house with Ned and Hugo; she likes her quick wit and her fondness for the two men. She and Hugo, especially, have a very easy relationship, which stretches back to their teenage years. And Rose is such a beautiful woman: amazing bone structure, tall and slim and strong. She must have been an absolute knock-out when she was a girl.

Dossie knows that Rose comes from generations of fishermen and guesses that there will be many of her family in that stony churchyard. She waves again and drives on.

Rose waves back as she crosses the churchyard, wondering if Dossie has been to see Ned and Hugo, whether she's met Jamie. So far as she can tell, Dossie seems to be handling Ned and Hugo with no difficulty, but Jamie will be a different story. Jamie's like his cousin Jack: he's trouble. Smiling to herself, Rose crosses the churchyard with its wind-bitten grass and dry-stone walls, to the corner where the Tremaynes are buried. Lady T and the Admiral together, Margaret alongside them and, beside her, a stone memorial to Jack.

"If I die," he said to her, one early autumn evening up here in the churchyard, "I want my ashes to be scattered at sea so that I can travel right round the world."

"If?" she queried, mocking him. "You mean you ain't mortal like the rest of us?"

He laughed, tugging her by the arm away from the quiet graves, out into the woodland where the trees were almost bare, flayed to the bone by the westerly winds. He pulled her down with him, rolling together with her in the crisp gold and scarlet leaves, holding her close. After they'd made love he always said the same thing. Raising himself on his elbow above her, he'd smile down at her, and say: "Here's looking at you, kid."

"I bet you say that to all the girls," she'd retort, pushing him off, straightening her clothes. "One in every port."

"You'll always be my first love, Rose. That's special," he said to her once. Serious, he was. Meaning it. "There's only ever one first love. Remember that."

That's all she's got of him now, as she stands in the damp churchyard. She drops a little spray of bluebells on to Margaret's grave, pauses before the headstone. Lt John Edward Tremayne RN. 1959–1982. "They shall not grow old . . ." His body lies in Blue Beach Military Cemetery at San Carlos in the Falklands.

Rose wraps Margaret's scarf more closely around her throat.

"Here's looking at you, kid," she murmurs.

She turns away and begins to hurry back to the village, her head bent against the rising wind and the rain, back to the small terraced cottage that has belonged to her family for generations. The door opens straight into the little sitting-room, with the small Victorian fireplace and her mum's old rocking chair. She passes through into the kitchen, wondering what to eat for supper. She guesses that Dossie has been with the Tremaynes and wonders how she and Jamie will get on.

"Trouble," she says aloud. And she smiles to herself.

Jack, Jamie, Hugo; she loves them all, one way or another. Her glance falls on a pink silk rose, beautiful, though faded now, which stands in a tall narrow glass vase on the windowsill, and she begins to laugh. How many years it is since Hugo sent her that rose all the way from London; sent it to Lady T because he didn't know Rose's address.

"It's from Hugo," Lady T said, puzzled, "to thank you for something special you did for him. Some ironing, was it?"

Rose still remembers it clearly, not long after Jack was killed and about the time that Jamie got engaged to Emilia. And it was nothing to do with ironing. But the next time Hugo was visiting, the subject was raised again. His mother was shocked that he should have asked Rose to do his ironing and Rose's pride, her anxiety that Hugo might be regretting that brief moment of shared intimacy, had made her quick to step back.

"It was just the once," she said to his mother, there in the Tremaynes' kitchen, and Hugo, smiling, answered, "And I wouldn't dream of taking advantage of it." Even now, she doesn't know if she hurt him.

It's good to have him back; home where he belongs. Rose touches the silk petals with a gentle finger and turns away to prepare her supper.

154

CHAPTER
SEVENTEEN

Each day Emilia walks: on the beach, on the moors, on the cliffs and in the lanes. And as she walks she knows, absolutely knows, that something wonderful and earth-shaking is about to happen. So certain is this belief that she is able to be calm, to wait. She goes to the Relish café and though she doesn't see Hugo she knows that it will happen, that one day she will walk in and he will be there and everything will change.

So she walks and revels in the miracle that is nature. Never before has she been so close to it, never experienced it at first-hand over a period of time so that she sees how it changes almost daily, how profligate it is. Here on the peninsula the weather can alter in moments from a Mediterranean warmth, with clear skies and exotic wild orchids blooming in a ditch, to gale-force winds driving streaming clouds that bring rain, and even hail, to beat down fragile blossoms and rip the sea to shreds.

She wanders in deep, hot lanes where the scent of bluebells is dizzying; sheep barge and jostle at a field gate and then scatter at her approach. She pauses, shielding her eyes, to watch the flight of swallows as they dart in and out of an old barn. Then she hurries aside as a tractor rattles past, raising her hand in response to the farmer's salute.

Down on the shore, on a wild windy morning, she stands in awe at the power of the sea; tall, green, glassy waves shouldering in to smash themselves against the high, granite cliffs, whilst gulls scream to make themselves heard above the tumult. She watches a dog dashing in and out of the waves, and then it stands on the sand, shaking itself, so that a million splinters of light sparkle in the sunshine. And later, on a calm sunny afternoon, the sea lies flat as a metal shelf whilst tiny boats painted like wooden toys rock gently across its smooth, shining surface. So warm, so inviting does it look that she takes off her shoes and socks, rolls up her jeans, and ventures into the shallows. Oh, how icy it is: her feet are numbed in seconds. Quickly she steps back on to the sand, sitting down to dry her feet and ankles with a handful of tissues from her bag and pulling on her socks, grateful for their warmth. Getting up, she stamps to and fro, laughing at her foolishness, and all the while this certainty, this expectation that something good is about to happen is like a bank of coals heaped around her heart, warming her.

As she crosses the sand to go back to the car she sees a child with its mother walking at the water's edge — "Please, Mummy, please can I paddle?" "No, it's much too cold." — and she suddenly remembers Lucy, at the playground, pleading to have one more turn on the swings, the slide, the roundabout. "Please may I go round again, Mummy?" And her own answer. "No, you can't. I'm afraid it's too late." Emilia smiles to herself, watching the mother and child at the shoreline.

She drives away towards the moors, which are so magical at this time on long, light summer evenings: a cobweb of a moon hanging in the east, a stampede of ponies appearing unexpectedly around a rocky outcrop, the wavering cry of an owl hunting in the woods below. She pulls on to the short cropped grass and gets out. She's learned to be prepared for these moments — to have a flask of tea or coffee, a few biscuits or some cake — so as to be able to linger when the magic is too strong to ignore.

She pours hot coffee into a mug and leans against the car. The rural silence is still a surprise to her: no traffic, no sirens, no voices. In a distant farmyard a dog barks, the owl cries again, and then silence. It's odd that she isn't afraid; that she would be much more anxious standing alone in a London street at sunset than she is here in this bleakly beautiful landscape.

Emilia sips her coffee and allows herself, at last, to look at her life: at the mess and the muddle, the triumphs and disasters, the lies and deceptions. How simple and clear it seems, out here in these empty spaces; here everything falls into perspective. Here she need not feel guilty or anxious. She is able to examine her actions, understand the motives, and be quietly calm.

How easy it would be now to sit with Hugo and talk to him about the past, to explain her regret over leaving Jamie, how she was simply overwhelmed by the loneliness, the emptiness, that assailed her; that she was too young to cope with the sudden change from her boho London life to existence on a married patch surrounded by unsympathetic women. He would understand her need to flee back to that familiar scene each time Jamie went away and, because she was so lonely, the dangerous attraction when she met Nigel. Of course she was foolish and selfish, but she was naive and inexperienced, and shouldn't youth be forgiven much? She longs to talk about Lucy; the shock of finding herself pregnant, the indecision, and the doubt. Surely Hugo would understand? She remembers his gentleness, his eagerness to please, and she longs to have his absolution . . . but there is more that she needs.

Emilia finishes her coffee, packs the Thermos and the mug away, and stands for a moment with her arms crossed, her hands tucked under them. The sunset glow is all around her and she is filled with confidence and hope. Her hope is simply that Hugo will bring her to Jamie. The time is right. She is alone and she longs to put things right. She tries not to dwell too much on whether Jamie might be married with a family; she doesn't want to think about that. It seems impossible that now, when she needs him, he won't be there. And she has so much to give him now: a daughter and a grandson. She hugs herself at the prospect of being able to offer him such a reward; to repay him for the pain she caused him. Nobody will be hurt; the timing is perfect. And Hugo is the person to lead her to Jamie. She can remember very vaguely that they had relations in Cornwall, some old uncle and aunt; somewhere they

158

used to go on holidays from school. She feels certain that this is where Hugo is staying and she wishes now that she'd listened more carefully, but it was so long ago and didn't seem particularly important at the time. She simply cannot reproach herself. It's odd, this feeling of absolute certainty that everything is working together for good: Tom and Lucy buying the cottage in Rock, Lucy meeting Hugo.

Emilia gives a great sigh of happy anticipation, climbs back into the car and drives slowly away towards Rock.

CHAPTER
EIGHTEEN

Jamie is playing the piano, jazzing Bach's Prelude and Fugue No. 2 in C minor, when the dogs begin to bark and he hears the front door close and a voice calling, "Hi, it's me." Prune must be home unexpectedly, he thinks, but he gets up and goes out, just in case. As he comes carefully down the stairs, holding the banisters, he stops in surprise. Dossie is standing in the hall with a cold box in her arms. They stare at each other almost in consternation and then Dossie says: "I've got the supplies to go into the freezer. Is that OK?"

"Of course," he answers. "It's just I wasn't expecting you. Hugo didn't mention it. He's taken Uncle Ned for his check-up at Derriford Hospital."

He leads the way into the kitchen, pushing the door open for her, shushing the dogs, and then takes the box. They smile at each other across it and he feels unusually self-conscious as his hands close over hers as she transfers the box to him.

"I'd forgotten about the appointment," she's saying quickly, as if to cover their moment of self-awareness. "Or I might not have known. I'm making deliveries all round today. With the Bank Holiday coming up the holiday cottages are filling up and needing supplies."

160

He stands the cold box on the table, and then grips the back of one of the chairs for support, feeling pleased that she's turned up unexpectedly but slightly less sure of himself without Hugo and Uncle Ned to make everything normal between them.

"I'm not sure what happens next," he says. "Do you actually put all these away or does Hugo do it? I mean, is there some sort of system I don't know about?"

She has a delightful way of smiling that is infectious, as if he's made some sort of joke.

"Are you kidding?" she asks. "Does Hugo even know what the word 'system' means? I usually put it all in so that he knows that main meals are on the left and puddings on the right, but I think he just takes things out randomly and they eat whatever it is that comes to hand."

"Like some kind of lucky dip?" Jamie suggests, amused.

"Exactly. They probably have banoffee pie three days running and then pheasant stew for a week."

"Sounds good to me," he says.

She's already unpacking the box and carrying the individual packets into the small utility room where the freezer is. He can see that each carton is clearly labelled: cottage pie, shepherd's pie, fish pie, beef stew.

"What's the difference between a shepherd's pie and a cottage pie?" he asks.

"Oh, come on," she answers. "One has a shepherd in it and the other has a cottage. Do keep up!" And then she laughs and says, "Shepherd's is lamb and cottage is beef. I can't believe you didn't know that."

He passes the containers to her, reading each label.

"What luxury," he comments. "Does Hugo do any cooking at all?"

"This is just basic stuff," she answers. "Things to fall back on. He makes all sorts of exotic things. Do you cook? Or did you just dine in the mess all the time?"

"Not quite all the time. I can do a few things but it's not really my forte."

It's odd how comfortable he feels in her company, as if he's known her for ever, yet with an extra dimension of excitement that leads him to say: "So since you do this cooking all the time, would you like to go out to lunch just for a change?"

Dossie pauses, her hands full of packets, obviously taken aback.

"Oh," she says blankly.

She glances up at him and then looks away again. Aware that he is standing very close to her in the small utility room, he moves back into the kitchen. She puts the last containers into the chest freezer and closes the lid.

"Well, that would be very nice," she says. "If you really . . . I mean, what about the dogs?"

He is rather touched by her sudden confusion — her jokey poise seems to have deserted her — and he gives a little shrug.

"I think they'll manage for an hour or two on their own, won't they?"

"Yes," she says, though rather doubtfully. "I expect they will. Well. Thank you."

"And you haven't any more deliveries to do?"

"A few. But they can wait a little longer."

"Good," he says. "In that case, I have control. We'll go to The Chough."

She looks at him and then starts to laugh. "Your car or mine?"

"Oh, mine," he says at once.

"Wonderful," she says. "I was hoping you'd say that. Mike had an MGB roadster back in the day. I haven't been in one since then. I loved that car. It was British racing green. Just like yours."

For a moment he is disconcerted. He doesn't know quite how to react, remembering how Hugo told him that Mike was killed in a racing accident, but it's clear that she knows what he's thinking because she's smiling at him.

"It's OK," she says. "It was all a very long time ago. But I shall still enjoy a ride in an MGB. Was it you playing when I came in?"

"Yes," he says, taken aback by the sudden change of direction. "Yes, it was. I was jazzing up some Bach."

"It sounded good," she says.

He feels almost embarrassed, pleased but not knowing quite how to react.

"I'm not as good as Hugo," he says. "Hugo could have been a concert pianist but he didn't have the encouragement at the right time."

Dossie nods. "I've heard Hugo play. He's amazing. Rather different from what you were doing, though."

Jamie feels a foolish momentary stab of jealousy, of competitiveness.

"Oh, Hugo doesn't approve of the way I mess around with it," he says lightly. "He's a purist."

"I liked it," she answers — and now he feels ridiculously pleased.

"Well, maybe I can play for you sometime?" he suggests casually. "So, shall we get going?"

He has a sudden fear that Hugo and Uncle Ned might appear and spoil his plan, though he knows that it's much too early for them to be back from Plymouth. He settles the dogs, gets his old leather jacket and picks up his stick, and they both go out. Dossie has pulled into the space where the Volvo usually is and they stand together looking at the MGB.

"We could put the hood down," he offers. "It's warm enough. What d'you think?"

"That would be great!" she says, and he opens the passenger door for her, and then goes round and climbs in. He feels happier than he's felt for months and he's loving it.

Leaning back in the passenger seat, Dossie breathes in the wonderful smell of leather, the tarry scent of the hood; she notices the gleam of chrome and walnut on the dashboard and listens with pleasure to that old familiar hubble-bubble of the engine. The air is soft and the sun is warm on her face.

"I suppose I should keep a scarf in the glove compartment for these occasions," says Jamie, glancing sideways at her, and she laughs for the sheer pleasure of it all.

"Silk," she says at once. "And Hermès, of course. No, you shouldn't. That would be totally naff."

"Thank God for that," he says at once. "Think how terrible if I'd done that. Would you have asked me to stop so that you could get out?"

"Definitely," she answers. "It would have been much too smooth. I'm glad we're going to The Chough. You'll be able to meet Ben. Then you'll be one up."

She sees his look of surprise, the raising of his eyebrows and the way his eyes crease up in that smile that doesn't touch his lips. She guesses that Jamie likes to be one up; that he is an expert in gamesmanship.

"One up?" he asks casually, and she laughs.

"You won't have to rely on Hugo or Ned or Prune to introduce you. You'll be able to say, 'Ben? Oh, I know Ben. I met him at the pub.' That only leaves Janna."

"And Adam," he says.

She shrugs. "They've already met Adam. Can't do anything about that."

Suddenly she realizes that she'd like to introduce him to Adam, and she wonders how her brother will react to Jamie.

"When will he be down?" Jamie is asking.

"On Saturday. He's down for the Bank Holiday week. You must come over to meet him."

"I'd like to do that," Jamie says, and she feels foolishly happy and excited.

She raises her face to the sun and closes her eyes.

"Don't you feel," she asks, "that there are some moments when you want to drive for ever? Just going on and on until it gets dark or there's no more road."

She opens her eyes and glances sideways at him, and sees that he is laughing silently.

"And then?" he asks.

Dossie knows that he is trying to wrong-foot her and she is delighted that they have so quickly moved into this easy bantering early friendship.

"Oh, then," she answers, shrugging. "Well, if you were the kind of man to have an Hermès silk scarf in your glove compartment I should feel very nervous. But then I wouldn't have gone driving into the dark with you in the first place."

She falls silent, surprised at herself, wondering if she has misjudged him and that he might be shocked at her easiness, her familiarity, but when she slides another glance at him she sees that he is still laughing.

"I know just what you mean about the driving," he says. "I'd love to drive to Land's End. But I have to think of the dogs so it'll just have to be The Chough today, I'm afraid."

She gives a snort. "Typical," she says. "Mike always said that you fly-boys had no sense of adventure. Oh, well. The Chough it is."

"You can drive home if you like," he offers.

She turns in her seat to look at him, to see if he's joking, and he glances briefly at her with that smile creasing his eyes, eyebrows raised.

Oh God, she thinks. I'm falling in love with him.

"I'll take that as a 'yes' then, shall I?" he's asking, and she settles back in her seat, smiling to herself.

"You're on," she says. "And no reneging on it later."

"Do I seem like a man who reneges on his word?" he asks as he drives into the pub car park, pulls on the handbrake and switches off the engine.

Dossie purses her lips, pretends to think about it.

"I don't think I know you well enough to answer," she says decorously.

"Well, we'd better remedy that," he says briefly, and gets out.

She follows him into the pub and there is Ben, grooving quietly behind the bar to Enrique Iglesias' "Bailando", and she smiles at him. His face lights up, and then looks surprised to see her with someone new.

"Hi, Ben," she says. "How are you doing? This is Jamie, Hugo's cousin. Have you got a table for us?"

He comes out from behind the bar, settles them at a table and hands them menus, and then goes off to get some drinks. Dossie looks enquiringly at Jamie, as if waiting for his reaction.

"So that's Prune's young fellow," he says. "It's nothing to do with me but I approve."

"Me, too," says Dossie. "So that just leaves Adam. I'm beginning to look forward to this party."

"Are you sure Janna won't join us?" asks Jamie. "At the moment the numbers, male to female, are a bit weighted in our favour, five to two."

Dossie shrugs. "Sounds good to me," she counters. "You know what Mae West used to say?"

Jamie shakes his head. "No. But I think you're going to tell me."

She grins at him. "'So many men. So little time,'" she quotes, and he bursts out laughing.

Ben brings their drinks and she thanks him and then raises her glass to Jamie. He lifts his glass and smiles at her.

"Next time Land's End," he says.

CHAPTER
NINETEEN

As soon as Ned walks in through the front door and hears Jamie playing the piano upstairs in the sitting-room, his intuition tells him that something of great moment has been happening. He couldn't say just why — he's heard Jamie jazzing up Bach many times before — but this time there's a little something extra about the speed and the energy, a whole vibe about the place, that alerts his sixth sense. And when he goes into the kitchen and sees the empty cold box standing on the table he knows that he's right.

"Hi," Hugo is shouting up the stairs. "We're back."

The arpeggios slow a little and then stop and the dogs come hurrying down the stairs. Jamie follows more slowly.

"Looks like we've had a visit from Dossie," says Ned, still looking at the box, which has Dossie's Fill the Freezer stickers on it. "Did you know she was coming?"

"Oh my God, I utterly forgot," Hugo says. "She did say she was doing deliveries over this way today."

"Well, I expect Jamie was able to cope with it," Ned says calmly.

"Cope with what?" asks Jamie, coming in behind them.

"I forgot to tell Dossie we were in Plymouth," says Hugo. "It's lucky you were in. Sorry."

"Nothing to be sorry about," answers Jamie. "We got the freezer filled but she left the box behind."

"And did you play to her?" asks Ned, settling himself in his armchair beside the Aga. He watches Jamie, noticing that he is in high spirits, which he is only just able to contain. He sees the quick glance Hugo gives his cousin: questioning, alert.

"No, I didn't, as it happens," replies Jamie casually. "I took her to the pub for lunch. It seemed the polite thing to do since she'd just supplied us with food for the next few weeks."

There is a tiny silence.

"So that's why she forgot her cold box," says Hugo.

He lifts it from the table and puts it into the utility room and Ned glimpses his resigned expression.

"We went in my car," says Jamie. "And when we got home she simply switched cars and went off."

"That's all good, then," says Hugo. "You must have enjoyed yourselves."

"Oh, we did. I met Ben and I let Dossie drive home. She's a bloody good driver, actually."

"But you didn't tell her that," says Ned, grinning.

"Good grief, no," says Jamie, shocked. "Don't want her getting any ideas."

"If you're not one up you're one down?"

Ned's laughing now. He can't help himself. Jamie's sense of well-being is a delight to behold. And, after all, the human heart instinctively turns to consolation. After the brutal end to his career, and the disability he now has to deal with, Ned cannot grudge him this pleasure. He knows that if Jamie had the least idea that Hugo had any hopes for himself with Dossie, he would have backed right off. As it is, Jamie can see no reason why he should not follow his instincts.

"Stephen Potter is my guru," Jamie answers, grinning back at him. "As you well know. So how was the check-up?"

"Everything is proceeding as it should be. Everyone was very helpful."

"So you didn't get the dogs out for a walk?" asks Hugo.

Jamie shakes his head. "No, but I can take them now if you like."

"I'll take them," says Hugo. "I'd like to stretch my legs after all that sitting about. I shan't be long. We'll have a drink when I get back."

He goes out, with the dogs clattering behind him, and Ned reaches for the newspaper. Jamie hesitates.

"Anything I can get you?" he asks.

Ned shakes his head. "No, thanks. You can go back to your playing. Leave the door open; I like to hear you."

Jamie goes out and up the stairs. Ned unfolds the newspaper but he doesn't read it. This isn't just about Jamie; it's about Dossie, too. He wouldn't want Dossie to be hurt. Ned gives a little sigh, and then a snort of contempt at his foolishness. Can't a man and a woman have lunch together without it being invested with high drama? But he's too experienced to be able to ignore Jamie's suppressed high spirits, and he suspects that

Dossie is a woman who might be susceptible to falling in love. He knows the feeling only too well.

Jamie is playing "Just The Way You Are". Ned gives a deeper sigh and opens the newspaper.

Hugo drives out of the village into the woods at the edge of the moor. He parks the car and lets the dogs out, standing for a moment before he shuts the door so as to breathe in the scents that drift on the currents of warm air. The dogs sniff around, smelling the passing of a badger or a fox, then a squirrel darts across the clearing and they are after it in a scuffle of dead leaves and dry earth.

Hugo follows, hanging their leads loosely around his neck. He is seeing Jamie's face, hearing his voice, studiedly casual, as he said, "I took her to the pub for lunch." Hugo gives a tiny bitter snort. It's rather like Emilia all over again except that this time it's clear that Jamie has no idea that his cousin's feelings might be engaged. Too often in London he's seen Hugo with attractive women with whom he's made good, deep friendships to be suspicious now.

"I think romance has been left out of my make-up," he once said to Jamie. "Occasionally I think I might want to follow up but I always lose my nerve."

He experiences a moment of anger, regret, sadness, and then the peace and beauty that surround him soothes his pain and he lets out his breath in a great sigh. If he's honest with himself he knows that he would never have made it with Dossie; that crucial spark is missing. And, deep down, he doesn't really want the

172

hurly-burly that belongs with passion or the life-changing decisions that go with it. He's really very happy with the status quo, and if Jamie is being distracted from his problems, if he can find a new happiness and structure to his life, isn't that a rather wonderful thing? On the other hand, he doesn't see why it should be made too easy for him. Hugo begins to smile as he thinks of the many ways that this might turn into rather a good tease.

His spirits rising, he hurries on after the dogs, climbing up towards the moor.

When Prune comes in she can hear the piano but no dogs come rushing out to meet her. She guesses from the kind of music that it is Jamie playing, and when she puts her head round the kitchen door and sees Ned asleep in his armchair, the newspaper falling across his chest, she slips out again and goes upstairs.

Jamie smiles at her, but continues to play, though more quietly lest she should want to talk.

"Ned's asleep," she tells him, "and I imagine Hugo is out with the dogs. I'm going to have a shower."

"I was giving him a recital," says Jamie, "but clearly it was more like a lullaby. Yes, Hugo's taken the dogs off for a walk."

"How did Ned's check-up go? Is everything OK?"

"As far as I could gather, it's all going according to plan. Guess who I met earlier?"

Prune looks at him, trying to think who it might be. He has an expression on his face that she recognizes from years of living with three elder brothers: it seems that a tease is about to take place. She shrugs, shakes her head. "I don't know. Kim Kardashian? Benedict Cumberbatch? I give up. Who did you meet earlier?"

Jamie gives a little flourish up and down the keys. "I met Ben," he says — and she has to make an effort not to show any interest apart from a slight raising of the eyebrows.

"Ah," she says, nonchalantly. "You've been to the pub. Did you go on your own, then?"

She sees that she's managed to disconcert him just a little and she grins to herself.

"No," he answers. "No, actually I went with Dossie."

"Ah," she says. "That was quick work. When the mice are away . . .?"

"*Touché*," he says, laughing. "Ben says he's looking forward to the party."

"Did he?" She answers a little too eagerly and tries to pass it off. "Well, he might have to wait a bit. I'm not sure when it's going to happen."

"When Adam's down," answers Jamie, "which is at the weekend, so I hope Ben can get time off. He's got very good taste in music."

She can't help the little glow of pleasure when she hears Ben praised.

"He likes all sorts," she says. "He always has to have music. When he works. In the car."

"Does he play an instrument?"

She shakes her head. "Well, the recorder when he was little but we all played the recorder, didn't we, at some time? Used to drive my mother round the bend."

174

"Don't knock the recorder," says Jamie. "It can make a remarkable sound."

She laughs. "My mum would agree with you but not in a good way. See you later."

Prune goes out and up another flight of stairs to her room on the top floor. She likes to be up here in this small bedroom that looks away across the harbour and the cliffs to the sea's horizon. She is alone up here with her own space, a small bathroom, and another tiny room where she can keep her belongings. It's rather like Ben's little flat at The Chough and she wonders how he will react to these quarters of hers, and to being here with this household of odd people.

It would be good if either of them had a place where they could go and chill and just do their own thing, but that seems a long way off at the moment. Meanwhile, she knows that she's lucky to be here, to have a job, to have Ben. She strips off her working clothes, checks her phone, and goes to have a shower.

Dossie makes her last drop at the little holiday complex of Penharrow on the edge of Port Isaac and sets off home. She is still on a high after her lunch with Jamie, and especially after driving his MGB back. It revived all sorts of memories, but they're good ones and she could almost believe that Mike's spirit was with them, encouraging her. Jamie is so like Mike: so easy, such fun to be with; quick, acerbic, but with an unexpected kindness.

She parks the car, decides to deal with the cold boxes later, and gets out. The thrush is singing in the apple tree and for a moment she experiences that little wrench of the heart, remembering how much Mo loved the thrush's song. Dossie opens the door and is greeted unexpectedly by the sound of clapping. She's taken Adam's advice and leaves the radio on, switched to Radio 3, just as Mo always did, and now she's getting used to entering to the sound of singing, a voice talking, a symphony. It was good advice. The house no longer feels empty, though there have been one or two bad moments. Once, the talking voice sounded just like Pa's and quite without thinking she called out in response before realizing what it was. She felt foolish: foolish and bereft. The second time was when she came in to the sound of Pergolesi's *Stabat Mater* with the glorious voices of Emma Kirkby and James Bowman. This was a favourite of Mo's and once again there was an ache of longing and sadness for times past.

Now, however, she has Adam's visit to look forward to, as well as the rather exciting development in her new friendship with Jamie. And even as she thinks about it, a text pings in and she reaches for her phone with a sense of expectation before she remembers that Jamie doesn't have her phone number. The text is from Hugo:

Check-up went well. I hear you had lunch at the pub! Let's make a plan for the party. xx

Dossie suffers a little pang of guilt whilst at the same time wondering quite how to act now with Jamie when Hugo and Ned are around. She feels nervous at the

176

thought of her next visit to the house on the quay but then suddenly laughs aloud. How good it is to have something like this about which to feel nervous: to feel young again. It's what Prune would call a First World problem. She sends back a text:

Adam here Saturday for the week so it will depend on Ben's time off. Looking forward to it. Glad all went well for Ned. xx

She feels confident; happy. Dossie thinks of her mantra and laughs. Her grip on events seems more secure; her life suddenly looks full of promise.

So now, she tells herself, all I need to do is to get a dog.

PART THREE

CHAPTER
TWENTY

Janna sits in her usual seat in chapel, tucked away at the end of a row, aware of the scent of the lilac, growing outside the open window beside her, and the sound of birdsong. It's just after seven o'clock, and the stone walls are washed with sunlight. A few retreatants have made it to this early service and Mother Magda, frail but indomitable, speaks the words of the opening prayer:

"'The night has passed and the day lies open before us . . .'"

And what, wonders Janna, will the day bring? The usual Offices, which give structure to the day; the domestic round. Her life is peaceful and fulfilling where once it had been chaotic, purposeless and empty. She longed for stability, for approval, until she arrived here with nowhere to live, no family, no work, and found a place to stop for a while. She travelled light, carrying her old tote bag with the memories of her childhood wrapped in it: the treasures her mother had given her when she was small. She kept them with her, taking them to the foster homes, from which she ran away at the earliest opportunity, never knowing her father, who'd abandoned them before she was born. These precious things, these symbols, were all she had to show of her mother's love for her. How fiercely she protected them: the Peter Rabbit mug, the *Little Miss Sunshine* book, and the pretty Indian silk shawl.

"'As we rejoice in the gift of this new day . . .'"

Janna remembers that when she told Sister Emily the lonely, unhappy story behind these precious things the elderly nun, rather than commiserating with her, smiled at her with a kind of radiance and said: "When you no longer need them you will be free," as if this were the goal Janna must be pursuing.

It didn't take long. First little Jakey accidentally broke the mug, then, because he loved it so much, she gave him the book, and finally dear old Sister Nichola appropriated the shawl. How easy it was, in the end, to let go.

"'. . . may the light of your presence, O God, set our hearts on fire with love for you . . .'"

Here in this beautiful old house, on the high cliffs of the wild north Cornish coast, she came home at last. They all — the Sisters, Father Pascal, Clem, even little Jakey — recognized her need for privacy; to live at the edge of the community life without committing herself. They respected it, enabled it, until at last she was able to move closer, to take some responsibility to herself. She felt part of this extended family, the Sisters, Clem and Tilly and Jakey, and even a few people beyond Chi-Meur's walls. Dossie of course was dearest, and best beloved, and very vulnerable just now.

"'Raise us up, O God, that we may live in your presence . . .'"

Janna knew at once; as soon as she saw her yesterday. She sighed and rolled her eyes as Dossie beamed at her, putting the usual offering of cakes on the small table in the courtyard, exuding happiness.

"OK," Janna said, resigned. "Don't tell me. Jamie, is it?"

She could see that Dossie was struggling to make a show of innocence but after a moment she began to laugh.

"Drop-dead gorgeous, darling," she said. "But don't tell anyone."

"I shan't need to," Janna said drily. She thought about Dossie's relationship with her unpredictable brother. "What's Adam going to say?"

"Ah, well." Dossie sobered up and looked anxious. "I hope that he won't find out just yet. I want him to be more, you know, like he was last time. Feeling he's at home. Confident."

"Then you'll have to do better than this," Janna said.

"Well, it's different with you," Dossie said defensively. "I don't have to pretend with you."

"And how are Hugo and Ned taking it?"

"There's nothing to take," cried Dossie. "Honestly. It's just that I went over with some food for the freezer and Jamie was on his own. Hugo had taken Ned for his check-up at Derriford. I'd met Jamie briefly, because Hugo texted me to drop in not long after he arrived, and so, because nobody was around, Jamie suggested we go to the pub and he let me drive his MGB home. Gosh, that was fun. It really took me back."

She was smiling again, like a teenager who'd been given an unexpected treat, and then her face changed and she added: "He reminds me so much of Mike." And suddenly Janna wasn't inclined to laugh or tease. Instead she felt profoundly touched.

"'You are the God of my salvation. In you I hope all the day long . . .'"

Now, in the chapel, Janna shifts on her chair, remembering Dossie's expression.

"Well, that's good, isn't it?" she asked tentatively.

Dossie looked at her quite seriously and nodded. "It was really odd. And really nice. I've never known anyone like Mike. He was such fun to be with. He would banter and josh but at the same time there was such a quickness to notice how I felt and to act on it. He was perceptive and kind."

There was a silence. Janna rarely heard Dossie talk like this about Mike and she was very much moved.

"I still miss him," Dossie admitted. "It doesn't get better. You just learn how to deal with it."

"So what happens next?"

Dossie shrugged. "Well, there's the party." She began to smile. "And you're invited."

Janna experienced her usual sensations of alarm at the prospect of being moved out of her comfort zone.

"What party?"

"Well, Prune wants to bring Ben home to meet everyone and show him where she lives, and they thought it would be nice to invite Adam, and then we thought about you. I've often mentioned you so they're dying to meet you."

184

Janna was already shaking her head. "No way," she said firmly. "Not a chance."

"I knew you'd say that," said Dossie. "I told them you wouldn't want to, but how would you feel if I were to bring them here? One at a time, of course."

"Here?" Janna glanced round as if Hugo or Ned might even now be advancing into the courtyard.

"It would be OK," Dossie said coaxingly. "I wish you would, Janna. They're my friends and so are you. It would be so nice for you all to know each other."

Janna reflected on it; after all, Ned and Hugo didn't sound too alarming and it would be very interesting, now, to meet Jamie.

"Maybe," she said cautiously. "Here, but not all of them at once."

"Of course not," Dossie said. She grinned at her. "But which one first?"

Janna surprised herself with her answer. "Adam."

Dossie's eyebrows shot up. "Adam?" she repeated. "Well, of course. Why not? He's driving down tomorrow very early."

"Well, bring him for a cup of coffee or tea some time. Whatever you think would be right."

"Adam doesn't drink tea," Dossie said.

But Janna could see that she was thinking about it; that for a moment she'd forgotten about Jamie.

"And you'd rather meet him here? You've been to The Court. It wouldn't feel strange to you there."

Janna shook her head. She had a strong feeling that she wanted to be on her own patch for this first meeting.

"No. If he wants to come then just bring him. I'd really like to meet Adam, though some of the things you've told me about him in the past make me a bit nervous."

"I know I have." Dossie looked anxious, puzzled. "It's weird, really. He's been so difficult, sometimes, that I've quite disliked him but I hadn't realized how hard it's all been for him. He's been damaged and his instinct is to strike first."

"We're all damaged," Janna answered grimly, "and we need to protect ourselves. Or at least we think we need to. Perhaps Adam is beginning to feel he doesn't need to any more."

"I think that's true," agreed Dossie slowly, "but it's just awful, somehow, that it's happened because Mo and Pa have died. It's so confusing. They were so good to me. I don't know how to handle it. I can't deny them, yet I want to help him."

"Perhaps you don't need to deny them," suggested Janna cautiously. She never felt comfortable offering advice but she hated to see Dossie looking so anxious. "Perhaps you just need to listen to him without attempting to justify them. Just to begin with. Go with the flow."

Dossie nodded. "I know you're right. And it helps now that he's met Hugo and Ned so that it won't be just me all the time. And you, too. I'd love it if you were to become friends."

"And Jamie," added Janna mischievously, trying to recapture that earlier happier mood. "Mustn't forget the old Drop-dead Gorgeous."

186

Dossie began to laugh. "And Prune and Ben. It's so important to feel part of a family, isn't it? I'm lucky. I've got Clem and Jakey, and now Tilly, but I think it would be good for Adam to have a few men of his own age when he comes down. It might encourage him to come and stay if there are a few more options."

"'In the tender compassion of our God, the dawn from on high shall break upon us . . .'"

Janna bows her head for the blessing. Even now Adam will be on his way, driving west, coming home.

Adam gets back into the car, refreshed after his break at the Exeter service station, and turns on to the A30. He left London slightly later than he intended but he's beaten the weight of the Bank Holiday traffic and he'll be at St Endellion before it builds up. It's good to make this journey so early in the morning; driving west, away from the rising sun, into the darkness, which every moment grows brighter.

It's odd to be travelling this road with a light heart, even with expectation, and he wonders why it need have been so bad in the past; why the sense of rejection should have affected him so much. Other people survived the experience of being sent from abroad to school at a very young age and by now, surely, he should have learned to deal with it. And for most of the time he has. He loves his job, and he's good at it; he has close friends. Only when he was going home, back to the inevitable questions, to the third degree, did the past resurface: the reminder that to come second was to be first of the losers. He can see how his own sense of inadequacy became a self-fulfilling prophecy and that it seemed better, simpler, to keep at a distance from his family. He knows that he allowed the rupture to happen, that he should have been tougher. The danger is that his feelings of guilt might colour his future relationship with Dossie. It's hard for her to see Mo and Pa from his viewpoint and he doesn't want her to feel in any way disloyal to them or obliged to defend them. There must be some way through without apportioning blame.

A drifting curtain of mist obscures the western slopes of Dartmoor and small fields are edged by banks of white and pink hawthorn. The cloudy sky diffuses golden light, then suddenly the sun breaks through so that the road ahead gleams and shimmers. Adam crosses the county boundary into Cornwall. He thinks about Dossie, wondering what is really best for her; whether she should stay at The Court. It's amusing to talk about decaying grandeur, but not so much fun when the roof is leaking and windows need replacing. He can't quite see Dossie in a modern house, or a flat, but she must feel lonely rattling about in The Court. Perhaps a dog might fill the gap, up to a point, but there's still the cost of the upkeep of such a big old house to think about. He can't help but see The Court as an investment that should be protected, as well as a home, and it's in Dossie's interests that it should be properly looked after. He feels protective towards her. When she first mentioned Hugo and Ned he suspected that she might be somehow romantically involved with one of them, but once he met them himself he knew at once that this was not the case. She behaved towards them as she might towards any of her close friends, knowing them well enough to laugh and joke, to share an easy affection that flowed between the three of them. Just at first Ned reminded him of Pa: that straight, critical look and strong clasp of the hand. He was glad he was able to recover from it quickly and to enter into this new friendship that Dossie seemed to want to share with him. And Ned and Hugo were so open, so ready to include him. He was touched by their warmth and is looking forward to meeting them again. And Jamie: Dossie has told him about Jamie. It seems that Jamie has been dealt a very tough hand and Adam wonders how it must be to lose one's career and health all in one turn of the cards.

How suddenly life changes, the old pattern giving way unexpectedly to something new and utterly different. He's glad that the old jealousy of his sister, which has gnawed for so long like a canker at his soul, seems quite gone. It has been difficult to see the approval, the love, flowing so readily towards her whilst his own life was so unimpressive in his parents' eyes; difficult to sustain a good relationship with her, though when Mike was alive they were closer.

It was incredibly hard for her when Mike died. Poor Dossie. Mike was so alive, so dynamic, his absence was a terrible thing for her. Adam shakes his head, remembering. It was tough for him, too. God, he loved Mike. He stood between Adam and his parents, defending him, approving him, encouraging him.

"It's like that sometimes between fathers and sons," he said consolingly, when Pa was dismissive about Adam getting the job in London. "It was the same with my old dad. He wanted me to follow the family tradition and go into the army. Nothing I did pleased him. Sometimes you can't do right for doing wrong."

Mike's kindness, his approval, was everything to Adam when he was in his late teens. His grief when Mike was killed paled into insignificance besides Dossie's; left so young with a small boy to raise. There was no room — nor did he know how — to show, to share, his own terrible sadness. He did what he could, tried to support them both, and then she took little Clem and moved back to Cornwall; back to Mo and Pa. In some foolish way he felt that he'd failed them, both her and Clem; failed Mike.

At Bodmin Adam turns west on to the Wadebridge road, heading for St Endellion.

"I shall have breakfast waiting," Dossie told him when they spoke earlier in the week. "No stopping off and pigging out on the way down."

"As if I would," he protested. "I shall want the full English breakfast, mind. None of your croissants and special granola from the farm shop."

"You shall have it," she promised. "Travel safely."

It's as if the wheel has come full circle; that he has another chance to support Dossie. He felt it when he was last down here: that she was looking to him to help her through this period of bereavement, and this time he simply mustn't let her down. He thinks about Mike,

190

and he smiles to himself and increases his speed. Soon he'll be home.

CHAPTER
TWENTY-ONE

Lucy lifts Dan out of his high chair and sets him down on the floor. He toddles away to his *Thomas the Tank Engine* railway set and kneels amongst the rails and the trucks. She watches him for a moment, then sits down again at the small table and picks up her coffee cup. It's too early for Mum, who is still in bed, but it's good to sit here, to look out at the distant horizon, and plan ahead for when the kitchen is finished and the cottage will be properly up and running.

Lucy sips at her coffee, thinking about her mother. There's something odd going on but she can't quite pin it down. There's a slight disconnect; a distraction in her manner. Of course, Mum can be a bit strange sometimes; she's not quite like other people's mothers.

"It's all that theatrical background. You have to remember that she had a seriously weird childhood," she tells Tom defensively when he comments on her mother's oddball behaviour. "You can't expect her to be like other grannies."

"I guess," he answers. "But there does seem to be a definite lack of reality sometimes. And it's all about her, isn't it?"

When Lucy thought about it later she could see what he meant. Her mother lives out of her own reality and anything she really wants to do she is able to justify before too long.

But perhaps, thinks Lucy guiltily, we're all a bit like that.

She looks at Dan, kneeling amongst his engines and trucks, and her heart is filled with love and anguish. She's seen how her colleagues beat themselves up when they can't get to the end-of-term play or the athletics day or a prize-giving. Generally one of the parents manages to show up but an awful lot of self-chastisement goes on.

"Nothing beats being there," someone said to her once, and she's never forgotten it.

Meanwhile, Lucy prays that it will all work out with the nanny so that she can have the best of both worlds. And since this is how she feels, it's unrealistic to expect her mother to be different. What is different, though, is that Mum doesn't seem to suffer from the guilt — or anyway, not for long. She gets over it very quickly by convincing herself that, whatever the outcome of a situation, however unfavourable it might seem to be for everyone else, it will be better for them in the long run.

Lucy finishes her coffee and gives a little shrug: nice work if you can get it. Nevertheless, none of this is quite relevant to her mother's behaviour just now. She's being really good about staying here at the cottage whilst the work is being done, despite several hitches and hold-ups. Usually she becomes restless if she's too long away from London but she's being very patient, though there's still this odd sense of distraction about her.

It's as if, thinks Lucy, she's waiting for something really good to happen; calm but excited.

Suddenly she remembers the old friend, the man she met in Relish, and she wonders if he is the reason for her mother's readiness to stay in Rock. It might be as simple as that. And if it is, well, that's all good.

Lucy thinks of her father, that genial, jolly, affectionate man, who was rather like a much-loved uncle or some other relative, rather than a parent. He exercised no fatherly rights, demanded nothing of her except her happiness and affection, and she'd loved him very dearly. He'd comforted her when she was unhappy, rejoiced in her successes, was continually amazed by her cleverness at passing exams, and told her how beautiful she was. Yes, OK, he was vain, insecure, and loved attention, but he hurt nobody and most people adored him. She is very sad that he never knew Tom or saw Dan. He would have been so proud of both of them; so happy for her. Nevertheless, if her mother wants to renew an old friendship Lucy feels quite cool with that. And he seemed such a nice man, very dishy; so struck with the resemblance between her and her mother. Perhaps he'd been in love with her, back in the day.

If she's honest, she knows that she's ready to encourage it because she feels just the least bit guilty about the way she and Tom have taken the opportunities offered in their work and moved away to Geneva. It's a bit tough for her mum to be left behind

194

but Tom's promotion was simply too good to miss. Maybe renewing an old friendship will fill a few gaps and will make the prospect of coming down to Cornwall to stay at the cottage even more attractive.

Lucy is suddenly aware that Dan has become very still and quiet. As she looks at him she sees his eyes grow round and thoughtful, his face turns a rather peculiar colour and he holds his breath. She knows that she is looking at someone who is about to do a gigantic poo. Leaping to her feet, she seizes him and hurries him out of the sitting-room and up the stairs.

Later, after breakfast, Emilia, Lucy and Daniel catch the ferry across to Padstow and wander in the town. Dan loves the ferry; loves to be on the water. He shouts at the seagulls and waves at people in the other boats that sail or motor past. The town is busy now that the Bank Holiday has begun and Lucy buys an ice cream for Dan, sits him in his buggy and pushes him towards the harbour.

"Watch out for seagulls," Emilia warns. "I'm going to buy a paper."

She's folding the paper so that it will fit into her bag, pushing it in, when two men come round the corner at the end of the street and stop, talking together, as if deciding on some course of action. As she looks up and sees them she gives an intake of breath so sharp it's as if she's cut herself. It's Jamie she recognizes first. Hugo is slightly shorter, there's a lot of grey in his hair and his face is fuller, though he's still a very attractive man. But Jamie looks tough, slightly dangerous, with the

195

familiar wary, assessing look, his head tilted very slightly to the left. He'd always stood like that; as if he were ready for action. She stares at them in amazement, unprepared for such a reaction, though this is something she's been expecting, waiting for, during this last week.

They finish conferring and Jamie turns away and disappears down a side street. Hugo is coming towards her but now panic overcomes her and she moves back into the doorway, head down, pretending to be searching for something in her bag. Hugo strides past and she watches him moving on amongst the visitors, and she wonders if he would have recognized her. If Lucy hadn't spoken of him would she have known him? All she can think of is Jamie. She hadn't expected to be so affected by the sight of him. And she knows now that she doesn't want him to be prepared by Hugo, ready for her, as it were. She wants to be able to pick her moment, to come upon him when he is alone. But how is it to be done?

It occurs to her that if Jamie and Hugo had walked round that corner a few moments earlier they might have seen Lucy. Hugo might have spoken to her, introduced them, and Jamie would have seen Daniel. Emilia's gut churns and she takes quick, deep breaths. Even now Jamie might come walking back; Lucy might be strolling across the road, pushing Dan in his buggy.

Emilia can see now how important it is to be in control, not just wandering about and leaving things to chance. She needs to be prepared. Her mind darts and flicks about, trying to see how a meeting with Jamie

196

might be managed but meanwhile she needs to get Lucy and Daniel on to the ferry. And all the while she's remembering how Jamie stood there, with his head tilted on one side, looking at Hugo. How could she have forgotten how he used to stand like that; how sexy he was?

Once again the memory comes out of the blue: Hugo's room in Bristol, the "*Widmung*" playing, the door opening and Jamie coming in, and the way she got to her feet in one quick, smooth movement. As she hurries across to the harbour, looking for Lucy amongst the jostle of tourists, she tries to remember why she ever left him. She loved him so much. Was it the separations, the dreary married quarters, the other wives with whom she had so little in common? It's difficult to remember now why she fled so often to the chaotic theatrical London life or why Nigel captivated her so easily. It occurs to her, like a blow to the heart, that Jamie might be happily married with a family, but she thrusts the thought away. It must all be as it was before, back then in Bristol. Hugo and Jamie, unattached and ready for love.

She spots Lucy standing by the harbour wall, pointing to something, and she sees Dan's arm outstretched, copying her. Emilia hurries towards them, calling Lucy's name, trying to think of a really good reason for going back to Rock so soon. Lucy sees her and waves, turning the pushchair so that Dan will see her, too.

"I was just thinking," says Emilia, as she gets into earshot, "that it's a bit busy here, isn't it? I was wondering if we might drive up on to the moor to see the ponies. We could take a picnic. What d'you think? Would you like to see the ponies, Danny?"

Dan's face beams with delight at the prospect and he shouts, "Ponies, ponies," and Lucy smiles and shrugs.

"OK," she says. "If that's what he'd like. It is a bit overwhelming, isn't it?"

"We'd probably have to queue for lunch," says Emilia, trying to hide her relief. "Let's dash back to the ferry and I'll make up a picnic and we'll get out of all these crowds."

Luckily there are only a few people waiting for the ferry, and soon they are on the boat and heading towards Rock. Emilia stares aft at the busy town, wondering where Jamie and Hugo are, trying to imagine how and where she might be able to effect a meeting. Luckily, Lucy and Danny are going back to Geneva tomorrow — this has been just a quick dash to check up on the work in the kitchen — and she will be free again to patrol the local places.

"What's the name of the pub you mentioned?" she asks casually, as they disembark and walk back to the cottage. "I haven't tried it yet."

"The Chough," Lucy answers. "We should go while I'm here. I saw that friend of yours there. Hugo, is it?"

"Yes," she answers calmly. "Hugo. Never mind. When you come next time, perhaps. It'll be nicer for Dan up on the moor today. You get Dan sorted while I do the picnic."

CHAPTER
TWENTY-TWO

"Poor Ben," observes Adam, as he and Dossie make the detour to the pub to pick up Ben. "Rather daunting, isn't it, to be confronted by all these people?"

"Well, he knows us all," says Dossie. "It's not as if we're strangers."

"It's a bit different, though, isn't it? He's only met you as customers in The Chough, not at a private party en masse."

"He'll be fine," says Dossie robustly. "Ben's a sweetie but he's tough. And Prune will be there."

"But isn't that worse?" suggests Adam. "To be there with your girlfriend and everyone looking at you. It's not as if we're their contemporaries. It's like having four fathers looking at you."

That's how he would feel, thinks Dossie, watching her brother's hands tighten on the wheel. And the terrible thing is that, even now, the memory fills him with a kind of dread. How sad is that?

"I can't quite see all of you in that light," she comments. "Well, Hugo and Jamie might tease him unmercifully but nobody's going to be judging him. We all love Ben. And Prune. It's a pity his car has let him down. It's a bit of a banger but at least he has wheels and he might have preferred to have the option to leave when he feels like it rather than being dependent on us. But there we are. And at least it's one less vehicle to park on the quay."

"I will admit," says Adam, "that I rather covet Jamie's MGB. I bet it costs him a fortune to keep it running. Those old classic cars just eat money. But I imagine he can afford it."

"I suppose he can," she answers casually.

Dossie's wondering why she has no wish to talk about Jamie, to discuss him. She's trying to work out how she feels about him. He drove over to The Court yesterday, early in the evening, following a text from Hugo:

We need more wine glasses. Can you help us out, please? x

She smiled at the request. Hugo is notorious for smashing glasses, dropping plates, and she tapped out her reply knowing it would make him smile:

As long as someone else does the washing up. x

She didn't expect Jamie to turn up, unaccompanied. She and Adam were in the garden when he drove in. She heard the engine, the slam of the car door, and walked round the side of the house to come face to face with him.

"Oh," she said inadequately. "Hello."

His eyes crinkled up with amusement. "Hello," he said. "I'm here on a glass-collection mission."

Furious with herself for allowing him to see her confusion she tried to pull herself together.

"Oh, gosh. Sorry. I didn't realize that Hugo needed them now. I assumed we'd bring them with us tomorrow."

"He's doing that housewifely thing," Jamie said. "You know? Prepping madly. Dragging out all the non-matching plates and tutting over them and counting the two clean spots in Roo's feeder."

She laughed then. "Wasn't it Tigger's feeder?"

"Damn," he answered. "I think you could be right."

"Come and meet Adam," she said. "We were just about to have a drink. Would you like to join us?"

Even as she asked the question she remembered what Hugo had told her about Jamie's problem with alcohol; how quickly even small amounts affected him. She was embarrassed, wishing she'd been more tactful, but he looked quite calm.

"Not when I'm driving, thanks," he said.

Adam was standing, waiting for her to reappear, and as she introduced them and they shook hands, she cast around in her mind for what she might offer Jamie to drink, hoping he wouldn't just take the glasses and go, but when he turned back to her she knew that he was aware of her dilemma.

"Do you have any tonic water?" he asked. "That would be good," and she was able to pull herself together and say, "Ice and a slice?" as Ben does at the pub.

"Ice and a slice," he answered. "Definitely."

She went inside, into the kitchen, and poured some tonic into a glass and added a slice of lemon and some ice. She then stood for a moment, telling herself that she was a complete idiot, before she went back to join them in the garden.

"I've got a boxful of a dozen wine glasses," she told him. "They come in useful when I'm catering for a party. They're not very special because of breakages but they should do the trick."

"Finish your drink," he suggested. "There's no hurry. I love your garden. This wisteria is amazing. It must be a devil to keep pruned."

She looked at him, surprised. "Are you a gardener?"

"Not much of one but enough to know that you have to look after one of these to get this kind of effect. My mother was a ferocious gardener and I learned never to make the same mistake twice when it came to pruning. She took no prisoners."

"Ours was much the same," Adam answered. "Three strikes and you were out."

They all laughed, and now, as they drive in The Chough's car park, Dossie remembers how pleased she was to hear Adam talk with amusement and affection about Mo. Ben is waiting, looking smart but casual in a pair of black jeans and a cotton shirt. He waves to them as they pull up beside him and he opens the back door and climbs in.

Prune waits anxiously for Ben to arrive whilst trying to appear cool. It's one thing everyone knowing Ben at the pub but it's a bit different inviting him here and having to behave naturally. Luckily, Adam's a bit of a new boy, too, and she's hoping that having him here will take the heat off a bit. Adam's never been to the house before so that will cause a bit of a distraction. She rather liked Adam when she met him at The Chough that time they all had lunch together, though she sensed that he wasn't quite so much at ease as he was acting. Once or twice she caught an odd expression on his face, as if he were surprised to find himself there; as if this were not a normal situation for him. She is so used to the super confidence of her older brothers that it is always rather sweet to see a man who is slightly unsure of himself. It was this touch of vulnerability that drew her to Ben: a sensitivity behind the ready laughter and the jokes. Sometimes it's good not always to be on your toes, ready for the quick response, though she enjoys the banter, too.

She likes listening to Jamie and Hugo, who occasionally behave like teenagers. Yesterday she caught them playing Rock, Paper, Scissors.

"Oh, honestly," she said. "I don't believe this. How old are you?"

They'd looked a bit embarrassed — but only a bit.

"We used to play it to see which of us would get the last Malteser," Jamie said.

"And don't say what good memories we've got," warned Hugo. "We're not that old."

Prune wanders out into the courtyard. It's going to be an early party with drinks and nibblies, and then a buffet supper. Rose has helped to organize it but Jamie and Hugo are surprisingly efficient, though they use different tactics. Hugo has a slapdash but creative approach whilst Jamie deals with it rather as if it is a military exercise. Between them everything is done and ready, Rose has gone home, and Prune glances at her watch again and wishes they could get started.

Hugo appears suddenly at her elbow, holding a bottle. "How about a few bubbles?" he suggests. "Just to get us started."

She nods, smiling at him. The front door opens, Dossie calls out and the dogs start to bark, and suddenly Prune relaxes. She knows that it's all going to be fun.

Ned sits at the wrought-iron table in the courtyard with his gin and tonic, and observes the scene. Hugo and Dossie have taken control and are making certain that everyone has a drink, and Ben seems very much at ease and is clearly enjoying being waited on for a change.

"You could have a job at The Chough any time," he says jokingly to Dossie, who shakes her head at him.

"I'd be useless," she says. "I'm OK working on my own but it would all be too fast for me."

"But Prune tells us that you're really into IT," Jamie says to him and, whilst he and Ben talk about modern technology, Prune begins to talk to Adam about the dogs who are milling about, hoping for attention, and Dossie sits down for a moment opposite Ned and raises her glass to him.

"I'm only allowed a small one," she tells him, "because I'm driving. I thought Adam might need an extra bit of Dutch courage."

"Oh, come on," protests Ned. "We're not that frightening, are we?"

"Definitely scary," answers Dossie solemnly. "I was terrified when I first met you."

He laughs at her. "Rubbish. I remember it perfectly well and you were entirely composed and made some very rude comments about the state of the kitchen."

"Did I?" She looks rather pleased; as if he has paid her a compliment. "Oh, good. That's OK, then."

Ned studies her, liking the pretty long skirt she's wearing; a change from her usual jeans. Oddly it makes her seem more vulnerable; feminine rather than sexy. She's such a pretty woman. Instinctively he glances at Jamie, who is still talking to Ben. He is quite certain that he is not deceived about the attraction between them but they are both playing it very cool. At this moment Hugo refills Ben's glass and Jamie turns away and catches Ned's eye. He strolls towards them and Ned tries to think of something that will keep Dossie sitting there, protected from the look on Jamie's face that has something focused and determined about it.

"I wondered," Ned says quickly, "whether you ever take a holiday? I don't remember you having one ever since we've known you."

"It's crazy," Dossie answers, unaware that Jamie is close behind her. "I never seem to get time for one. And I'm always at my busiest at holiday times because of the visitors."

"But where," persists Ned, "would you like to go most if you had the time? If you could choose?"

As Dossie deliberates Jamie moves a little nearer.

"She'd go to Land's End," he says, smiling down at her. "Wouldn't you?"

As she glances up at him her cheeks flush bright with colour and Ned feels oddly excluded, almost as if he is eavesdropping on some private moment between them. To his relief Mort barges up, breaking the spell, and Dossie hastens to bend to stroke him, almost as if she is grateful for the interruption. Ned experiences a whole mix of emotions: irritation, confusion, envy. It's clear that Jamie is in control here and Ned resents it whilst also sympathizing. He was just the same when he was younger — ready to seize an advantage — unlike Hugo, who is now suggesting that some food might be a good plan.

"Shall I bring some out to you, Uncle Ned?" he suggests.

But Ned shakes his head, irritated by the implication that he's too old to fetch his own supper.

"Thanks, but I can manage to get to the kitchen," he answers, and then regrets his grumpiness. "I need to see what's on offer," he says.

He picks up his stick and smiles at Hugo, who follows him with Mort at his heels.

Jamie looks at Dossie. He draws down his mouth at the corners and gives a tiny facial shrug. He knows that she has noticed Ned's sharp retort and he invites her complicity but almost at once regrets it. Ned is her host and an older man, and he knows he's behaving just the least bit childishly. He can't seem to help himself. Her presence acts on him like a stimulant and he wants to impress, to amuse. The reference to Land's End was to remind her of the moment in The Chough; to build on their budding relationship. It's just so good to have something positive and exciting in his life that he's in danger of behaving foolishly. But she smiles at him as she gets up.

"You're quite right," she says, as she brushes past him to follow Ned and Hugo into the kitchen. "It would definitely be Land's End."

He wants to grin and punch the air but Prune and Ben are beside him and he stands aside to let them go ahead, then falls in step with Adam.

"So do you think that Ben feels like Daniel in the dragons' den?" he asks. "I think he's handling it very well, poor chap."

"Well, I did wonder," answers Adam. "I said to Dossie that it's rather like having four fathers checking you out, but he seems very calm. I like him."

"I don't think he'll stay in hospitality very long," says Jamie. "He's just saving some money before he goes on his IT course. Hugo and I promised Prune that we wouldn't josh him too much. And we wouldn't mess with Prune, I can tell you."

Standing together, looking into the kitchen, Jamie is aware of Adam beside him. He feels his tension: not the assessing wariness that a military training instils but a nervousness. It's as if Adam is waiting to be judged — and found wanting.

"It's a damned nuisance," Jamie says randomly, "this not being able to have a vodka or a glass of wine. It would be easy to forget to keep track, but you feel such a prat at a party, standing there with a soft drink."

Adam gives him a quick glance. "Dossie did just mention . . ." he begins awkwardly.

"It's not a secret but it's a bit of a fall from grace, if you see what I mean. From pilot to loser in six easy lessons."

Adam frowns. "Oh, but come on. You've still done more than most people would ever dream of. I wish I'd done anything so . . . well . . ." He shrugs, as if embarrassed that he's being over the top.

"I gather that you're in a good job at an estate agency in London. That's impressive, too."

Adam sighs and Jamie can hear bitterness, frustration and disappointment in that sigh. "My old pa wouldn't have agreed with you."

So here it is, thinks Jamie. All these years on and it still has the power to hurt. And the fact that he was disinherited isn't going to make that any better.

"My dad was a bit like that, too. He was with the British Council so he and Mum were always abroad. Hugo and I were at school here together, which is why we're so close. More like brothers than cousins."

"Lucky you," remarks Adam. "Wish I'd had someone like that."

And then Hugo calls, "Come on, you two, or there won't be anything left," and Adam steps back to let Jamie go ahead into the kitchen.

★ ★ ★

As Adam watches Jamie join the group around the kitchen table, suddenly the connection is made. Jamie reminds him of Mike. He's very charismatic but there's something more than that. There's that quick kindness that Adam had found so comforting all those years ago. He remembers the remark Mike made when they'd talked about difficult relationships with their respective fathers and how Mike had said: "You can't do right for doing wrong." In that moment it was as if they'd been allies and, just now with Jamie, it was as if he'd allowed Adam to see the damage to his self-esteem so that they might also share something.

It's clear that Jamie and Dossie are attracted to each other — he'd noticed it when Jamie arrived to fetch the wine glasses — and Adam wonders how that might work out. After all, Jamie lives in Oxfordshire, and it's almost impossible to imagine Dossie leaving Cornwall.

Adam catches Ned's eye across the kitchen and almost instinctively he straightens up and moves forward to join the group. Ned's one of the old school, like Pa, and Adam can't quite shed this response to him. It's interesting that Ben doesn't seem to share this reaction to these older men but just calmly carries on, talking easily, joking, and presently he says to Prune, "So what about some music?" and everyone laughs.

"I told you," says Prune, resigned. "At work, in the car, wherever. We have to have the music."

As Adam watches, he sees that Hugo and Jamie are struck by a similar idea. Hugo looks at his older cousin and shrugs.

"OK," he says. "You first."

Jamie grins at him and goes out of the kitchen, leaving the door open. Presently there is the sound of music: jazz piano. It's very good and Adam sees Dossie raise her eyebrows in approval, and the way Hugo smiles to himself in a slightly bitter, "So here we go again," grimace.

Ben says, "Wow. Is that Jamie playing?"

"Yes," says Ned after a moment. "That's Jamie."

"Cool," says Ben happily, and the party continues.

In the morning, Rose looks around at the remains of the festivities with a jaundiced eye. Hugo and Jamie are still sitting at the kitchen table finishing breakfast, drinking coffee.

"It's always the same," she mutters. "There's them that play and there's them that clears up after."

"We've done a bit," says Hugo placatingly.

"And Dossie offered to stay on last night and clear up but we wouldn't let her," adds Jamie quickly.

Rose smiles to herself at his quick defence of Dossie and raises her eyebrows at him. He's looking irritated, as if he suspects he might have given himself away, and she grins at him to let him know he has.

"Good party, was it?" she asks brightly.

"Yes," says Hugo happily, unaware of any byplay. "Ned's still sleeping it off. So we'll stay down here, shall we?"

"Looking at this lot I doubt I'll get further than the kitchen this morning," agrees Rose amiably. "So are you two going to hang around and get in my way or are you getting out from under?"

They look at each other.

"We thought we might help," begins Hugo.

"But we could take the dogs for a walk instead," says Jamie. He grins at her. "Whatever would we do without our Rose?"

And just so, she thinks, Jack would've looked — that same grin, the challenge in his eyes, and tilt of the head — and her heart twists with pain, even all these years on.

"Oh, and I was hoping you might help me out," Jamie adds, finishing his coffee. "I suppose you wouldn't consider doing some ironing for me, would you?"

Hugo chokes on his coffee, Rose begins to laugh, and Jamie looks at them, puzzled.

"Are you OK, old man?" he asks Hugo.

Hugo nods, unable to speak, and Rose shakes her head at Jamie.

"Sorry," she says. "I only do ironing on very special occasions. Now, just go, the pair of you, and take those dogs out of my way."

When they've gone, and it's quiet again, Rose makes herself some coffee and sits down at the table. She's thinking about an afternoon many years ago, not long after Jamie announced his engagement to Emilia. She came in, knowing that Lady T and the Admiral were at one of their bridge afternoons, and heard the sound of the piano. She stood at the bottom of the stairs, listening, and then she began to climb, as if she were being drawn upwards by the music. It moved her, touched her heart, made her feel all sorts of things she couldn't explain, and she hesitated outside the drawing-room door where she could just see Hugo, his eyes closed, his hands flying, his fingers moving so quickly over the keys. He didn't look like the Hugo she knew; he looked different, almost frightening in his strength and confidence. She was so rapt, drawn in by the sound, that she moved closer, hypnotized, so that when he stopped she was just a few feet from him.

He opened his eyes and stared at her, slow and dreamy, as if he were coming back from somewhere far away. To her distress she saw that he had tears in his eyes and she felt guilty, as if she'd spied on him, seen something she shouldn't.

"That was beautiful," she said. "I couldn't help myself. I'm sorry."

"No," he said at once, getting up and coming round to her. "No, I was just . . ." he hesitated, shaking his head, "just saying goodbye to someone. Something."

Instinctively she thought about Jack and put out her hands to him. He took them, holding them tightly as he tried to blink away his tears.

"I'm being a fool," he muttered. "Sorry, Rose."

"Come here," she said gently, and she released her hands from his grip and put her arms around him, holding him against her. "There. There, now."

He clung to her, and as she thought about Jack, so recently dead, and her own grief, combined with the mood the music had wrought in her, her hold tightened. She turned her face and touched his damp

212

cheek with her lips, tasting the salt of his tears, kissing them away. Blindly, eyes closed, he began to kiss her in return and, after a moment, she gently disengaged herself, took him by the hand and led him into his bedroom just down the landing. Quickly, lest he should lose confidence, she pulled him down with her on to the bed and began to make love to him: whispering to him, helping him, guiding him, enfolding him, until he cried out and then collapsed sideways beside her. Tenderly she pushed back his untidy dark curly hair and smiled down into his blue eyes. He seemed incapable of speech and she began to laugh. At last he began to laugh, too.

"That was amazing," he said.

She could see a whole variety of emotions in his face: delight, shock, confusion. Now was the dangerous moment. She gave him one quick last kiss, slipping away from him; reaching for her discarded clothes. She dragged on her jeans, pushed her feet into her shoes, and gave him one last, brief smile. He stretched out his arms to her, and she could hear him calling after her as she hurried away down the stairs. On an impulse she left the house, so as to give him the chance to recover. She ran all the way home, wondering what she'd done, how it would be in the future.

He went back to London the following morning.

"Hugo sent something for you, Rose," Lady T said, a few days later, slightly puzzled. "A little present for doing something very kind for him. Some ironing, I think he told me?"

She pushed the package across the kitchen table to Rose. Cautiously, fearfully, Rose unpacked it whilst Lady T watched her.

It was a perfect, long-stemmed pink rose, made of silk.

"How very nice," Lady T said coolly. She sounded faintly surprised.

Rose wrapped it up again quickly and put it with her bag.

"It was quite a lot of ironing," she said, trying to control the need to laugh.

When she got home, Rose unrolled the wrapping paper again and smoothed it out. Two words were written on the inside: "Thank you". Underneath was a telephone number. That touched her, somehow; showed her that Hugo was there should she have need of him. She knew she wouldn't telephone him but the relief was very great when she saw the blood on her knickers a few days after their brief sharing of love and grief.

It was several months before Hugo returned to Cornwall. When she came into the kitchen she saw at once that he was at a loss as to how he should behave towards her and she grinned at him.

"Hello, stranger," she said. "Nice to see you back again."

"You too, Rose," he said awkwardly. "Are you well?"

"Couldn't be better. Ready for anything. Must have been all that ironing I did last time you were down."

Margaret came in behind her.

214

"Ironing?" she repeated. "Has he been making you do his ironing? Honestly, Hugo. As if poor Rose hasn't enough to do in this big house."

"It was a nice change," says Rose, laughing at Hugo's discomfiture, "but I did warn him that it was just the once."

"It was definitely a rather special occasion," Hugo said, beginning to smile, "but I wouldn't dream of taking advantage of it."

After that, things were easy and natural between them. Hugo was mostly in London, Lady T and the Admiral died, visits were few and far between . . . And now Hugo is back again. Luckily, time and distance has removed any embarrassment between them, but earlier, when Jamie mentioned the ironing, there was just a spark of awareness in Hugo's eyes, an exchange of something shared when she grinned at him, acknowledging their private joke.

"Don't even go there," Rose tells herself as she stands up and begins to clear the table. "Let sleeping dogs lie."

But she can't prevent herself remembering.

CHAPTER
TWENTY-THREE

Lucy and Danny have gone back to Geneva and Emilia begins to think about where she might see Jamie again. She plays patience on her laptop: if this comes out I'll meet him in Relish; if this comes out I'll see him in The Chough. She takes the ferry to Padstow and wanders around the narrow streets and the harbour. She googles The Chough and phones to book a table, then drives herself over for lunch.

The tall, attractive boy behind the bar smiles at her, shows her to her table and hands her a menu. Foolishly she's tempted to ask if he knows Hugo or Jamie but casts the thought aside. Even if they use the pub occasionally this boy is hardly likely to know them by name.

She eats her lunch slowly, alert to each newcomer, but neither Hugo nor Jamie appears. What, she wonders, would be Jamie's reaction? Her biggest fear is that he will no longer recognize her. Each day she stares at her reflection in the mirror, almost willing herself to see the resemblance to Lucy that Hugo noticed. It's rather sad that, having seen Jamie, her plan to ensnare Hugo has vanished almost as quickly as it did in Bristol all those years ago. It's as if she's fallen quite madly in love with Jamie all over again, and she longs to see him.

Various scenarios occur to her. She's certain that he'll still be in the RAF and will be living near one of the bases or maybe he'll be at the MOD in London. In which case he might have already left Cornwall and gone home. This could simply have been a short visit to see Hugo — assuming that Hugo is living in Cornwall or has a holiday home here — and she's missed her opportunity. As for Jamie being married, having a family, she can't face the thought of it. She is quite certain that this is all meant to be happening: it's fate.

Neither does she want to think too much about Lucy's reaction if she were to be told that Nigel wasn't her father. Emilia takes a deep breath. She remembers those last few days with Jamie, her flight to London, and then the letter attempting to explain why she was leaving him. She sees now, with the clear vision of hindsight, that she should have got some kind of job, trained to be something, bought a little house, but back then it was always so much easier, each time Jamie was away, to get into the little car and go driving back to London. Back to the parties, the backstage dramas, and, of course, to Nigel . . . It was so much more fun, it was what she was used to, and being seen around with Nigel at that time when the sitcom was top of the TV viewing lists was simply magic. Rather like it had been at first with Jamie, she thinks, until the realities of being a service wife began to chip away at the glamour.

Nevertheless, each time she looks at little Danny she knows exactly from whom he has inherited those brown eyes and that black hair. Even if she were able to persuade herself that Lucy was Nigel's child, there's no doubt about Daniel. And surely, she says to herself, surely Jamie would want to know that he has a daughter and a grandchild? He wanted children so much. He has a right to know. And Lucy . . .? Well, Lucy must be told the truth, gently, of course, but firmly. One way or another she'll be able to persuade Lucy how impossible things were back then. Emilia shrugs away the difficulties. She'll think about them later. Meanwhile she'll make another plan of action.

A text pings in from Lucy:

Hi Mum. Just heard that the things I ordered from the Steamer Trading Cookshop in Pydar Street in Truro have arrived. Could you possibly pick them up for me? Thanks. xx

Emilia sighs, slightly irritated. She remembers from her trip there with Lucy that it's quite a long drive, but it's a lovely little city and it will be a change. She'll go in the morning. In the meantime she'll take the ferry to Padstow, and maybe she'll see Jamie again. But this time she'll be prepared.

"So was it a good party?" Janna shakes her head at Dossie's blissful expression. "Looks like you've got it real bad, my lover. Hopeless, you are. Hopeless."

"No, I'm not," protests Dossie, but she can't help smiling. "Yes, it was really good. And you should have come to it. Everyone's longing to meet you."

218

"Scarcity value," says Janna. "That's the secret of my success."

Rain pours from an unrelenting grey sky and the two of them sit inside at Janna's little gate-leg table watching the drops bouncing amongst her tubs and pots of flowers and herbs.

"Adam stopped off to see Clem but he's going to come to meet you any minute. Are you ready for him?"

Janna thinks about it. She feels quite calm, here in her little room, with all her things around her, and anyway, she has no real fear of Dossie's brother. Meeting a group of strangers in someone else's house might be a bit of a test but if she's truthful, she's looking forward to seeing Adam. And before she can answer, or think about it further, there's a knock on the door and suddenly Adam is here, brushing drops of rain from his hair and smiling at her as Dossie introduces them.

"It's chucking it down," he says, shaking Janna's hand, slipping off his jacket. "And it's cold with it. Thought it was supposed to be summer."

"Cast not a clout till May is out," she tells him, thinking how like Clem, and how like Dossie, he is.

"Ma used to say that," he answers her, "but is it the month of May or the hawthorn blossom? Not that it matters. It'll be just as cold and wet in August."

"That's Cornwall for you," she agrees. "D'you want some tea? Oh, wait. Dossie says you only drink coffee."

He looks at her as if he is surprised and pleased that she's remembered that, and she warms to him.

"I'm afraid so. Is that a problem?"

"'Course not. Sister Emily runs on coffee. But it has to be Fairtrade."

Janna goes behind her little breakfast bar to make his coffee whilst he continues to stand, looking out at the little courtyard. He seems at ease, hands in his jeans pockets, feet apart. Janna realizes that it was set up like this; that Dossie should appear first, followed quite quickly by Adam so that there's no awkward introductions, standing about being polite, just this sudden entrance. It all seems easy and natural.

"Dossie was just telling me about the party," she says. "Says it was good."

"Well, it was." He turns to look at her, taking a few steps towards her. "Doss and I are thinking of a return match at The Court. Would you like to come to it, if we do?"

And suddenly she knows that she'd like it. That she'd feel comfortable with it.

"We thought we'd try to get Clem and Tilly and Jakey over for it, as well," Dossie is saying. "They're always so busy but we're determined to get everyone all together."

This convinces Janna that she'll enjoy this party at The Court. With Clem and Jakey and Tilly there she won't feel outnumbered.

"Perhaps they'll give me a lift?" she suggests casually, as she pushes Adam's mug of coffee across the breakfast bar towards him.

Behind his back, Dossie turns to look at her with a surprised smile and raises her teacup in salute.

220

"Or," offers Adam, "if that's a problem, I could come and fetch you?"

Janna begins to laugh. "I'm not going to get out of this one, am I?"

"And why would you want to?" asks Adam.

"Exactly," says Dossie with satisfaction. "That's settled then."

"But won't you have to get back to London?" Janna asks Adam, coming to sit at the table.

"It might have to be on my next visit," he answers, "but I can get down at the weekends. It's no sweat."

And, just briefly, Dossie's eyes meet hers with a glint of delight and relief: a battle has been won.

"Well, that went off really well," says Dossie as she and Adam drive home together. "It's silly, really, because she's such fun. But she gets these odd ideas in her head and then it's difficult to shake her. She thinks Ned and Hugo and Jamie will be posh and out of her league and she gets nervous. Did you like her?"

It's important to her that Adam should like her friends; to feel really at home here. It's been such a good few days.

"Very much," answers Adam. "She's very unusual. That wonderful Cornish lilt to her voice and those Bohemian clothes. Not someone you'd immediately associate with nuns and a retreat house."

"You haven't met the nuns," retorts Dossie. "You need a bit of an oddball to take care of people like Sister Emily and Mother Magda. They're very lucky to have her and they know it. Janna feels safe there after years of being on the road as a child, then foster homes. I think she knows when she's well off. It works both ways. And I love it that she and Clem are such good mates."

"She's lucky," says Adam, "to find a place where she really belongs and where she can be what she's supposed to be."

There's a little silence whilst Dossie thinks about what he's said and hears the slight note of wistfulness in his voice. Is it possible that, after all these years, Adam is still searching?

"And so," she says, after a moment, "you and Jamie are going to Truro tomorrow?"

Adam chuckles. "He offered me a ride in the MGB and I couldn't resist. When I told him I was meeting an old mate for lunch who was working in Jackson Stop Start he said he'd like to have a look at some local properties, so he suggested we went together."

Another silence. Dossie thinks about Jamie looking at local properties and her spirits rise.

"I suppose," she says, with a show of indifference, "now that he's retired it would be nice for him to be near Ned and Hugo. He doesn't seem to have any other family."

She glances sideways and sees that Adam is grinning.

"What?" she asks sharply. "What's funny?"

"Nothing," he says innocently. "Who's laughing?"

She stares out of the window. The rain has almost stopped and silvery grey curtains of mist shake and drift in the wind. Adam drives carefully.

"It's a pity you can't come too," he adds. "He'll be on his own for lunch. But it would be a bit of a squash for three adults. Do you remember how I used to squeeze in behind you on the little seat in Mike's?"

"Oh, yes," she says, smiling with pleasure at the memory. "Oh God, what fun we had in that car," and just as suddenly she is seized with a sense of loss.

"Sorry," says Adam, glancing quickly at her. "Sorry, Doss. Didn't mean to make you sad."

"You didn't," she says. "Well, you did, but in a good way. I wouldn't want to forget a minute of it. It was the best time of my life."

Something makes her want to add, "Until now," but it seems silly, so she doesn't, and Adam drives in through the gateway, and they are home.

Hugo packs Dossie's wine glasses back into their box and stands looking at it. A little plan is forming in his mind. He knows about the jaunt to Truro in the morning and he's wondering if Dossie might be home alone after Jamie and Adam have left. He's trying to decide whether to text her now and offer to bring the wine glasses or to wait until Jamie and Adam have set off. It would be rather nice to have Dossie to himself for an hour or two. She might even invite him to lunch. Uncle Ned's got one of his bridge days so it's a perfect opportunity.

"Why Truro?" he asked Jamie.

"Adam's going," he answered. "There's an estate agency that he calls Jackson Stop Start and he knows someone who's working there."

Hugo snorted with amusement. "That's a silly nickname for Jackson-Stops & Staff. It's in Lemon Street."

"Well, Adam used to work with this guy in London and then he transferred down here. Adam thought he'd look him up and I offered him a lift. He's like a kid about the MGB."

"*You're* like a kid about it," retorted Hugo. "Two big kids together."

But Jamie refused to rise and simply grinned back at him.

"Should be fun," he said.

"I wonder," Hugo said, irrelevantly, "what Jack would have made of Dossie?"

There was a brief, surprised silence.

"Neither of us would have stood a chance," Jamie said. "He'd have knocked us both out of the contest like he did with Rose. What a bloody tragedy it was. He was so young. Twenty-three. Much too young to die."

"When I think of him — try to imagine what he'd be like now — I always think he would look like you. You were always so alike."

Jamie smiled a little bitterly. "But perhaps he'd have made a better fist of things than I have."

Now, Hugo puts the box on a shelf in the boot room. He wonders what happened to Lucy and the little boy and where they are now. Are they still in their holiday cottage in Rock or have they returned to Geneva? He knows that he should mention the meeting to Jamie but the moment never seems right and he can't think of the words: "You'll never guess who I saw . . .?" or "Look,

224

this might come as a bit of a shock . . ." And he can't get the memory of that little boy out of mind: those dark eyes and black hair. A few days ago, he turned out a few photographs, looking for ones of Jamie as a child, just to confirm his suspicions. And there it was. A small black-and-white snapshot with Jamie staring out at him: the likeness was undeniable. He wonders why she never told him — or did that actor, Nigel Kent, really believe that Lucy was his child? If Emilia was having an affair with him it was perfectly possible, and Lucy is so like her mother that he might not have suspected. Emilia wouldn't have wanted to rock any boats and Jamie certainly wouldn't have made it easy for her. He always longed for children — though not enough to remarry. The betrayal hit him hard and he kept his relationships casual.

Hugo crosses his arms across his ribcage, fists clenched. How will Jamie react if he comes up against his daughter and his grandson with no warning? Hugo sees all the pitfalls opening before him and knows that he's been a fool. Yet it's been so good to see Jamie as he's been for this last couple of weeks. This wretched vertigo, the migraines, the fear that it might strike at any time, is disabling and Hugo knows that his cousin feels emasculated, unviable. Every car journey Jamie takes is hedged about now with the threat of having to stop, to wait until the dizziness passes, to be constantly aware. For someone whose whole life has been lived in perfect control it must be like a death sentence. And now, just when for the first time in nearly two years Jamie is happy, enjoying life, having fun, it is necessary

225

to take him to one side and tell him that he almost certainly has a daughter in her late twenties and a small grandson of whom he knows nothing at all.

Hugo groans aloud. Yet he knows he must do it. Not tonight, because Uncle Ned has invited some friends to supper, but when Jamie comes back from Truro tomorrow he will talk to him. He'll ask him to come out with the dogs and he'll tell him as they walk across the cliffs. The prospect of it makes him quail. He's been a dilatory fool. Jamie could bump into Lucy in Wadebridge, in Padstow. It was just wishful thinking that she'll be back in Geneva, and, anyway, it looks as though Jamie is going to be a regular visitor here from now on so the moment must be seized. And it's possible that Emilia, too, might turn up to visit her family, though Rock isn't at all her natural habitat. Even so, Hugo's spirits sink even lower. He must speak to Jamie tomorrow before something disastrous happens.

The front door opens and he hears Rose's familiar call. Surprisingly, he is washed with relief at the prospect of her company and he steps back into the kitchen just as she enters it from the hall.

"Morning, Rose," he says.

"What's up?" she asks, staring at him. "You look in a right old state."

Hugo smiles involuntarily. Foolish to think he might be able to hide anything from Rose. She has become very dear to him over the years but he is always cautious lest she feels he might be taking advantage of that afternoon, long ago, when they shared that very

226

precious and unexpected moment of intimacy. He longs to tell her his fears and anxieties but that would be very unfair to Jamie.

The dogs are demanding her attention and he is able to pull himself together, to smile, and say: "I'm fine."

"Good," she says cheerfully. "In that case you can make the coffee while I see what a mess you've all made since I was here last."

Hugo begins to laugh. "You ought to be available on the National Health, Rose," he says. "A daily dose of Rose to keep the doctor away."

"I'll take that as a compliment," she answers.

He longs to put his arms around her, simply to take comfort from a hug, a kind of sharing, but he hasn't the courage. She watches him quizzically for a moment and then turns away.

"Kettle," she says, resigned. "Mugs. Coffee. Milk. Want anything done I s'pose I'll have to do it myself."

"No," he says, laughing. "No. Even I can manage that much."

And as he begins to make the coffee he feels more confident again: more equal to the prospect of talking to Jamie.

Rose sits across the table, watching Hugo. She's aware of his inner turmoil but she won't push or press. In her experience people unburden themselves when the time is right and it doesn't do to probe, but she guesses that it is to do with Jamie.

"Ned and Jamie out?" she asks casually.

"They've gone to visit an old oppo of Uncle Ned's," he answers. "How do you think he's looking?"

She knows that he means Jamie and takes her time to answer. Hugo's not looking for meaningless reassurance but for her genuine opinion.

"He looks stretched," she answers after a bit. "Oh, he's still a looker and all that, but it's taking it out of him, isn't it? Must be hell for him."

Hugo nods. She can see that he seems relieved that she's on his wavelength but she's aware that he's struggling with something else: something he'd like to tell her but can't for reasons of loyalty, or because it's someone else's secret.

Rose drinks her coffee thoughtfully. She can't encourage him to break a confidence but she would like to give him some kind of consolation, some reassurance that he can rely on her if he needs to. She casts around, trying to think of a way back to that long-ago sharing; something that might bring them closer again. It needs a trigger — maybe some light-hearted remark about ironing.

She gives a spontaneous little chuckle at the thought of it but, even as he looks at her, eyebrows raised, ready to be amused, the telephone begins to ring.

"Damn," says Hugo. "Sorry, Rose."

He gets up to answer it and the moment passes.

CHAPTER
TWENTY-FOUR

On the way to Truro, Jamie resists Adam's attempts to make him talk about his flying career.

"Pilots are the most boring people in the world," Jamie says. "Anyone will tell you that. Tell me about Mike."

Jamie is intrigued by Mike. What was it about this man? Why does Dossie remember him with such warmth and love? It's interesting, too, that Mike had such an effect on Adam.

"Oh, well, Mike," Adam says, as if he is remembering a famous explorer. "He was just everything I wanted to be. I was about sixteen when they got married and he was so confident, so good at anything he turned his hand to. Everything I wasn't. I aspired to be him. I had no idea what I wanted to be but I longed to work in London. He knew someone at one of the top estate agencies and got me an interview."

As Adam talks about Mike, Jamie is touched by the fact that the dead man is clearly still so alive to him. Gradually, he guides the conversation so that he discovers what happened to Dossie after Mike died; how she and her small son managed. It is interesting to learn about her like this, to discover more about her.

"It seems a big place for her to be all on her own," he suggests lightly, after Adam has talked of the death of their parents. "But it's obviously very much your family home."

He is aware that Adam is struggling with a huge sense of grievance — Hugo has already told him about the situation with The Court — and he waits to see if the younger man wants to talk about it. How hard it must be to be disinherited, cut out of your parents' will in favour of a sibling.

"I was bloody angry about it, actually," Adam says suddenly. "To be honest, it seemed incredibly unfair simply because I suggested that they should downsize a few years back. I was in a rather difficult relationship at the time, my parents didn't like her or her children, and I think they simply didn't want to hand over half of their estate to her. Well, I can sort of see that, but when the relationship broke up I thought they might have reconsidered."

"That's tough," agrees Jamie sympathetically.

"Yes. Well, I think my mother didn't like to go against my father's wishes, though I know that Dossie tried to persuade her to change her will after he died. He left half the property to Dossie to soften the blow of inheritance tax later when Mo died. But it's not about the money. I've done well. It's about being disinherited."

"Must be tricky for Dossie, too," suggests Jamie.

"I think it is. And I don't want her to feel pressured about it. I was so angry to begin with that I wondered how I would ever be able to have any kind of relationship with her. She was always the golden girl, if

230

you see what I mean. Coping with Mike dying, bringing up Clem, starting her business and making it a success. Then, when they wanted to restart their own bed-and-breakfast business, which I thought was crazy at their ages, she agreed to help them and, naturally, they made a huge success of it."

Jamie can hear the bitterness, the envy, in his voice.

"I can see," he says rather drily, "how extraordinarily irritating that must have been for you."

Adam begins to laugh. "Well, it was," he admits. "And at the time I was behaving like a complete arsehole with this woman and getting it all wrong. It was just dire."

Jamie laughs with him, admiring his honesty, liking him for it.

"But now," he says, "you seem to get on very well."

"Well, that's the weird thing," says Adam. "It was as if, once my parents had died, all the resentment died with them and I could see Dossie clearly. I'm not proud of this but I have to admit that it's a relief. I don't have to pretend any more, to feel guilty about never quite making the grade."

"I can understand that, too," Jamie says. "It's like friendships. I think family relationships should be viewed on their own merits. People earn respect and love. Just because they're family doesn't mean you automatically love them. Well, at least if Dossie decides to sell you're the right man to advise her."

Adam smiles. "I asked her the question. It'll cost a lot to keep The Court in good condition. She said she'd

231

rather live in decaying grandeur than in a modern bungalow."

"Is there no middle course?"

"Well, there might be, but she needs to take time to think about it. I think she's more concerned about which dog she might have than which house she might like."

"I approve of a woman who gets her priorities right," says Jamie. "Now remind me where I need to park and then you can show me where we'll meet up after you've had lunch."

They park near the cathedral, buy a ticket, and then wander away into the town. Adam shows him a bistro called The Place, in a narrow lane near the cathedral, and they agree a time.

"We're lunching at Bustopher Jones," Adam tells him, "and I wish I could suggest you join us but I know we'll just be talking about old times and you'd be bored stiff. It won't be that long. He has to be back by two fifteen but I'll text you if there's a problem."

"I shall be fine," Jamie tells him. "I haven't been to Truro for years. I shall enjoy myself. See you later."

They part, Adam heading off towards Lemon Street while Jamie turns and walks back up the street, collapsible walking stick tapping the ground in that efficient cadence that he has developed since he started using it. At the estate agents on the corner of High Cross he stands quietly, leaning on the stick, reading the property descriptions. There are houses, cottages, apartments, all across the south-west of Cornwall; in the Roseland peninsula, Helston, Falmouth, St Mawes.

But what is it he is really looking for? Unquestionably he knows he is ready to move, to put the air force and his former life behind him. To run away? The thought is uncomfortable. Say rather to put distance between him and the constant reminders of the life he used to live. But why, then, buy a property on the south Cornish coast? Surely his place is in the wild north of the county, within striking distance of Hugo, Ned, The Chough . . . Dossie? He suppresses a grin: steady boy, early days.

What then has drawn him to Truro? He turns and looks up at the cathedral, towering over him like a cliff, and he walks west, struck by the contrast between the stark, concrete, oppressive ugliness of the BHS store on his left and the mellow, pale, almost white-gold stone of the building on his right. He pauses in the west square and stares back at the towering face with its twin towers soaring above him. So much smaller than Wells, he thinks, but so extraordinary in its ambition. Now, unthinkingly, he steps forward to the left-hand door and enters into the quiet. A few people are moving around the building, gazing at the stained glass or craning their necks to take in the immense space under the vaulted ceiling. Sunlight spears down from the south windows so that he can trace the beams in the dust motes that rise and fall at the whim of unfelt air currents. Jamie is drawn forward to the Quire, to the Willis Organ, one of the greatest instruments in the world. As he approaches, out of long habit, he bows his head to the cross on the high altar and then stands looking at the ornate wooden pews, which he had once occupied. How many years ago was it when he and Hugo came here from Wells to sing choral evensong, accompanied by that organ?

He can almost see them, those half-forgotten faces of boys long grown up. It was never easy, being a chorister; so why does he remember it with such fondness? And what is it about cathedrals?

Is it because I was happy then? thinks Jamie. Was life really that simple; uncomplicated, untroubled by thoughts of the far future?

The thought is poisonous, unhelpful, dangerous. Abruptly he turns and walks briskly away down the nave, out through the west doors and into the pedestrian precinct. The weather has changed; clouds shield the cathedral from the sun. He finds little to spark his interest as he circles through the bustling shopping centre. The familiar, uninspiring shops that are replicated in every high street of every large town and city leave him longing for the quirky individuality of Cathedral Lane. He begins to walk back towards his starting point. The crowds, the lack of horizon, the cluttered sight-lines, the narrow streets, all combine to destabilize him. He can feel the onset of the dizziness, the increasing unsteadiness of the pavement. He moves slower now, keeping his head still, avoiding looking into the shop windows to his left and right as he reaches, and turns into, Cathedral Lane. The Place is quite busy and he is vastly relieved to find a corner table where he can settle. Out of habit he folds his stick and puts it out of the way in his overcoat pocket, as if he were removing his disability from view. He orders a baguette

234

because he knows he must eat, and an Americano, then he leans back with eyes half closed to reduce the visual distractions and to allow the impending storm to pass. He can rest here, recover, replenish his energy, while he waits for Adam.

His meal arrives and he eats slowly, keeping his head still, as far as possible. He takes his time, relieved that the dizziness is receding and that the worst is past. He's nearly finished when the door opens and he looks up, checking to see if it is Adam. It's a woman, about his own age, wearing jeans and a loose shirt under a suede jacket. Her reddish-brown hair is cut in a short bob and she's attractive, slightly boho, and somehow familiar. He stares at her, frowning slightly, and, as her glance meets his, her eyes fly wide open and she claps her hand over her mouth. In that moment he recognizes her and as she approaches his table he rises automatically to his feet, as if he is pulled up by strings.

"My God," she's saying, beaming now. "How amazing. Oh, I can't believe it."

He stares at her. "Ems?" he asks, and he realizes that the really odd thing is that she isn't truly surprised. Pleased, yes, but it's as if she's half expecting to see him.

"Yes," she's answering. "It's really me. Hello, Jamie."

They stand staring at each other until he pulls himself together, struggling with several different reactions that he always associates with her: love, anger, resentment, jealousy. He loved her, trusted her, and she walked out on him, giving no real reason except foolish muddled excuses that made no sense — apart from the fact that she'd met Nigel Kent and wanted to be with him.

Quickly she slides into the chair beside him and makes a gesture that pleads with him to sit down. Her expression has changed and he knows that she's seen his reaction and understands that this is not going to be a happy reunion.

"Sorry," she says. "Honestly, I'm really sorry, Jamie . . ." and he's not certain if she's apologizing for dumping him way back or for the shock this meeting has caused.

He sits down, too, pushing the plate with the remains of his baguette to one side. He can think of nothing to say that isn't banal. It's totally impossible to greet her as some old friend, which it seemed that she was quite prepared to do right in that first moment. At the same time he is acutely aware of his situation, of the danger that the maelstrom will return. Please God, he prays, not now, not in front of her. He fumbles for words.

"Are you in Cornwall on holiday?"

She shakes her head but then nods. "Sort of."

It seems as if she's trying to decide on what she is going to say, mentally trying out various plausible reasons to explain her presence in Truro, and suddenly he knows that she is no more in command than he is. He slowly and carefully leans back in his chair and picks up his coffee cup, watching her; waiting.

"The thing is," she says, and hesitates, and then hurries on. "Actually, I'm staying at a cottage in Rock."

He raises his eyebrows: that's very close to home. "In Rock?"

"Yes." Once again she seems to be trying out phrases in her head, which puzzles him. But he waits. "And there's something, Jamie. Something I need to talk to you about. It's really important."

"Really?" He looks disbelieving. "After all this time?"

He drinks his coffee, fighting the urge to grip the table for balance as she opens her bag. She takes out a small notebook, scribbles down an address and a number, then tears the page from the book.

"Would you come and see me?" she asks. "Please."

He watches her coolly, drawing on years of professional training to hide his inner turmoil. He doesn't trust her but his interest is aroused. He makes a negative face: why would he want to?

"Please," she says again, insistently but pleadingly. "I don't really want to talk about it here."

She glances round her and he is intrigued, if irritated, by all this secrecy and silence. His instinct is to get up and walk out, but now that presents a problem. His stick is folded, in his pocket, and he has the strongest desire that she should not know; not know anything about what has happened to him, what is happening to him. Ems reaches out and quickly pushes the piece of paper into his hand. Glancing down, he realizes, with a huge shock, that he can't see the writing on the paper in front of him. The maelstrom is on him; he is falling into a full migraine attack.

"Please," she insists, looking pleadingly at him.

Just for a second, as he looks up into her anxious face, there is a treacherous revival of all he once felt for her and he hesitates, assailed from every side, battling a long-suppressed desire for companionship, for love . . . for help. Em closes his fingers round the paper. But Jamie is past caring. He is becoming desperate to leave; to leave now.

"Sorry, I have to go," he says gruffly.

He rams the piece of paper into his trouser pocket and stands, grabs his old leather jacket and pulls it on using the wall at his shoulder to keep stability. The weight of the stick is like lead in his pocket. The floor seems to pitch beneath him and it takes a supreme effort to start moving. He navigates from chair-back to chair-back towards the door. He doesn't look back. Somehow he makes it without stumbling, turns right and moves unsteadily until he knows that he is out of her sight. He leans against the wall, his hands fumbling in his pocket for the stick. It flicks open as he jams it into the ground. He knows what is coming. As the migraine takes hold he will lose a large part of his vision and he needs somewhere to rest, somewhere to hide. Lurching forward, he heads towards the cathedral.

Somehow he forces himself to walk calmly, controlled, even as the first traces of the crescent that characterizes his visual disturbances begin to sparkle in his mind's eye. The dizziness is acute, but he is well practised in dealing with what once would have laid him out on the floor.

"Keep moving," he mutters.

Part of him dreads and expects a voice calling; feels certain that Ems will follow him and will see him like this. His fists clench in frustration. Jamie makes his way back to the west entrance of the cathedral. He pushes open the heavy door and walks into the nave. The cathedral is darker now, with few lights on. The visual turmoil is robbing him of his sight. He reaches the first row of seats and moves further down the aisle till he can turn right and feel his way to the end of a row where a chair is close by a pillar. He sits, laying the stick on the seats beside him and bowing his head as if in prayer. The migraine aura is fully on him now, growing, growing in his vision like a pulsing, jagged, sparkling crescent moon till it obscures all of the central part of his sight. He fumbles in his pocket for the emergency strip of pills that he keeps with him always. He takes two and swallows them with his saliva. But the pills will not relieve the turmoil in his mind.

Emilia! What in heaven is she doing here, in Cornwall, in Truro? And what was that feeling that had assailed him, of need, of desire, of hope? He curses his frailties, railing silently at his vulnerability. But he also allows himself a sense of relief. He made it. For now he is safe.

Emilia sits quite still, her hands clenched into fists, her eyes screwed shut. Her heart beats fast and she takes deep breaths as she rewinds the scene that has just played out. "Ems," he said. Just that: "Ems". Funny how it really struck her to the heart. Nobody but Jamie called her "Ems". And that way he looked at her, just at the end, for a moment it was as if he was remembering how it was all those years ago.

Someone is standing beside her and she looks up quickly, hopefully, but it's not Jamie come back to her, it's one of the waitresses.

"Are you all finished here?" she asks politely.

Emilia stares at the remains of Jamie's meal and nods rather reluctantly. The waitress hesitates and then begins to clear the table.

"Can I get you anything else?"

Emilia thinks about it. She feels shaky and not quite ready for the drive home, but at the same time she knows she couldn't eat a thing now.

"Coffee," she says. "Could I have a cappuccino?"

The waitress nods, smiles, and goes away, and Emilia reruns the scene in her head: the shock of seeing Jamie in the one place it never occurred to her that she might. He still looks good; tough, attractive. She wonders what he thought about her. How typical that, after all those times she'd got herself dressed up — hair looking nice, a bit of slap — to go to Relish or The Chough or Padstow in the hope of seeing him, she has to bump into him after an hour's shopping in her old jeans.

Her coffee arrives and she ladles sugar into it to help her cope with the shock.

But will he come? she asks herself, stirring the coffee. And what will I do if he doesn't?

She wonders who Jamie was with and where he was going. She tries again to remember where the Cornish part of his family — some old aunt and uncle or perhaps grandparents — lived but shakes her head. Back in the day, Jamie's parents were abroad a great deal but they met up from time to time, generally in London.

He must come, she tells herself, sipping her coffee. He must.

The hot sweet liquid strengthens her and she grows calmer. He's got the address of the cottage in Rock and her mobile number. Thinking of this, she instinctively grabs her bag, rooting about for her phone, lest by some miraculous chance he's already been in touch, but there's nothing. She puts the phone on the table beside her, watching for the way it lights up when a text arrives, and drinks more of her coffee. It occurs to her that he might turn up at the cottage unannounced. What if he should go there later today? The thought causes her to swallow the rest of her coffee hurriedly, pay the bill and rush back to her car.

Jamie sits quietly in his seat waiting patiently for the attack to recede, as he knows it will. If he is lucky then he might escape the worst of the headache that follows an episode like this; the pills are strong, and effective if taken early. It is only now, as his turmoil lessens, that he begins to be aware of his surroundings; only now that he begins to hear the voices ahead of him in the Quire. He observes the quiet discipline of the red-cassocked boys, attentive to the instructions of the master of choristers. Then the organ begins to play, and the voices harmonize as the rehearsal begins.

He is summoned back to that summer's evening years ago. In his mind's eye he sees Hugo opposite him in the front row, the earnest expressions of his chorister colleagues, the feeling of command and of control. He revels in the rhythm of the rehearsal, in fragments of psalms and responses, of the Magnificat and the Nunc Dimittis. And then the choir begins rehearsing one of the most majestic anthems in the whole chorister repertoire. It is by John Ireland. Jamie listens in rapt silence, listening for the phrase that has resonated with him since childhood. "Greater love hath no man than this, that a man lay down his life for his friends." As the pure voice of the young soloist rings out — as he, Jamie, sang so many years before — he realizes that he remembers every word and every note. The choir joins the soloist, carrying forward the musical theme, building the piece to its dramatic climax, and Jamie is once again a young boy, his soul soaring as he sang "That ye should shew forth the praises of Him who has call'd you, out of darkness, out of darkness, into His marvellous light". The sublime final organ chord fills the spaces, swirling through the cathedral before it changes and quietens. And then, as the choir begins the slow, quiet, achingly moving final lines, Jamie crosses his arms and lowers his head. Nobody must see his tears.

CHAPTER
TWENTY-FIVE

"I'm going to have to chuck you out," Dossie tells Hugo. "I've got a children's party in St Breward and I need to get a move on. But thanks for coming over and for bringing the dogs. I love it when you bring the dogs."

"Still no decision about a puppy?" he asks her.

He doesn't want to go. It's been so nice to have her to himself, but he doesn't want to make her late.

"It's crazy," she tells him. "Why should it be such a big deal?"

"Because there's a lot to think about," he answers. "It has to fit in with your work. Like this afternoon, for instance. How would you manage?"

"Well, this is my difficulty," she agrees. "You can leave an older dog for a while but a puppy is more tricky. We always had two dogs so that they had company. One older, then when the older one died we'd bring in a puppy and the other dog would help to train it. It worked very well. But then Mo and Pa were here most of the time. I'm not very happy about leaving dogs in the back of a car."

She's moving round, getting her things together, and he helps her to carry ice boxes and polythene containers out to the car, the dogs running ahead.

"What's the theme this time?" he asks, amused.

She rolls her eyes at him. "*Frozen*," she says. "Don't ask. I'm more at home with *Thomas the Tank Engine*. Thanks, Hugo. See you soon."

She gives him a hug and a quick kiss and watches as he encourages the dogs into the car, climbs in and drives away. He gives a little toot, watching her in his mirror as her car comes out of the gateway and turns left, and she gives an answering toot. He pauses for a moment at the junction, fiddles about with his CDs and puts in Samuel Barber's *Toccata Festiva*.

The rain has stopped and the mist is clearing. The ditches are bright with colour: yellow celandine, red campion, bluebells, creamy cow parsley. Each year the miracle that is spring occurs, yet each year he is taken aback by it. He drives slowly, his window down, breathing the sea-salty air and thinking about Dossie: how easy it is to be with her. Perhaps, after all, it's like a brother and sister relationship without the sibling rivalry; rather like his relationship with Jamie.

At the thought of Jamie, at the prospect of his plan to talk to him, Hugo's gut churns a little. He still hardly knows how he will frame the words. The familiar music, the sound of the organ, stirs him and gives him some kind of courage. How would it be if he and Jamie were to bump into Lucy and she were to greet him, talk to him, and then have to explain to his cousin why he'd never thought to mention meeting her before? It's unthinkable. He must tell Jamie as soon as he comes in.

Hugo drives down through the village and parks, but he has only just let the dogs into the house when the

244

MGB slides in beside him and Jamie gets out. Hugo stares at him. Jamie looks grim, not terribly well, yet in some way excited.

"Good day?" Hugo asks apprehensively, as Jamie locks the car.

Jamie doesn't answer. He steadies himself and then hustles Hugo into the house and along the passage to the kitchen.

"Is Ned out?" he asks almost peremptorily.

Hugo nods. "It's his bridge day. Won't be back yet."

Jamie takes a deep breath. "Good. Listen. You won't guess who I unexpectedly met up with today in some bistro in Truro. Wanna try?"

Hugo shakes his head, but his heart beats fast and his gut lurches. "Who?"

"Only Ems." Jamie flings himself round, strides down the kitchen and back again, grabbing at chair backs for support. "Ems! Can you believe it? I'm having a coffee and in she walks. Recognized me straight off." He pauses. "It was odd, actually. She didn't seem that surprised. I still can't get over it. And what's more, get this, she wants to see me again. She says she has something to tell me that's very important." He raises his shoulders, his hands, his eyebrows, miming amazement. "Like, seriously? After twenty-eight years? Actually, I was bloody glad Adam could drive me back as far as The Court, though he had no idea what I was really feeling."

Hugo lets out a very slow breath. He didn't know that Emilia was in Cornwall and he experiences an overwhelming mix of apprehension and a bittersweet remembrance of things past. This is the worst that could have happened and what's frightening is Jamie's reaction. His normally cool, calm approach to any kind of surprise has vanished. He's edgy, excitable, seeking a reaction.

"We need to talk," Hugo says, aware of the total inadequacy of this remark. "I should have told you something before."

Jamie stops striding up and down, sinks down on to a chair and stares at him. "What? Told me what?"

"I was in Wadebridge," Hugo begins quickly. "I was in Relish when I saw this girl. I thought I recognized her and then I realized that it was because she looked so much like Emilia. She saw me staring at her and I thought she might think I was trying to get off with her or something so I said this silly thing about how much she reminded me of someone I'd known way back." He shakes his head. "Forget all the conversational flim-flam. It turned out that she was Emilia's daughter."

Jamie is watching him intently. "So Ems has a daughter living in Wadebridge?"

"No," says Hugo quickly. "No. She lives in Geneva but she and her husband have just bought a holiday cottage in Rock."

Jamie raises his eyebrows. "You got off pretty quick on one short glance." His expression changes slowly, as if he is working something out; his eyes grow cold. "Are you going to tell me that you've seen Ems and didn't think it was worth mentioning to me?"

246

Hugo shakes his head. "I haven't seen her, no, but it was on the cards and I should have warned you."

"Yes, you bloody should have," Jamie shouts. "So Ems' daughter has bought a cottage in Rock. OK. It's a bit of a shock. But I can't see Ems spending much time in Rock." He takes a breath, shrugs. "Well, that explains why she's around."

"I suppose so." Hugo hesitates.

Should he go further, declare his suspicion?

"She didn't talk about her family," Jamie's saying. "But why should she want to see me again? There was something weird about it. Not just, 'Let's try to heal old wounds and mend bridges' stuff. Something more than that. She was very insistent." He roots in his pocket and drags out a piece of crumpled paper. "Look." He smooths it out. "She's written an address and a mobile number. See?"

He shakes his head, trying to work it out, and Hugo knows that he must take the risk.

"This is going to sound bizarre," he begins, staring at the piece of paper. "The thing is, Lucy has a little boy of about — oh, I don't know — eighteen months? Two? I'm not good at babies' ages. Anyway, when I looked at this little fellow, little Daniel, I thought I could see a kind of likeness . . ." He risks a glance at his cousin, who is staring at him, baffled.

"What?" Jamie asks impatiently. "Get on with it. What are you saying?"

"He reminded me of you," Hugo blurts out. "He looks just like you did at that age. Same colouring. Same way of holding his head. It's probably nothing but I'm just saying . . . and that might be what she wants to tell you," he finishes feebly.

There is a silence. When he speaks, Jamie's voice is almost unrecognizable.

"Do you mean that Ems wants to tell me that she had a daughter twenty-seven years ago and that the child was mine but she didn't bother to mention it? Are you really suggesting that?"

Hugo looks away from the anger on Jamie's face and quite suddenly is calm. He turns to face him squarely.

"Yes," he answers coolly. "I am suggesting that. If Emilia seems so insistent on seeing you I suspect that, now Nigel Kent is dead, she thinks it might be time to tell the truth."

"That I've had a daughter for the last twenty-seven years? And now a grandson? Christ, Hugo! Can you possibly be serious? And why the hell didn't you tell me before?"

Never has Hugo seen Jamie so angry. This cold rage is much more frightening than a violent loss of temper.

"Remember that I know nothing. But I've seen the boy. Daniel." It seems important to keep repeating the child's name. "To begin with I didn't put two and two together but it nagged at me. The likeness is undeniable. But, yes, I put off mentioning it because it's so bizarre and I was afraid that it might . . . cause problems for you." He glances at Jamie and looks away again. "It might possibly be that Emilia believed that Lucy was Nigel's child. She looks so much like her mother and I imagine that . . ." He hesitates, not quite knowing how to go on. ". . . that she could have been Nigel's child."

"You mean that she was running us both at the same time?" Jamie's voice is icy. "Yes, I think you can assume that."

"Well," says Hugo helplessly. He raises his hands and drops them again. "You see where I'm going with this?"

"Absolutely. The child pops out looking just like her, huge relief, and no forward thinking like, 'OMG, supposing she should have a baby twenty-five years from now who looks just like that bastard Jamie?' Yes, I get that."

His rage and bitterness are so palpable that Hugo is silent. He cannot begin to imagine what Jamie must be feeling and his main concern is that this will make Jamie ill; precipitate a vertigo attack, the dizziness, the headaches.

"Will you go to see her?" he asks at last.

"Oh, yes! I'll bloody go!"

Hugo knows that he must try to bring Jamie back from the edge and he casts around for something that will speak to Jamie's natural instincts for reason; that will help to regain his instinctive coolness.

"What worries me, too," Hugo says at last, "is how Lucy will feel? Assuming that all this is true, of course. I imagine that she won't know either. It will be a terrific shock to her, too."

He looks at his cousin and he sees that Jamie is regaining control, the peak of his fury is past and common sense is taking hold again. Hugo glimpses the military man back in charge. Jamie is attempting to catalogue and file all the data he's been given in the last seismic half an hour. But he is still very angry.

He stands up, turns away from Hugo; picks up his leather jacket.

"I'm going to take the dogs for a walk," he says abruptly. "Come on, boys."

"Do you want me to come with you?" asks Hugo diffidently. "I'm just thinking . . . Are you OK?"

"I expect the dogs will come home if I fall over in a fit," Jamie answers. "And then you'll have to come and find me."

He and the dogs go out together. Hugo drags out a chair and collapses into it, his head in his hands. He feels that he has somehow let Jamie down, that he has misjudged the situation and he has no idea how to go forward.

Adam waves goodbye as the MGB pulls out of the drive. He's forgotten that Dossie is in St Breward. In the kitchen he finds a note propped against a plastic bag with a tin in it.

Just in case you're at a loose end when you get back, I promised to take this over for Jakey. You might like to drop it off for me. Thanks. Hope you had a good day. Back about seven-ish. If there's nobody around (it's half term and they might have gone off somewhere) just leave it at the back door and drop in and have tea with Janna!!

Adam thinks about it. He might as well go. It would be nice to see Jakey, Clem and Tilly, and the rain has stopped. He feels extremely restless after the day out and further distraction would be good. He dashes off for a pee, grabs the bag, and goes out again.

His car feels very dull and ordinary after the MGB and, as he drives towards Chi-Meur, he thinks about Jamie. The disabling effect of the migraine attack has shocked Adam. Although Jamie recovered on the way back, Adam wishes he was able to summon up the courage to insist on driving him home. But there's something just the least bit intimidating about Jamie that keeps you slightly at arm's length.

When he drives in through the gates, Adam sees at once that Clem's car is missing. He gets out anyway, knocks at the front door, wanders round to the back, but there's nobody about. A football lies on the path and a trampoline is parked in the middle of the small lawn. Adam smiles as he remembers how he and Jakey played football out in the lane; running, barging, Jakey shouting, "Pass! Pass!" He's a tall boy, and very like his father, though he doesn't show any signs of Clem's stillness; his austerity. When they came in to tea, Clem grinned at Adam, noticing his breathlessness, his heightened colour.

"That was fun," Adam said, almost defensively, whilst Jakey disappeared to wash his hands. "I really enjoyed it."

"Good," said Clem. "Great. So that's the next few weekends booked out for you, then. And if you throw in going to the beach and up on the moor I might even let you have some time off for good behaviour."

Tilly appeared then, smiling at Adam, asking how long he was staying with Dossie, laughing at his dishevelment. They were so welcoming, so accepting, that Adam could hardly believe that his visits hitherto had been so few and far between. He saw how easy and happy Tilly and Clem were together, and how Jakey and Tilly were rather more like brother and elder sister than stepson and stepmother. Briefly, he was gripped with the old sense of being the outsider, of not belonging, until he realized that he didn't have to be — if only he could put the past behind him and look forward.

Then Jakey reappeared with Bells, and Adam crouched to accept her enthusiastic licks, while Jakey said: "Can we play football again after tea? Please? Can we?" So he'd said: "I don't see why not," and Jakey cheered whilst Clem grinned at him once more.

Adam puts the plastic bag with the tin in it outside the back door, but once he's in the car again he hesitates, remembering the rest of Dossie's note, and on an impulse he drives along and round to the Coach House. The sun is out now and Janna's courtyard is a pretty, peaceful place, raindrops glittering on the petals and leaves. As he stands looking at it all, an elderly nun in a blue habit comes in at the gate behind him and smiles at him.

"Welcome," she says with a little bow towards him, her hands folded together.

She says the word almost as if it is two words "Well come," and he returns her smile.

"I was wondering if Janna might be around. Dossie told me to drop in on her."

"Dossie!" The Sister's face lights with love at the mention of the name.

"I am her brother," he tells her. "Clem's uncle."

"How wonderful," she exclaims.

He is warmed by the sincerity of her delight. "Clem's not in," he explains, "so I just thought I'd check on Janna. It's probably not a good time. I'm Adam."

"Now that is a good name," she says, taking his hand in hers. "And I am Sister Emily. Janna has driven Mother to a doctor's appointment. She will be sorry to miss you. Would you like a cup of tea?"

"Well," he glances around. "I wouldn't want to be a trouble."

Sister Emily looks puzzled. "Is it a trouble?" she asks, genuinely surprised.

He can't help laughing. "Not if you say it isn't. Except that I only drink coffee."

"And so do I," she says serenely.

"Oh, yes, I remember now," he exclaims. "Janna said that. You drink coffee but it has to be Fairtrade."

"Quite right," she agrees. "Sit there in the sun and I shall fetch us some."

He decides to do as he is bid and not make an offer to help, and sits at the wooden table and relaxes in the sun. He closes his eyes and tries to make out the scents that drift around him: lavender, wallflowers, *Daphne odora*. Still with his eyes closed he stretches a hand sideways and ruffles some leaves in a nearby pot and then smells his fingers: thyme. A blackbird is singing.

There is a clink and a rattle and Sister Emily is back, putting a tray on the table. She places a mug of black coffee beside him and smiles down at him.

"If Dossie were here there would be cake," she says. "But I have biscuits."

She says this proudly, as if biscuits are a special treat, and he sits up straight and accepts one, smiling his thanks.

"I'd like to stay here for ever," he says randomly, because just at this moment this is what he would like more than anything else in the world. "Not just here in this courtyard," he amends quickly. "Just here. In this amazing part of the country. It's so beautiful."

"And can't you?" she asks innocently, as if it would be quite easy to throw everything up and move to Cornwall.

"Well," he says, slightly taken aback. "It's not quite that simple."

"Isn't it?" she asks, interested. "Why isn't it?"

He gazes at her, knowing that she isn't making fun or trying to be clever but just wants to know the reason. And he can't think of one. He can't think of a single reason why he should not leave London and move to Cornwall.

"Best thing I ever did," his old friend Barnaby said earlier, over lunch. "You should give it a try. Swimming, surfing, coastal path walking. What's not to like? And you've got family here . . ."

"And how nice that would be," Sister Emily is saying, as if she has read his thoughts, "for your family. For Clem and little Jakey. And for Dossie, of course."

Adam picks up his cup and sips the hot strong coffee, remembering that game of football out in the lane.

"Maybe I should," he says. "After all, I've nothing to leave. I haven't exactly done a lot with my life."

There is a little silence. The late afternoon sun is warm now, and the little courtyard is full of light and shadows and an odd kind of magic.

"It depends," says the patrician old voice, "on how you define doing a lot with your life, I suppose. How do we know how much we might do when we touch people's lives?"

He looks at her, puzzled, and she smiles at him.

"People feel that their lives must be dramatic, successful, to achieve anything of importance, but think of Jesus Christ. He was born in a stable — not a very inspiring beginning, despite the rumours of wise men and angels — and then nothing is heard of him for twelve years. Next we hear briefly that he has been a very naughty boy, run away from his parents on that visit to Jerusalem, and they find him showing off in the Temple. Another silence for eighteen years. And then this thirty-year-old man appears. No money, no property, no transport, no job. Rather odd friends: itinerant fishermen, tax collectors, ladies of dubious reputation. He is rude to his mother at Cana, he loses his temper with spectacular violence in the Temple and finally dies a criminal's death. And all in three short years. Yet here we are talking about him more than two thousand years on. And loving him. So it depends, you see, on what you mean by 'I haven't done a lot with my life'."

There is a silence: a bee drones. Adam has never heard the life of Christ described in quite these terms and especially not by a nun. Sister Emily sips her coffee reflectively. She is not afraid of the silence that stretches between them.

"I suppose there was a bit more to it than that, though, wasn't there?" he suggests at last. "Making people see and hear? That sort of stuff?"

"Ah, yes. Opening people's eyes to realities, making them listen to unpleasant truths." Sister Emily nods. "Inculcating a true sense of awareness. That's always miraculous. Mind you, I don't think the Pre-Raphaelites did Jesus many favours portraying him with all that long fair hair and blue eyes. 'Gentle Jesus, meek and mild.' I imagine him as young, tough and charismatic. Have you noticed that he always answered a question with another question? Leading people forward? Making them think? He would have made a first-rate barrister."

Thoroughly confused now, not knowing what to say, Adam finishes his coffee and puts the empty mug back on the tray. He glances at her and she smiles that delightful smile, full of joy and the expectation of good things.

"Thank you," he says. He hesitates and an idea occurs to him. "I suppose you don't go to parties? Only

256

we're hoping to give one soon. Me and Dossie at The Court. Janna's coming. And Clem."

If he's imagined that he might disconcert her he is disappointed. She beams at him mischievously.

"I should love to. I so enjoyed the last party Dossie gave at The Court, though your parents were alive then. Thank you."

He begins to laugh as he stands up. "I shall very much look forward to seeing you there. I shall come and collect you and Janna, and bring you home afterwards. We have a date."

"We have a date," she repeats, as if relishing the phrase.

He doesn't quite know the form when it comes to taking leave of a nun, so he simply smiles at her, gives her a little bow.

"Thanks for the coffee."

"Happiness is always on the road ahead," she says. "*Courage, mon brave.*"

He stares at her for a moment, then he gets into the car, reverses, and drives away. Clem's car is not there so he carries on past the Lodge and turns into the lane. After a mile or two he begins to laugh again.

CHAPTER
TWENTY-SIX

As the days pass after the trip to Truro, Ned watches his nephews with growing unease. The atmosphere is strained and it is clear that the two of them have fallen out. Jamie is preoccupied, irritable, and Hugo is anxious, treading warily where his cousin is concerned. He's stopped whistling the theme tune from *Mission Impossible* each time Jamie mentions Dossie. She and Adam are looking after Jakey for the last few days of the half-term week and she hasn't been over recently. Prune's presence helps to keep things on an even keel but it is Rose who precipitates a reconciliation between Hugo and Jamie. Nearly a week after the Truro trip she comes in just as they are finishing breakfast, drops her bag on a chair and stares at them.

"It's been like a fridge in here this last few days," she observes. "Am I missing something? It reminds me of when we were all kids and you two and Jack were having a strop about something. Put me out of my misery and tell me what it is."

Ned is almost inclined to laugh at Jamie's expression of surprised indignation but Hugo visibly relaxes, as if he welcomes this opportunity to put things right. Rose looks at him questioningly, eyebrows raised, and Ned is reminded of a mother's impatience with two small children. It's clear by Hugo's response that he thinks so, too.

He glances at Jamie's frowning face and begins to grin. "We had a row and he threw all his toys out of the pram," he says.

Rose looks at Jamie. "Got your cue?" she asks affably. "Now it's your turn to say, 'He started it.' Then we can all get on."

"Well, he bloody well did," Jamie begins indignantly. Despite his patent irritation he begins to smile — and they all burst out laughing. Hugo heaves a silent sigh of relief and Ned is filled with gratitude. The worst is over even if all is not well.

The next day, Jamie drives Hugo to the station to catch the train to London. One of his friends is having a birthday and Hugo has been invited to the party and to stay for a few days. Jamie's mood is still heavy, anxious, and Ned is worried.

"Is Jamie quite well?" he asked Hugo, the evening before his departure. "Does this wretched disability make him depressed?"

"Only in the usual frustrated kind of way," answered Hugo at once. "Not in a clinical kind of way. No, he's just heard something that's preying on his mind a bit. He's fine."

Nevertheless, Ned knew that Hugo was hedging, not telling the whole truth, but he decided to wait; to choose the right time to speak to his nephew in the hope that he might be of some use to him. So he nodded and told Hugo to enjoy himself.

After Hugo and Jamie have gone, taking the dogs so that Jamie can walk them on his way home, Ned paces the courtyard, wondering what his nephew might have heard to cause such a change of spirits. As he often does at moments like these, he thinks about Jack, wondering what he'd be like now, what kind of life he might have had. How terrible to die before he'd barely begun to live; to be unable to fulfil his potential, to experience love, to have children. At least, he thinks, Jack would have had plenty of opportunity to have some fun before he died. He was a good-looking boy, and girls were attracted to him. At one time he'd even wondered if Jack had been tempted by Rose, but it was unlikely. There were too many barriers, and Margaret would have been horrified, of course.

Ned sits down at the table and pours the last of the coffee into his cup. It wouldn't occur to Margaret that her son could be attracted to their cleaning woman's daughter, however beautiful the girl might be. Anyway, to her they would have seemed barely more than children.

The thought of his wife is accompanied by familiar sensations — loss, sadness, guilt — and Ned shifts uncomfortably on his chair. Fortunately, Margaret wasn't the kind of woman to listen to gossip: she was always so composed; so good and kind. It's odd that he should feel much more guilty about his extramarital adventures now that she is dead than he ever did when she was alive. Does he really believe that she is watching him; seeing his weaknesses and knowing his secrets at last? It's too late now to admit his guilt, confess his sins to her, but the shame is there. She was so true, so loyal, that it would never have occurred to her to suspect him of disloyalty. Ned grimaces ruefully: somehow that thought doesn't bring much comfort. A phrase lodges in his mind: "A guilty conscience needs no accuser."

He finishes his coffee, sets down his cup. The house is so quiet, so empty without Hugo or Jamie or the dogs. It's a relief to hear Rose's familiar call, her footsteps in the passage. Ned gets to his feet and goes to meet her in the doorway.

"Morning," she says cheerfully. "Sitting in the sun?"

"Jamie's taken Hugo to the train. He's off to London," he tells her. "I was finishing my breakfast coffee out here in the courtyard."

She hands him the newspaper. "I'll clear up," she says.

He takes *The Times*, glad to be distracted.

"I'll be in the drawing-room," he tells her, and makes his way out of the kitchen and up the stairs.

Rose looks around the little court. There is a mug on the table and an empty cafetière. She picks them up and stands in the sunshine, staring up at the back of the house, remembering a summer thirty-five years before when she hid out here, praying she wouldn't be discovered, listening to Margaret's voice as she came down the stairs with Toby.

Rose gives a tiny choke of laughter. What a shock it was, arriving at what she expected to be an empty house, knowing Lady T and the Admiral were in

London, and seeing an unfamiliar car parked outside. Then, once inside, hearing voices from upstairs. She didn't call out but went up to the drawing-room, wondering if they were home early; perhaps driven down from London in a rented car. But the voices came from Ned and Margaret's room, the door was ajar, and Rose had a glimpse of a rumpled bed and naked limbs.

She backed away, puzzled, knowing that Ned was abroad, and then Margaret's voice, amused and happy, could be heard.

"This was such a good idea of yours, Toby. Travelling down through the night, creeping in, behaving like a couple of teenagers. Why don't I feel guilty?"

Standing immobile, Rose could hear a voice, mumbling as if its owner's mouth were pressed against soft flesh, and then Margaret's laugh, warm and infectious.

"I'm going to have to chuck you out, though. It's a Rose day, though she might not come, seeing that the oldies are in London. No. Wait. I've had a better idea. Let's go and find some breakfast in Padstow. Much nicer. Come on, Toby. Quick. In case Rose turns up. Get a move on. Show a leg or whatever it is you say in the navy."

There was more laughter, a flurry near the bedroom door, and Rose turned and fled, down the stairs, through the kitchen, and out into the courtyard. She pressed back against the wall, close to the window but out of sight, and minutes later Margaret and Toby came down together.

262

"I haven't shaved and I smell like a badger," he was complaining, and she was laughing at him, saying, "I've always loved badgers," and then the front door slammed and there was silence . . .

Rose still remembers how shocked she was by Margaret's behaviour, that morning long ago, and then how she began to laugh, after the two of them had rushed away in Toby's car; how she stood just here, in the courtyard, exulting in the way Margaret had seized on some pleasure for herself after her husband's betrayals and her son's death. Rose experienced a fierce exultation on her behalf.

As time passed it was amusing to note that, occasionally, when Ned was at sea and Margaret came to visit his parents, Toby also happened to be down in Cornwall to see his mother. Walking the dog, driving to the shops, Rose would see his car parked in different places: in the old quarry up on the moor, on a deserted beach. It didn't take long for Margaret to guess that Rose knew and was not judging her. Nothing was said but they grew closer.

"Jack was very fond of you, Rose," Margaret said to her, not long after he died. "You were almost like brother and sister, wouldn't you say?"

It was a test question, and she looked at Rose intently, not wanting to ask, but longing to know. Rose stared back at her, thinking of how young Jack had died and what he'd never have, and answered the unspoken, almost wistful, question.

"Fond, yes, but I wouldn't say brother and sister. Weren't like that at all, our fondness."

"Oh, good," Margaret said, as if she were relieved, happy. "Oh, I am so glad, Rose. Thank you. And you? Are you . . .?"

She didn't know what to say, and once again Rose took the initiative.

"I miss him," she answered simply. "There don't seem to be nobody else quite like Jack."

"Oh, Rose." Margaret's eyes brimmed with tears, she held out her arms, and they'd clung together, grieving for Jack and all that they'd lost.

For the few years that followed, before Toby was posted abroad, life remained much the same. Rose nursed her mum through the terrible cancer, then stayed on at home to look after her old dad, continuing to work for Lady T and the Admiral in their retirement. Meanwhile, Margaret visited her in-laws at regular intervals and, when she disappeared for a few hours to catch up with a local friend, they asked no questions. Margaret had so many friends.

Rose carries Ned's empty mug and cafetière into the kitchen and grins to herself.

Poor old bugger, she thinks. All those years and he never suspected a thing.

It's early evening before an opportunity presents itself to Ned to confront Jamie. They decide to have one of Dossie's casseroles for supper and Jamie puts it into the Aga to heat it through. Aware of the importance of creating the right kind of atmosphere Ned has already opened a bottle of pinot noir, he's lit the tea-lights in their small glass containers that Hugo scatters around the kitchen table, and now he pours two gin and tonics — very weak for Jamie and a stiff one for himself. This is going to require tact and forethought. He has a huge respect for his nephew; for his career, his operational experience in the Gulf, in Bosnia, in Afghanistan. But he has just as much respect for the way Jamie is dealing with this brutally unexpected change of circumstance. Coping with loss of health, loss of career, will need a great deal of strength and courage.

"You don't know how strong you are," the naval chaplain said to him after Jack was killed, "until strength is the only option left."

They drink their gin and tonics whilst the dogs shift and groan in their beds, sleeping off a long walk in the woods and over the moor, dreaming of their adventures. Then Jamie takes the casserole from the oven and shares it out on to the warmed plates.

"Hugo would have done some kind of vegetable," he comments. "Sorry about that."

"Dossie stuffs these things with vegetables," answers Ned. "I'm sure we'll survive."

He pours wine for them — just a fraction of a glass for Jamie — picks up his knife and fork, and prays for some kind of guidance. He hates to see the look on Jamie's face, that withdrawn, anxious expression: baffled, angry. What could possibly cause it? Then suddenly all his plans for tact and caution fall away from him and he speaks out in his usual forthright manner.

"What is it, Jamie?" he asks. "I can see that you're brooding over something. Good grief, man! I know you have plenty to brood about but this seems to me to be something new. I've no right to question you, and you can tell me to go to hell, but if there's anything I can do only say the word."

Jamie sits staring at his wine glass. He turns it gently so that the wine shines and gleams, bright as blood in the candlelight. There is no disclaimer, no embarrassment; only the sense that Jamie is searching for the right words.

"I've seen Ems again," he says at last. "I bumped into her in Truro."

Slowly, haltingly, he speaks about the encounter, about Hugo meeting unexpectedly with Emilia's daughter, Lucy, and her child, Daniel, in the Relish café. Just briefly Ned recalls the girl he saw a few weeks back at The Chough, and the small boy, and how he'd experienced a flicker of recognition. But Jamie is talking on, in that same flat voice, explaining how Ems is very anxious that she should tell him something, explain something. When he told this to Hugo, his cousin reluctantly admitted that he'd been struck by the likeness between the small Daniel and Jamie at the same age. Extraordinary and unlikely though this sounds, Jamie says, it would go some way to explaining Ems' urgency to talk to him.

"So," says Ned at last. "Let me get this straight. Your understanding of the situation is that the daughter, Lucy, is your child and Daniel is your grandson?"

He shows no kind of emotion and Jamie looks at him, relieved.

266

"Yes," he says. "We're rather jumping the gun but it seems to add up. Why else would she be so desperate to see me again?"

"Still. It seems quite a pretty big assumption, just based on Hugo seeing this small boy and thinking that he looks like you did at the same age. Are you going to see her again?"

Jamie sits back in his chair; he sips some wine and then begins to eat. Ned follows his example. The casserole is perfect: hearty, comforting and full of flavours.

The two men eat in quiet appreciation until Jamie says: "This sounds a touch bizarre but she gave me her mobile number and the address of the cottage in Rock, but I don't want to contact her. I don't want her to have my phone number. Or the landline here."

Ned nods. He totally understands this. Emilia walked away from Jamie once and he has no intention of allowing her to hurt him again.

"And would you contact her, if there were any other way of doing it?"

"Probably. Supposing it's true? That I've had a daughter all these years and nobody told me?"

Ned looks away from the pain and anger in the younger man's face.

"Use my phone," he suggests.

Jamie stares at him and Ned shrugs.

"Why not? It won't hurt me if she texts or rings me. I shall ignore her. But you could at least set up a meeting."

"What . . . What d'you think?" Jamie asks uncertainly.

Ned is oddly moved — the younger man suddenly looks like a boy, young, vulnerable — but he answers strongly.

"I think you should go and hear what she has to say. If you have a daughter and a grandson you need to know about it. Don't let anger and pain get in the way. They might need you — who knows? If you don't go you'll always think about it, wonder about it. Don't be blinded by a sense of injustice. This is not to do with Emilia. This is to do with Lucy and Daniel. Perhaps they don't know about you, either."

On an impulse he gets up, roots about on the dresser, finds his phone and hands it to Jamie.

"Do it," he says. "Send her a text and set it up. Don't speak to her. Text her."

His nephew takes the phone; he looks shocked. Then he puts the phone on the table, pulls out a piece of paper from his pocket and begins to tap a message into the phone. Ned watches him for a moment, then he puts the pudding into the Aga to heat up and sits down again at the table, and refills his glass.

"Good," he says. "Now we wait. Your food will be cold."

Jamie shrugs. "After six weeks under canvas on ration packs it's amazing how your tolerance to any kind of food improves."

Ned is silent. Jamie has never talked of his flying missions during operations in the Gulf, or in Bosnia and Afghanistan, and Ned has no intention of encouraging him to break his silence now. They've both signed the Official Secrets Act.

"Thirty years in the submarine service had much the same effect," he answers lightly — and just at that moment the phone's screen lights up. "I think you have an answer."

Jamie picks up the phone. "D'you want to check it's not for you?" he asks diffidently.

Ned shakes his head. "Most unlikely. Hugo is the only one likely to send me a text but he'd probably send it to you rather than me. He knows I'm very bad at checking my phone. Go for it."

Jamie opens it and reads the message aloud:

"Hi Jamie. Thanks for this. Could you manage tomorrow morning around eleven? Do you need directions to find the cottage?"

Ned raises his eyebrows. "No hanging about, then. Will you go?"

Jamie sits staring at the message. His expression is unreadable and Ned waits for his reaction.

"Yes," he says at last. "I shall go. After all, I've got nothing to lose."

He says it with an air of bravado and Ned silently applauds him.

"Good," he says casually. "Well, confirm it and then we can get on with our supper. Dossie makes a mean sticky toffee pudding."

Jamie sips his wine and then, quite suddenly but with the air of a man making up his mind to something, takes his own phone out of his pocket, and dashes off a text. Ned wonders if he has decided to keep Hugo in the loop but he doesn't ask. Jamie returns his phone to his pocket and leans back in his chair. The decision has been made and he looks calmer.

But what a blindsider, thinks Ned. What bloody awful timing.

He can't begin to think, just at the moment, of the details and ramifications of the news. All he can hope to do is to keep Jamie focused and calm. He gets up, pauses for a moment to get his balance, and then goes to the Aga. The pudding looks good and he gives a sigh of thankfulness. Food can be a great comfort. Thank God for Dossie.

"Sounds like yours," says Adam, not glancing up from the newspaper. "Did you remember to bring Jakey's DS down?"

"Yes, or the little toad would be watching it under the bedclothes."

Dossie goes out into the hall, her hand over the phone in her pocket, and into the little office. Quickly she brings out the mobile and looks at the text. It's from Jamie. She takes a breath of relief and pleasure. It was on the morning of the trip to Truro that he gave her his phone number.

"I've given it to Adam, too," he said. "Just in case."

He didn't say in case of what and she didn't want to ask the question. He read it to her and she typed it in.

"Now you can send me a text," he said, "and then I'll have yours."

"Just in case?" she asked, raising her eyebrows, and he smiled at her.

She waited, though, not wanting to look too keen. And, anyway, there was no point while Jamie was driving. But even after she knew they must have arrived she hesitated, trying to decide whether it should just be a very brief message or something witty, until in the end she just sent:

Hope you enjoy Truro. Dossie.

She dithered over whether she should add an x and decided against it. She wasn't here when they got back, though Adam told her he'd driven them home because Jamie had suffered a migraine attack. And since then Jakey's been staying and, rather to her disappointment, there's been no further communication.

Now she stares at the message on the small screen:

Thank you for my supper. Really enjoying it J x

She feels elated, relieved, and she wants to dash off an amusing remark but fears that it looks a bit too keen to reply immediately. After all, it's been nearly a week since that first text. She's been here before and she's so afraid of giving herself away. Instead she puts the phone in her pocket and goes back into the sitting-room. Adam is still reading the paper, with Bells stretched at his feet, exhausted by her day down at the beach.

"So you invited Sister Emily to our party?" Dossie says randomly. "Brilliant. She really loves having a moment. The thing is, when are we going to do it? We ought to get a date in the diary. Can you come down again soon or are you all booked up for the next few weekends?"

"I'd need to check my diary. I sometimes do viewings at weekends. I've got one coming up in Berkshire."

He hesitates, as if he is going to say something else, but then says: "So it wasn't someone telling you that they've got just the right puppy for you?"

"No, it wasn't," she replies. "And I'm not going to tell you who it was so it's no good worming."

He laughs at the old childhood expression. "I wasn't worming. Just wanting to keep you on the right track. You're dithering, Doss. Just get a dog. It's not right without one here. It's been lovely having Bells, hasn't it? You've been in your element."

At the sound of her name, Bells raises her head, her tail beats the floor, and then she collapses again.

Dossie sits down on the long sofa, tucking up her feet. "I know. Honestly, I do know it, but to tell you the truth, I'm wondering whether I ought to stay here in the long term, Adam. I know what I said about decaying grandeur, and part of me does really feel like that, but it's crazy, really. This place is far too big, and I can't afford the maintenance of it."

He folds the newspaper and puts it on the table beside his armchair. He remains silent and she hurries on, glad to be able to tell him her thoughts at last.

"And if I were to sell up we could share the money between us. I'd really like to do that."

Even as she speaks she remembers Mo's warning words, but she can't help herself. It's as if a high wall

272

between her and her brother is crumbling at last and she has no desire to prevent it from falling or to allow anything else to divide them. It's been wonderful to have him here this week with Jakey and Bells. They've had such fun together and Jakey has made his uncle promise he'll come down again soon. Adam has been so happy, so free, and Dossie doesn't want anything to be a barrier to this new unfolding relationship.

The silence seems to go on for ever. Bells stirs, as if she is aware of the change of atmosphere, gets up and pads across to Dossie, who bends to stroke her soft head, kisses her on the nose.

"So how about this for an idea?" says Adam. His voice is strained, nervous. "How about I move down, here to The Court, and help you keep the place going?"

Dossie stares at him in amazement. "Leave London?" Adam nods. "But your job? You're one of the top men."

Adam shrugs. "There are estate agencies down here. Jackson-Stops in Truro, for one. No, I haven't asked anyone but I expect I could get a job somewhere. I can sell my flat . . ."

He lets the words die away on the air, still not looking at her, as if he is afraid to see something negative on her face, and Dossie is overwhelmed with affection for him.

"It would be utterly amazing. I can't believe you'd even consider it. I mean, why would you? There's so much for you in London. You love the concerts and the theatre, and your friends. What's here for you?"

"My family."

Then she really does want to weep but she knows that he'd hate it and instead she buries her face briefly in Bells' coat and then lifts her head.

"I can't think of anything I'd like more. I'd love it."

She really means it, and because it is a genuine response Adam looks at her at last and makes a face.

"Bit of a shock all round."

She doesn't pretend to misunderstand him. "Yes, it is. But in a good way."

"Mo and Pa wouldn't be pleased."

Dossie shrugs. "OK. There were misunderstandings and differences. But that was then and this is now. I'd love us to share The Court. To be together and to have a dog. Let's start there."

Briefly she thinks about Jamie. How might that relationship develop? But she can't legislate for that right now. There's room for everyone; it's a time for healing and growing.

"In which case," Adam stands up, "I might have a word with Barnaby. Get things moving this end."

She looks up at him. He looks taller, confident.

"You do that, and I'll get the ball rolling with the black Lab rescue society." She grins at him. "By the time we have that party there might really be something to celebrate."

Through the open door they hear the light tread of footsteps. Adam grins at Dossie, points upward, and she looks resigned.

"Dos-sie!" The wail is uttered on two notes and Dossie responds in the same way.

"Ye-es?"

274

"I can't sleep, Dossie. It's too light."

"I'll go," says Adam. "I remember what it was like trying to sleep on these long summer evenings. I'll read to him for a bit. We've started *The Hobbit*."

He goes out and Dossie sits listening, hearing Adam's voice and Jakey's treble answering him, and gives a great sigh. She thinks of Mo and Pa again.

"But how can this be wrong?" she asks them, still holding Bells' head between her hands. "It seems so right. OK, so my track record isn't great with men — well, not since Mike — but all my instincts tell me that this is the right thing to do."

Bells slides down and curls up on the rug beside the sofa.

There must be no rush, thinks Dossie. Adam must find a job, give in his notice, and I shall have a dog. It will all fall into place if we give it time.

She lies along the sofa, her head on a cushion, one hand still reaching down to fondle Bells' ears, and by the time Adam comes back she is fast asleep.

He stands looking down at them. Dossie's face is untroubled, one hand tucked under her neck, the other lying loosely on Bells' head. He is still trying to grasp this new reality; the way the world has turned and shown him a whole new landscape. He is afraid of it, not knowing if he can trust it, yet something within him is willing him on; willing him to seize it and run with it.

How quickly and generously Dossie responded to his suggestion. He knew at once that this was a genuine reaction, not pity or guilt, and his relief was out of all proportion; he hadn't known how nervous he was until she spoke. Ever since that day in Truro — the time with Jamie in the car, his lunch with Barnaby — the idea had been building. Then that incredible moment with Sister Emily in Janna's garden had put the seal on and given it a truth; a reality.

He sits down opposite, quietly, not wanting to disturb them, and tries to understand this new sense of homecoming; of being somewhere he truly belongs.

"I wish you'd come more often," Jakey grumbled earlier. "Why do we hardly ever see you?"

Adam murmured something about things being different from now on, that he would be around more often. They'd gone to the beach, to the moors, to the Padstow Bookseller to buy books to be read at bedtime. They were both loving every minute of it.

At the same time there is a shadow of guilt, the knowledge that Mo and Pa didn't want this to happen.

"I'm not taking The Court from her," he says silently to their shades. "Just enabling her to keep it. Don't worry. I shan't try to cheat her out of it."

Adam rests his head on the cushion and stretches out his legs. He gazes at the bookshelves packed with his parents' books; at the familiar watercolours hanging on the walls. He realizes that bitterness still clings to his thoughts of them, that he believes that somewhere they are disapproving his behaviour, but he won't give up. He will show them that they are wrong; that he will be here for Dossie, and for Jakey, Clem and Tilly, should they need him. And there are other friends now: Jamie, Hugo and Ned. Prune and Ben. Janna and Sister

Emily. He feels overwhelmed by his good luck. But there's a long way to go yet. First he must find a job. He raises his wrist and glances at his watch. It's too late now but tomorrow he will telephone Barnaby. He remembers the conversation he had with him about moving, and, just before he falls asleep, he wonders about Dossie's text and who sent it.

CHAPTER
TWENTY-SEVEN

Emilia paces anxiously. She was awake early, out on the beach before breakfast, and now she waits, watching the clock, rehearsing what she will say to Jamie. For three days she waited for him to contact her, her spirits gradually sinking into despair and then, just when she'd almost given up, the text arrived. She was almost mad with relief and joy when he got in touch with her, though she tried to show restraint with her response. And now he is due at any minute. She has no doubt that he will be exactly on time. She remembers that he hates to be late or early but somehow he will contrive to pull into that parking space across the lane at exactly eleven o'clock.

And here he is, his beautiful classic car sliding alongside the wall and then his long legs thrusting out of the open door and the rest of him following. Emilia stands well back so that she can watch him without being seen. How strange that he should be so little changed: that same wary expression, the tilt of the head. Danny has that same look, that same trick of putting his head very slightly on one side. Her gut churns with panic and she hurries to open the door.

"Hi," she says brightly as he comes up the path.

"Morning," he says.

He doesn't comment on the cottage or its location and she stands aside so that he can enter the little hall, and then shows him into the sitting-room. For some reason he seems to dominate the space and she indicates a chair at the drop-leaf table.

"Coffee? Black? No sugar?" She tries to make it into a little joke, showing him that she hasn't forgotten how he likes it, but he merely nods, says, "Thanks" and turns to look out of the window.

She goes into the kitchen and makes coffee with Lucy's new and complicated machine and carries it back on a tray to the sitting-room. She sees now that she is going to get no help from him and she feels very nervous. As she puts the mug down in front of him and sits opposite, she knows that small talk is utterly pointless and he will respect her more if she simply tells it like it is. She's rehearsed this, just in case, and now she takes a steadying breath and begins.

"Thank you for coming over, Jamie," she says, calmly. "It was a bit of a shock meeting you like that in Truro, though since Lucy told me that she'd met Hugo it wasn't totally out of the blue. So let's start at the beginning. When I left you all those years ago I had no idea that I was pregnant. I was having an affair with Nigel, and because it was at least two months before I even suspected that I was having a baby I imagined that it was his."

Jamie lifts his cup to his lips, watching her all the time over its rim, and she looks back at him. She will not let him see how nervous she is but she doesn't lift her own mug because she is afraid her hand might shake.

"When Lucy was born she looked very much like me. My colouring, my features — well, Hugo probably told you how alike we are — so it wasn't until after Daniel was born that I began to have doubts. The more he grows the more I begin to wonder if, after all, I was wrong and that Lucy might be your child."

Still he watches her. He shows no surprise at this revelation and she is slightly thrown off balance. Surely by now there should be some reaction?

"So," she goes on, less sure of herself. She hesitates. "Well, when I saw you in Truro I felt that it was time to be up front about it. Of course," she adds quickly, "Nigel is dead now and so . . . and so . . ."

"And so," he says, "you decided to take the opportunity to tell me that I've had a daughter for twenty-seven years and a grandson for how many, two years, or is it three, and you'd like my reaction?"

"He's two," she says, confused. "Dan's two."

"And if you hadn't bumped into me in Truro?"

She stares at him. He has completely wrong-footed her. She'd expected either absolute anger or amazed delight but not this cool almost derisive reaction.

"I don't know," she cries. "It's all so . . . well. It's not as if it's a cut-and-dried thing. How can we know for sure? It could be . . ."

She stops, seeing where she's leading herself, and he nods.

"It could be either of us who is the father. Me or Nigel, because you were running us both together."

280

She can feel the blood burning in her cheeks but she tries to hang on to her self-possession.

"I'd already planned to tell you that I was leaving you," she says quietly, determined to show some dignity, to appeal to his chivalrous side, "but when you got back that night you were in quite a state, you know. It was hard. I still loved you. It was just . . ."

She flounders and he smiles that secret, inner smile that infuriates her.

"How very generous of you," he says lightly. "To be ready to comfort the warrior on his return from battle despite your divided loyalties. So, to cut to the chase. Lucy might be my child or she might be Nigel's. It would need a DNA test, I suppose. Does she know that this doubt hangs over her origins?"

"No," says Emilia quickly. "No, there was no need . . ."

She stops again, seeing her mistake.

"Until Nigel died and I showed up?" he suggests.

"It occurred to me," she says, trying to be dignified, "that if there has been a mistake about Lucy's paternity then perhaps now is the time to put it right."

"And how do you think she will react to this spectacular revelation?"

Emilia searches about for the correct response. She hasn't, actually, thought too much about Lucy. She's been too obsessed with the prospect of seeing Jamie again and telling him this. It was as if she had something she could offer him to make up for walking away from him, and it was to do with the hope of beginning again; having a second chance. It's so odd that he seems neither very angry nor very pleased. Instead, there is something slightly edgy, scary, about him.

Belatedly she asks: "Do you have children?"

He smiles then, almost pityingly.

"Do you ever think anything through to a logical conclusion, Ems? Or do you still just simply react?"

His query, his smile, the affectionate use of the nickname, all restore her spirits at once. There is still hope here but she must be careful. She grimaces, a kind of "Aren't I hopeless?" face and smiles at him.

"Probably not. It's just that since Danny was born, I've begun to wonder, and seeing you like that . . . well, it just seemed meant, if you know what I mean?"

He looks at her. Is that affection or pity in his eyes?

"OK," he says. "Then the next step is to talk to Lucy about it. That's your call, I'm afraid. Be in touch if she wants to go forward. Thanks for the coffee."

He stands up and walks out, striding down the path to the car, and before she can follow him, she hears the engine rumble into life, and he's gone.

Jamie pulls in next to the Volvo, switches off the engine and drops his head into his hands. He massages his scalp and tries to put his feelings into some kind of order. Hearing Ems talk like that was extraordinary. It was as if this is a perfectly rational process: Nigel has died. Lucy might be Jamie's daughter. Let's sit down and have a discussion about it.

Thank God Hugo alerted him. Imagine if all that had come out of the blue — however would he have dealt with it? Even being warned, discussing it with Uncle Ned, he had only just enough strength to listen to her without allowing his anger and pain to show. Can she have any idea what it might be like to be told that you've had a daughter for twenty-seven years and haven't known it? To know that you'll never see her as a baby, watch her as a toddler and a small child getting to understand the world around her; never know the schoolgirl, the teenager. He's missed all that. How he enjoyed walking out on Ems! A sweet revenge for that letter all those years ago.

Jamie gets out of the car and slams the door. He goes into the house, ignoring the dogs who swirl about him, and into the kitchen. Ned looks up from his chair. He doesn't speak, he just raises his eyebrows. Jamie strides to and fro, allowing his anger free rein at last.

"The woman's out of her mind," he cries. "It's as if she thinks she's giving me some bloody consolation prize for buggering up my life twenty-eight years ago. 'Oh dear, I think I was a bit naughty, wasn't I, so here's a lovely surprise for you. A daughter and a grandson. Doesn't that make you feel better? Now we can start all over again.' Thank God Hugo warned me. Christ! I might have killed her otherwise. I still might."

He can see that Ned isn't convinced by this threat and he sits down at the table, pushing newspapers and empty mugs aside with a sweep of his arm.

"So she just came straight out with it?"

"When she saw I wasn't in the mood for small talk, or in the mood for some kind of grisly reunion, yes, she told me that she'd never really suspected that I might be Lucy's father until Daniel came along. But now she's pretty sure that it's on the cards. Oh, and Nigel's dead so isn't it all very convenient?"

"And you remained calm? That must have surprised her."

"Yes, I think it did. It took her off guard. She probably remembers how very much I wanted children and was counting on a positive response. I think she actually believes she's making some kind of amends for walking out on me."

"And what happens next?"

Jamie is grateful for the older man's cool reactions. He doesn't need sympathy, or anger on his behalf, he simply needs to know how to proceed.

"She will speak to Lucy. Christ!" He shakes his head. "And how will she do that, I wonder? 'Oh, darling, you'll never guess. A lovely surprise. You've got a new daddy.' How is she supposed to respond to that?"

He can hear the bitterness and rage in his own voice and he stops, biting his lips. He begins again.

"If Lucy can begin to accept that this is a possibility then Ems will contact me. I simply can't imagine how she will react."

"But how do you hope she will react?" Ned's voice is still calm; prosaic.

Jamie takes a deep breath. "I can hardly bear to think about it," he admits. "Part of me longs for it to be true. To believe that I have a daughter. And a grandson. But I have no idea how she, Lucy, and I could ever make a start. How is it to be done? And apart from a DNA test how would either of us be really sure?"

284

"So you made no plan to see Emilia again?"

"No," says Jamie abruptly. "This is not a happy family reunion. If there is any relationship from here on in it will be between Lucy and me. And Daniel and me."

Ned purses his lips. "There might have to be some sort of crossover sometimes if they're just down the road at Rock. No doubt Emilia will be visiting from time to time."

Jamie shrugs. "OK. But you know what I mean. And if Lucy is my child then let's hope she'll have enough of me in her to understand, too. Even if she does look like Emilia. If," he repeats, "she is my child."

Ned remembers that glimpse he had of her in The Chough, of the little boy, with black hair and brown eyes, who was running ahead of her.

"I saw them," he tells Jamie. "In The Chough. I saw that extraordinary resemblance but I couldn't place it until you mentioned it. And I saw Daniel."

Jamie stares at him. He feels choked up, breathless. "And?"

Ned smiles at him; a tender smile. "I think you'd better begin to believe it."

The sound of a text pinging in makes them both jump. Jamie gets up, rescues Ned's mobile from the clutter on the dresser and hands it to him.

Ned shakes his head. "I suspect it's for you."

Jamie reads the message aloud:

"It was so good to see you again Jamie. I shall talk to Lucy later and then be in touch. Please can we meet up again though? There's still so much to say. Will you still be around for the rest of this week? Any morning will suit me. xx"

He frowns at the two kisses, and slams the phone back on the dresser.

Ned grimaces. "I'll take that as a 'no' then," he says.

"Too right it's a 'no'," answers Jamie. "I told her how I was going to play it. Thank God we used your phone."

A thought occurs to him and he takes out his own phone to check it: still no answering text from Dossie. He considers this for a moment.

"Fancy lunch at The Chough?" he asks casually. "We could invite Dossie and Adam."

"They've got Jakey with them," Ned reminds him.

"So? He's eleven? Twelve? Old enough to have lunch at the pub. I know it's a bit late but we could still make it in time. Shall I text her and ask the question?"

Jamie glances up at the older man and sees that he is smiling, complicit.

"I think you should," Ned says. "You need to keep your priorities right."

Jamie taps out the message and waits. The answer comes back quite quickly.

Here already. What's keeping you?

He begins to laugh. "Suit up, Uncle Ned. We're going on a mission."

PART FOUR

CHAPTER
TWENTY-EIGHT

How hot it is, even though it's still early in the morning. Prune stands outside the greenhouses breathing in the scents of growing things, looking around at her handiwork. There are pots of varicoloured peppers, aubergines and cucumbers. She's managed to raise some pak choi in trays, and she'll be able to plant out squash and pumpkin now.

This hot weather, following a wet, cold May Bank Holiday is very welcome, and Prune is distracted by the birdsong, the azalea blossom, and the colour of the copper beech leaves. She stands and stretches, her fingers stained with earth, and she feels happy and sexy. She and Ben made love last night down on the beach, moving to the rhythm of the sea, listening to the waves, and they'd clung together in the cliff's shadow and watched the moon setting. Although it was late, the sky was still light.

"Not long till the solstice," Ben said, his arms around her. "Longest day. Let's go up on the moor and watch the sunrise. We can sleep in the car."

She shivered, pressing close to him, wondering what Ned and Hugo might say. Oddly, she had a feeling that old Ned would probably say, "Go for it," and she gave a little chuckle, which Ben felt and he looked down at her and kissed her. She wrapped her arms around him, holding him tightly and they made love all over again whilst the moon disappeared below the horizon and the world grew dark.

Later, home again, she let herself in quietly but at once heard the sound of the piano and knew that she wouldn't be able to creep away to bed. She listened for a moment. She guessed it was Hugo playing, probably Chopin. He was in a contented mood after his visit to London but there was something going on; some new atmosphere in the tall, old house. She stood for a moment, listening, checked that all her clothes were straight and braced herself to go upstairs and enter the drawing-room. Thank goodness the dogs would detract attention from her.

Mort and Brioc came to greet her so that she was able to avoid the looks of all three men. She buried her face in Mort's furry ruff, reached a hand to Brioc, hoping that making love didn't somehow show, and then said "Hi," quite naturally. Hugo stopped playing, smiling at her, asking if she'd had a good evening, and the question made her want to burst into giggles, which was just so childish. Ned's expression was a mix of amusement and a kindly knowingness, which confused her, but it was Jamie who got to his feet and said: "Just in time for a nightcap. A nice brew of dock leaves?" And then it was all right and everyone was standing up and moving around and she was able to feel composed and calm.

"Hot choc, please," she said to Jamie, as they went down together.

He was being a bit odd just lately: kind of preoccupied but something else as well. A kind of battened-down excitement, as if he were waiting for something, but anxious, too. And Hugo has been slightly distracted. She wondered what might be going on but doesn't feel she can ask. They were talking about the party that Dossie is planning. Adam has gone back to London and they're waiting to know when he can get down again. Everyone wants to make a contribution and they are discussing what they might bring.

Jamie made the hot chocolate and then Hugo said, thoughtfully: "It crossed my mind . . ." and paused, considering.

"And that," Jamie said quietly to Prune, putting her mug of chocolate beside her on the table, "is neither a long nor complicated journey." Ned burst out laughing, Hugo gave his cousin a swift blow to the ribs, and in that moment everything seemed easy and natural again.

Now, as she stands in the sunshine, Prune rubs her hands together, relishing the gritty feeling of the earth. She needs to sow the French climbing beans in the border and bed out some tomato plants. But all she can think about is Ben. She wants to be back on the beach with him, watching the moon set.

Prune can hear voices on the paths screened by azalea and rhododendrons. She has no idea how long she's been standing here, dreaming, and she turns quickly and goes into the greenhouse, back to work.

*   *   *

Up on the cliffs, Lucy stands watching the gulls circling below her. She's had a shock that has rendered her unable to think clearly.

"The kitchen's all finished," Mum said, calling her a few evenings ago. "You have to come and sign it off, darling. I must get back to London and there's something I need to talk to you about."

"Well, you can go back," Lucy answered. "I've got a key. You needn't worry, Mum."

"No, no." Her mother sounded agitated. "I mean, if there's something not quite right or you want changed I can stay on for a day or two, if you can make a quick dash."

Actually, it was quite good timing. Tom's parents were over, which meant she could leave Dan for forty-eight hours, so it was probably a good idea.

"OK," she said. "Can you pick me up from Newquay?"

So it was agreed, and she'd made the journey, arriving in the early evening. The kitchen was everything she'd hoped for: the new slate floor, the dark blue Everhot stove, the Belfast sink. They'd just sat down to supper when Mum started on this whole new thing about Dad probably not being her father. To begin with she simply couldn't take it in and Mum was behaving like this might actually be good news; like, now that Dad was dead, suddenly here was this other guy back in her life again, who could stand in for him and be a grandfather for Dan.

"Wait," she shouted at her mother at one point. "Just wait. What are we saying here exactly? Were you and this man still lovers while you were with Dad?"

And then Mum had explained that, though she was leaving Jamie, he and Dad had briefly overlapped, as it were, and so it was possible that either of them might be Lucy's father.

Remembering, Lucy shuts her eyes and wraps her arms tightly round herself. It was as if Mum could have no perception of what it might be like to hear this. Tom is right. Her mother lives out of her own reality; there's some kind of disconnect.

"Can you hear yourself?" she asked her coldly. "Am I supposed to be jumping up and down with joy? As I see it, you have no proof except that you think Dan looks like . . . Jamie." Odd how hard it was to say his name. "And why didn't you mention it before?"

So then there were more explanations, more excuses.

"It doesn't matter," she said at last. "I don't want to know," and Mum had just stared at her in amazement.

"But you can't just ignore it," she said pleadingly. "Think about Dan. He has a right to know his grandfather."

"Then he can decide for himself when he grows up," Lucy shouted. "And now I'm going to bed and tomorrow I shall book the flight home and you can go back to London when it suits you."

She stormed upstairs, crashing around, slamming doors, and finally falling into bed, though not to sleep. She was unable to look at the furniture and linen she and Tom have chosen together; to feel pleasure in the things that were so important to her. She longed to talk to him but simply couldn't bring herself to shout all this shocking information across the very patchy connection between Rock and Geneva. How could she possibly explain it all — and what could he do about it? She dozed and woke again many times through the long night, then this morning she got up early, made herself coffee. There was no sign or sound of Mum, so she grabbed her jacket and let herself out of the cottage, walking through the village, out across the coast to the beach at Polzeath. She climbed up the path to the cliffs, trying to clear her mind, striding out, rounding the point where she can look along to the little fishing village further up the coast and out to sea towards The Mouls. Suddenly she remembered how Hugo said: "We're neighbours. Across the cliff in Port Quin Bay."

Now, Lucy stands still. Thinking about Hugo. Mum explained about him, too. How she'd actually been going out with him when she met his cousin. Jamie. Christ! She could almost laugh, if she weren't so near angry tears. What is Mum like! Hugo, then Jamie, then Dad . . . except it seems that he might not be Dad any more.

She begins to walk again, instinctively drawn across the cliffs towards Port Quin Bay, though she can't quite think why, except that she feels that it would be a comfort to see Hugo again. He seemed so stable; so nice. He'd remembered Mum after all those years, noticed the resemblance, and Lucy wonders how badly he was hurt; how hard it must have been to lose out to his cousin. She wishes now that she'd spoken to him in The Chough; made her number with him and reminded him of their meeting in Relish. Perhaps, if she had, she might have someone she could talk to about all this.

She has no idea how far she's walked, nor how long it's taken her, but at last, exhausted, she sinks down on the grass at the edge of the cliff. She sits, ankles crossed, clasping her knees and resting her head on them. What is she to think? Is it possible? How do you cope with this kind of thing: a father she's never known about suddenly appearing into her life? How would he fit in? How does it work? She doesn't need this . . . but then, what if it's true?

She is so preoccupied that she doesn't hear the shouts, or the pounding of paws, and she screams as a dog suddenly snuffles in her ear and licks her face. As she struggles to her feet, the dog whines, as if apologetically, and slumps to the ground. A man is beside her, steadying her, apologizing, and it is Hugo: the man she met in Relish, Mum's friend, but she finds that, after all, she is unable to speak naturally because of the man who is with him. He has black hair and brown eyes, and he is leaning on his hiker's stick. His expression is wary, assessing, and his head is tilted just very slightly to one side. It is as if she recognizes him because of Dan, and her heart sinks.

"Lucy," Hugo is saying gently. "Are you OK? Sorry about Brioc."

She shakes her head. "It's fine." She won't look at the other man again. "He just took me by surprise."

"This is Jamie," Hugo goes on, quite naturally, quite calmly. "He was married to your mother quite a long time ago." He turns to the tall dark man. "Jamie, this is Lucy."

She is covered with confusion, trembling with anger. She wants to run away but pride keeps her rooted to the spot. She knows that Jamie has been to see Mum and that Mum is waiting for some reaction from her before making any further gesture. Mum has made it clear that it is all up to Lucy. She forces herself to look at him. Once more she is struck by the resemblance to little Dan: that colouring, that stare, the way he puts his head to one side. She takes a deep breath and summons up all her self-command.

"How do you do?" she says politely. "You couldn't make it up, could you?"

She sees the flash of amusement in his eyes, the way his smile touches the corners of his eyes but not his mouth, and once again she feels a tug of recognition; swift but real.

"So Ems has spoken to you?"

It's more a statement than a question and she is oddly touched by the use of the nickname, an indication of intimacy that stirs her, and unsettles her.

"Yes," she answers briefly. "It's a lot to take in . . . Sorry."

"No," he says swiftly. "You have absolutely nothing to be sorry about. This is your call. And just for now this is between you and me."

She looks at him, frowning a little, and he nods at her.

296

"Just you and me. And Daniel, if it gets that far. No go-betweens."

She understands him at once, and feels grateful. How awful it would be to have Mum present at this moment, or at another meeting. Perhaps later on . . . She catches herself up.

"I'm going back to Geneva later today," she tells him. "I shall be back to Rock, of course, but I don't know when. Do you live locally?"

He points down into the harbour, to the house at the end of the quay, and she raises her eyebrows.

"Really?" She glances at Hugo, who is watching her with sympathy. "You were right. We're pretty close neighbours."

"And if you want to leave it like that I shall understand, but should you want to be in touch, for any reason, I could give you my phone number."

"Hasn't Mum got it?" she asks coolly.

He shakes his head. "No. She has a number that I can be reached on."

She sees exactly what he's saying and once again she feels that treacherous shaft of liking for him. She wants to smile but she doesn't want to give anything away. Not yet.

"This is between you and me until you say otherwise," he repeats. "If I give you my private number then, should you decide to do so, you can get in touch with me."

She hesitates, then nods, and pulls out her phone. He takes his out and reads the number to her. She types it in, reads it back, he nods.

"Have a good flight home," he says, and turns away, calling the dogs.

She looks at Hugo who smiles, says, "Goodbye, Lucy," and hurries after him.

Lucy waits, watching them go, and, as they begin to descend, Jamie glances back. He hesitates, just fractionally, and then raises his hand. She lifts her own in response, and then he disappears from view. She stands for a moment, quelling a strong longing to run after him, then she turns and begins the long walk back to Rock.

Emilia is packing. Slowly and methodically she checks each room, makes certain that nothing is left in the fridge. Lucy has gone, rushing back to Geneva, though she seemed very slightly less abrasive when she returned from her walk.

"Thanks for all you've done here, Mum," she said. "I don't want to talk about the other thing. Not yet. Sorry. Way too much to think about."

Emilia had to hide her disappointment; her need to make something happen. She could tell from Lucy's face that discussion was not an option. She caught herself thinking: she gets that stubbornness from Jamie, and then wondered how many times she's had that reaction through Lucy's life but squashed it at once. Now she can allow herself to think about it: the way she convinced herself that the baby was Nigel's. After all, she had no desire, then, to go back to Jamie, and she knew just how he would react if he thought she was carrying his child. He longed for them to have a baby but it would have tied her down, committed her to that life of rules and regs and the separation and loneliness. So much easier to convince herself that it was Nigel's baby, to blot out any other possibility. Until now. Now she is alone again. Now she has met Jamie again and remembers why she fell in love with him. Now she wants another chance and, through Lucy and Danny, she thought she might have it.

But Lucy has gone with vague promises of being back sometime in the summer, though making it clear that the next time she comes to the cottage it will be with Tom and Dan and that they will want some time to themselves.

Emilia carries her bags downstairs and out to the car. She goes back in for one last check around, picks up her handbag and her jacket, and pauses. She breathes in, puzzled, looking around her. That drifting miasma of bitterness, of disappointment, insistent like the faint smell of damp, seems to hover in the air. Emilia shrugs, locks the front door behind her and gets into the car. She fastens the seat belt and then sits staring despondently before her. In a last desperate bid, she takes her phone from her bag and checks it. Nothing. Though she has texted Jamie three times, made a call, which was not answered, there has been no message from him since that very first one. She sends one more text and waits hopefully.

Presently, she puts the phone away. Just for a moment she hears Lucy's voice: "Please may I go round again, Mummy?" and her own voice in response: "No, you can't. I'm afraid it's too late."

She wants to scream, to shout that it isn't fair, just as Lucy did all those years ago, but instead she starts the engine and drives away.

The three men sit in the drawing-room after lunch, the dogs stretched out beside them.

"It was a shock," says Jamie. "She's so like Ems as she was when I first saw her back in your rooms in Bristol. I can't get over it."

The other two wait, not knowing what to say, how to respond.

"I felt exactly the same," says Hugo, after a moment. "I think we all did. Even Uncle Ned in the pub. It's not that unusual, I suppose, but . . . she's such a pretty girl . . ." His voice trails away.

"I like her," says Jamie. "I liked the way she handled it. Meeting us like that with no warning. She has courage."

"So," says Ned, "you hope she gets in touch again?"

"Yes." Jamie nods. "I hope so. But I don't dare think about it, really."

Hugo watches him anxiously. He's afraid that the shock and the emotion might trigger Jamie's vertigo, make him ill, but the damage has been done . . . if it is indeed damage. Maybe it will all come good.

"And you were right," Jamie says to Ned, "to let me use your phone. Another text this afternoon. She says she's going back to London."

300

"Thank God," says Ned. "Now we can all sleep easy in our beds."

Hugo feels a pang of sympathy for Emilia, and it seems that Jamie senses it.

"It was necessary to be tough," he says. "Ems could ruin everything because she'll only ever see it from her own point of view. Can you imagine what Lucy must be feeling right now? She must hate me, dammit. The shock of being told something like that. She needs time. She doesn't need to be harried and pushed. Maybe in the future, when we've all got used to the idea . . ."

Another silence.

"It was odd," says Hugo thoughtfully, "wasn't it, that Brioc went up to her in that way? He never does that to people as a rule. It was as if in some way he recognized her scent, that it was familiar to him."

Jamie raises his head, frowning, thinking about the implications of Hugo's remark.

"It'll be OK," says Hugo encouragingly, knowing that it means nothing but longing to be of comfort, and Jamie smiles.

"Yes. Maybe it will. Play for us, Hugo. Play the 'Widmung'."

Hugo stares at him in surprise.

"Are you sure?" he asks.

But Jamie nods at him. "That's where it all started."

Hugo gets up and goes to the piano. He sits for a minute, his head bowed, and then he begins to play.

Rose lets herself into the house, hangs up her jacket, but before she can call out she hears voices from upstairs and then music. She knows at once that it is Hugo playing and, as she listens, she is drawn towards the sound of it, her head tilted upward, trying to catch every note as she hesitantly climbs the first few steps. She remembers how, once before, she did this; finding Hugo at the piano, watching this stranger, this hitherto unknown Hugo, controlled, passionate, remote. Rose holds tightly to the banister to prevent herself from hurrying up the stairs and going in to the drawing-room. The music is unbearably moving, and she wants to weep, to love, to share all her emotions. She remembers how Hugo looked as he played; how they'd made love, and now, foolishly, she longs for it to happen again.

The music stops; there is a murmur of voices. The drawing-room door opens and Hugo is there at the top of the stairs, with the dogs behind him. He hesitates when he sees Rose, his expression alters, and in that moment she knows that he, too, is remembering. They look at each other.

"Funny, isn't it," she says, hearing her voice tremble, "how music takes you back, like you're right there, however many years ago?"

He descends the stairs, still watching her.

"I hope it was in a good way?" he says. "What it was you were remembering, I mean."

Rose's heart beats fast but she mustn't go too quickly. She must be sure of him.

"Oh, it was very good," she says. "I had this pile of ironing given to me. Unexpected, different from what I usually do. Just what I needed right at that moment."

He's smiling now and, to her delight and relief, he stretches out a hand to her and she takes it and follows him into the kitchen.

He turns to look at her, still holding her hand.

"I never said thank you properly, back then," he said. "I was just a callow boy. What was I? Twenty? Twenty-one? You were so beautiful and generous and exciting. I couldn't believe my luck. And then the time passed and I still didn't know how to tell you. Sometimes I wondered if I'd dreamed it."

He releases her hand, opens his arms and Rose walks into them. She puts her own arms around his waist, looking up at him.

"There were too many barriers," she says quietly. "Lady T and the Admiral. Me a fisherman's daughter . . ."

"And there was always Jack, wasn't there?" he says gently.

She holds him a little tighter. "Not that afternoon," she says. "That was just you and me."

"Jack told me and Jamie that if we even so much as looked at you he'd kill us," Hugo murmurs. "But I didn't think he'd mind. Did you? Not then."

He hesitates, his head bent, his breath warm on her cheek and she thinks of Jack, laughing down at her: "Here's looking at you, kid."

"I've still got that rose," she tells Hugo. "Perhaps you should come and see it sometime. To remind you."

She can feel him begin to chuckle.

"I couldn't help it," he says. "You know? When Jamie talked about the ironing? It just took me right back there."

"Me, too," she answers. "And your aunt Margaret coming in and being cross with you."

"And you," he reminds her, "said very firmly that it was just the once. So I took the hint, though it's been tough, sometimes."

"And there was me," she says, "thinking you were glad to be let off the hook. You'd definitely better come and see that rose you sent me. It's time we cleared up any misunderstandings."

"You can't imagine," he says, "how nice that would be. I think there might be a few rocks and stormy weather in the months to come and it's good to know that there's a safe harbour somewhere."

"You're right." She reaches up to kiss him, then pushes him away, laughing back at him. "And a man always needs to get his ironing done."

Hugo pulls her back to him so as to hug her, and then gestures at the kitchen.

"I came down to clear up the lunch things. We left it all in a bit of a muddle. Slight crisis. Shall we do it together?"

"No. I'll clear up." She gives him another push towards the door. "Go back and play to them. I like to hear you play while I work."

"I'll play for you one day, Rose," he promises her. "One day I shall play the 'Widmung' just for you."

He hesitates, and then goes out, and she crouches to embrace the dogs, who lick away Hugo's kisses, just as once, long ago, she kissed away his tears.

CHAPTER
TWENTY-NINE

Dossie stands in the kitchen, the table and the work surface covered with the results of her working day: pies and puddings, soup and cakes. Soon things will be divided up into cartons and foil containers, labelled and packed away into the huge industrial freezers in the utility room.

She's listening to a CD Adam has given her: Tom Odell's *Long Way Down*. It's odd how music has always played a large part in her love affairs and now the track "Supposed To Be" makes her think of Jamie, replaying in her mind the few times they've spent together alone. Generally either Hugo or Ned — or both — are with him. The last time she saw him was at The Chough when he texted to suggest lunch and she replied that she and Adam were already there.

Dossie wanders to the doorway and out into the garden. How odd Jamie had been that day: edgy, witty, almost hyper. She wanted to believe that it was for her benefit, a kind of showing off, but it went deeper than that. Occasionally she caught Ned glancing at him, a watchful, slightly anxious glance, and briefly she wondered if it might be the effect of Jamie's disability or maybe it was to do with medication. She noticed that he didn't drink, though his appetite was normal, and that he took care to have a chair back available to hold on to when he was standing talking to Ben. She's begun to be aware of these small things: his collapsible stick that he always has with him, the proper walker's stick he used when they strolled down the lane to the church when he and Hugo came over for supper, that he drinks very little alcohol. She wonders now if he had an ulterior reason for offering to let her drive back from The Chough that day; just as he'd asked Adam to drive home from Truro.

Like Ned, she feels angry and sad that Jamie's career should end so suddenly. She thinks about him — his wit, his courage, his bloody-mindedness — and has little fear that he will control his disability. She feels real respect for him — and much more than that. But she is frustrated by not knowing how to proceed. She cannot seem to move beyond a general friendship with all three of them, though she wants to believe that there is something more between her and Jamie. She doesn't think she's misread the signs but she is too nervous to proceed. Given his situation, does he want a relationship? Her growing love for him makes her too aware, too cautious. She knows it but she is unable to help herself. She can't bear to get it wrong again. And suppose there's someone else? Another woman back in Oxfordshire?

Dossie turns and goes back inside. As she dumps a pile of container lids on the table she sees that she has a new message on her phone and she seizes it hopefully. The text is from Hugo.

Jamie has taken Ned to the dentist in Wadebridge. Are you working or shall I come and share a cuppa with you? xx

Dossie is ashamed that she is disappointed that the text is not from Jamie. How easily she and Hugo might have slipped into a quiet, happy relationship if his cousin had not turned up. But here she is again, heart beating fast when a text comes in, needing to see him, to hear his voice. She remembers the old test of love: "Do you need to see him? Do you need to touch him? Do you need to hear him?" and she shouts: "Yes, I bloody do!" and then bursts out laughing at her foolishness and taps out a text.

Yes please. Do come over. Just finished work.
Kettle on. xx

She doesn't stop to wonder if she should send kisses to Hugo. How perverse life is, how complicated. She begins to pack and label the food she's prepared and is nearly finished by the time she hears Hugo's car. He comes in, the dogs running ahead, and she quickly wipes her hands and then crouches to greet them, kissing their silky heads, hugging them.

"Adam not here?" asks Hugo.

As she looks up at him — tall, good-looking, that sweet smile — she wonders why she just didn't keep her life simple. She stands up and hugs him, too.

"Sorry, I'm all doggy now," she says. "No, Adam is in Truro. He's got an interview at Jacksons this afternoon. He's very twitchy but I think he'll walk it."

She washes her hands, puts water down for the dogs. Hugo walks about, hands in his jeans pockets. He looks thoughtful, preoccupied, and she is suddenly filled with apprehension.

"Let's have tea outside," she says.

"If you like," he answers, but she can see that he's not thinking about the tea and that this is not the usual jolly visit.

"What is it, Hugo?" She leans back against the Aga, watching him. "There's something. What is it?"

He doesn't argue or deny it; he sits down on one of the chairs at the table.

"I want to talk to you about Jamie," he says.

Adam walks up Lemon Street, crosses the road and turns into the little twitten where he knows there's the excellent bistro near the cathedral. He feels elated, excited, and he wishes he had someone with whom he could share this moment. He's texted Dossie, but for once she hasn't responded as quickly as she usually does, and he decides he'll stop for a coffee and calm down a bit before he drives home.

It's that quiet time in The Place: lunch long finished, dinner a way off yet, a few people having tea, reading the papers. He orders a double espresso at the counter and sits down. The woman at the next table glances briefly at him, smiles, in that friendly, easy way that they do down here; it would never happen in London.

He smiles back at her and looks at his phone to see if Dossie has responded: nothing.

Adam feels restless. He glances around the bistro and then sideways at the woman. She's probably in her early forties, thick blonde hair wound into a knot, a pretty profile. He longs to speak to her, not with any attempt to pick her up but simply to connect, to release some of this pent-up happiness. As if she guesses his thoughts she turns and looks at him, smiles again. The waitress brings Adam's coffee, the blonde woman asks her if she might have some more hot water, and this frail connection makes Adam brave enough to say: "The last time I was in here it was packed."

"You need to pick your moment," she answers. Her voice is nice; friendly, on the edge of a smile. "I dash over here for my tea break sometimes because it's so quiet."

"You work here? In Truro?" he asks, pleased.

"Uh-huh," she nods. "Not a grockle."

He laughs at the West Country word for tourist and feels the need to justify himself.

"I'm a local boy," he tells her, "though I work in London. At least . . ." He hesitates and she looks at him enquiringly, eyebrows raised.

"At least . . .?"

"I think I might have just got myself a new job."

"Here? In Truro?"

She's almost parroting his words and they both laugh. Her hot water arrives and she pours it into the teapot.

"It's an amazing stroke of good luck," he tells her. "Can't really believe it."

She purses her lips, consideringly.

"So nothing to do with having the right qualifications, being good at the work, fantastic track record, then?"

He laughs — he can't help it — struggling with this new sensation of being approved, assessed as being viable, and having this odd conversation with a beautiful woman.

"There might be something in that," he admits, "but it was all a bit on the spur of the moment. I decided I'd like to move back and I thought I'd chance my arm."

She nods her agreement. "Don't ask, don't get," she says and raises her teacup. "Shall we drink to it? Or would that be premature?"

"No," he says quickly. "Not premature. Well, I've got to go back and give in my notice and sell my flat, but they're OK with that."

"'They' being? Or am I being pushy?"

He shakes his head. "No, you're not. Jackson-Stops, in Lemon Street."

"Really?" Her face lights with pleasure. "That's great. I'm with the holiday cottage letting company round the corner." She stretches out a hand to him. "My name's Jemima Spencer."

"I'm Adam Pardoe," he says. Her hand is warm and her clasp is firm. "That's good. I shall come and look you up when I start work. Be afraid. Be very afraid."

"You do that," she says. "We can come here and have our tea breaks together."

She finishes her tea, stands up. "Back to the grind. It's not really, though. I love it. See you, Adam."

She walks out, hitching her bag strap over her shoulder, and he watches her go, enchanted; hoping that he'll see her again. He finishes his coffee in a daze, wondering what else the day might hold in store for him, and glances at his phone but there's still no answer from Dossie.

Hugo drives home, following the familiar lanes, still wondering if he's done the right thing, but fairly confident that he has. It's been easy to see that the shock Jamie has sustained has dulled his perceptions to life around him; that he's preoccupied, full of conflicting hopes.

"And if she does decide to contact me?" he asked suddenly, bitterly, "what's it going to be like when she finds that the glamorous pilot Ems has probably told her about is, in fact, disabled, unviable and unemployed?"

Hugo was dismayed, unable to think of words to sustain or comfort. And, anyway, Jamie wouldn't want them. Everything he could think of to say sounded trite.

"You'll just have to leave that up to Lucy," he answered casually, almost indifferently. "She doesn't come across as shallow or stupid to me. Rather the contrary. Isn't it who you are that counts?"

It was at that moment that it occurred to him that Jamie might also be feeling anxious about how Dossie would consider him in the long term. Hugo noticed that, though she continued her flow of messages to him, she never texted Jamie except in response to one of his. Was Jamie playing it cautiously because he feared she might see him in the light that he'd just described: disabled, unviable, unemployed?

This could become a self-fulfilling prophecy if something were not done about it. Each might lose confidence, grow doubtful, let the moment pass. He'd seen them together: the spark was there. It needed to be nurtured not extinguished.

And so he took the decision, grabbed the moment, and went to see her.

"My God," she said, when he explained about Emilia and her bombshell. "Good grief." And later, "Does he know you're telling me?"

"No," said Hugo. "I know. It might seem disloyal, or as if I'm breaking a confidence, but I'm worried about him. It's 'taken him aback all standing', as Uncle Ned would say, and he's not quite thinking straight. You need to know this. You need to behave with him in the old way. Just . . . Oh, just crash on, making jokes, sending texts, inviting him over. Once you become anxious, wary, the dynamic changes. Trust me, Doss. I know what I'm talking about. I've known Jamie all my life. Cut him some slack while this is going on but just act like nothing's happened. The thing is, I didn't want you to think that there might be anything else . . ."

She looked at him then, smiled a very small smile. "You mean someone else. Another woman?"

"Yes. That's just what I mean. You hardly know him, his past, his friends. I do. Trust me."

"It did cross my mind a few times." A pause. "Am I allowed to tell Adam?"

"Yes, I don't see why not. It's not so much a secret, as Jamie finding the right moment to mention it to you. And the thing is . . ." He hesitated. "I'm hating this," he suddenly burst out. "But I just am so afraid of a misunderstanding between the two of you and I'm sure that we can support him better this way. Anyway. He's had a text from Lucy."

"Oh my God!"

"Yes. Just saying that she and Tom and Dan will be at the cottage for a fortnight at the end of June. Nothing else."

"What did Jamie do?"

"He showed me his answer. It said, 'I'll be here.' So we'll just have to play it by ear. But it's going to be a difficult time. For all of us."

Dossie crossed her arms, head bent. "Poor Jamie," she said at last. "It's a lot to handle . . . But then it could all be so good, couldn't it?"

And at that moment Hugo knew his gamble had come off, that Dossie was equal to Jamie's disability and to the prospect of a family he hadn't known he had. Hugo let out a huge breath of relief.

"Yes," he answered. "It could all be so good. Bless you, Doss. Let's have that tea."

But, now, driving home, he knows that nothing is certain. Jamie is at a crossroads: who knows what direction he might take?

After he's gone, Dossie walks back into the garden and sits down on the seat on the terrace outside the drawing-room windows, looking south-west across the

314

garden and the fields to the low line of hills behind St Austell. In the escallonia hedge a robin is singing. A small part of her mind registers that the long border beneath the stone wall needs weeding, and that she ought to cut the grass, but really she is thinking about what Hugo has told her and is trying to remain unaffected by it. She knows that he has come in order to reassure her, to explain why Jamie might be behaving oddly, but instead he has made her very nervous. Her experience, except with Mike, has given her no cause to be confident in her relationships and she can't prevent herself from imagining the worst. After all, Jamie was once married to this woman; this Emilia. He must have been in love with her back then, and it was she who left him. So this indicates that he was still in love with her when they broke up; he hadn't tired of her. Supposing that those old emotions should reignite, especially now that she has his daughter and his grandson to add weight? It's fine for Hugo to imply that this won't happen but how does he know that? How can he be so certain?

Surely, in this new relationship, Jamie's ex-wife is bound to play a part? There will be family moments, intimate moments, and Jamie and Emilia would be a natural pairing. And they are all going to be just down the road at Rock. Dossie groans in despair. Just when it was all being so good; such fun; what Sister Emily always describes as "lovely joy". And now this happiness is threatened. After all, why did Hugo come to see her, to tell her all this, unless he feared that there actually might be some complication?

Dossie hears the sound of an engine, a car door slams, and Adam walks round the side of the house. She's lost track of the time and feels guilty that his interview in Truro has slipped to the back of her mind since Hugo's visit.

"Hi," Adam says. He looks happy, confident. "All good?" He frowns as he comes closer. "Are you OK? I texted you but you didn't reply. What's happened?"

She shakes her head, pulling herself together. "Nothing," she answers. "Honestly. How did it go? Tell me all about it."

He sits at the end of the seat, still watching her. "Doesn't look like nothing to me. It went well. Job's mine if I want it. So, what's up, Doc?"

She smiles reluctantly at the old childhood expression.

"I'm being silly, that's all. That's great news, Adam. Well done. But I knew that they'd leap at the chance. When can you start?"

He looks pleased at her enthusiasm, though not convinced by her denials, and she wills herself to greater self-control.

"Next month," he answers. "But I've got to sort things out in London and they are quite happy with that. It's a huge stroke of luck."

"No, it's not," she says at once. "They know a good thing when they see one."

He gives a little involuntary laugh, as if her words remind him of something else, and heaves a great sigh of relief and pleasure.

316

"So then," he says. "That's that. Now tell me, what's bugging you?"

She turns away from him and stares down the garden, pulling her heels up on to the edge of the seat, wrapping her arms round her legs and resting her chin on her knees. Presently, she begins to tell him about Hugo's visit, what he's told her and why. There's a silence when she's finished and she wonders what Adam might be thinking.

"It's good rationalization, isn't it?" he says after a while. "Silly misunderstandings can cause such huge problems. We're always needing a response, aren't we, and we panic when we don't get one?"

"You mean to a text?" she suggests, thinking of her caution in contacting Jamie.

Adam shrugs. "Or to a present, or to an offer of love. The trouble is, our timing isn't necessarily another person's, so we're left thinking 'If they really loved me they'd have responded by now,' because that's what our time frame would be. But everyone has a different way of receiving acts of love and generosity, depending on character, history."

She laughs. "But we continue to watch our email inbox or our phone and doubts creep in."

"Exactly. And I guess that's what Hugo was worrying about."

"Yes, I get that," she answers. "But why did he feel the need to mention it at all?"

"Because Hugo is observant, aware, and extremely fond of his cousin. And of you. He can see that with this huge shock Jamie might be thrown off balance and, because you have no idea what is going on, you might misread certain things. Is that a possibility?"

"Yes," she admits reluctantly. "Yes, it is."

"Well, there you are. Hugo is used to dealing with people. Camera crews, assistant producers, actors, presenters. It's his job to keep everything running smoothly and get a result. He's always one step ahead. It's good advice, Doss."

"The trouble is," she says frankly, "that it's made me anxious in case Jamie and Emilia decide to get back together again. She left him, you know, not the other way round. Supposing it all starts up again? Especially now there's a daughter and a grandson. Part of me wants to be happy for him. After all, I'd hate to be without Clem and Jakey."

"And did Hugo give the least impression that you should be fearful of this woman? What did you call her?"

"Emilia." Dossie shakes her head, wondering why she finds it hard to say the name. "No. In fact he said something like: 'You hardly know him. I do. Trust me.' And that I should go on in the same way as if nothing has happened."

"Sounds pretty good advice to me," Adam says. "And he said it was OK to tell me?"

"Yes. I asked him. It's not a secret, it's just a difficult thing to explain to people, isn't it?"

"Poor bugger," says Adam feelingly. "As if he hasn't got enough on his plate. And now he's got a whole new family just suddenly out of the blue."

318

"Yes," agrees Dossie, rather bleakly. She rather resents this ready-made family turning up, if she's honest.

"But then," says Adam, "Jamie has to learn to cope with Clem and Jakey. And Tilly. And me."

He looks sideways at her and she makes a face, shrugs.

"OK," she says. "You've made your point. I'm over it now. So, new readers start here. How did it really go in Truro? Tell me everything."

"I enjoyed that," says Ned, as Jamie comes round to haul him up out of the passenger seat of the MGB. "Took me back a bit. Made me feel young."

Jamie passes him his stick, waits until Ned is steady on his feet. He sympathizes with that sense of imbalance and insecurity.

"Looks like Hugo's off somewhere," he says. "I wonder if he's taken the dogs."

But the house is empty when they go in and Ned pauses at the bottom of the stairs.

"I'm not allowed to eat or drink for a couple of hours after that filling," he says. "So I think I might go up and have a zizz. See you later. Thanks, Jamie."

"I'll go out for a walk," Jamie tells him. "Will you be OK?"

Ned nods, almost impatiently. "Of course I shall be OK. It's only a filling. See you later."

Jamie watches him mount the stairs and then goes into the kitchen and scribbles a note for Hugo on the pad kept on the kitchen table. He pauses in the hall, takes Ned's shooting stick from the stand and goes out into the increasingly hazy sunshine. The stick is heavy but it has its uses and slowly he climbs the path out of the village to the clifftop. When he reaches the spot where they'd met Lucy at the edge of the cliff he drives the metal point into the earth, opens it up, and sits on the seat looking out towards The Mouls. The clouds have thickened during his walk, the visibility is falling and the misty white light merges with the silvery sea. Legs braced, arms folded across his breast, Jamie stares out beyond the rocks below him towards the obscured horizon. The sea's skin is stretched smooth as aquamarine silk, lifting and falling as it breathes, reflecting eternity: calm, untroubled, utterly ambivalent.

"Eternity's a terrible thought. Where's it all going to end?"

Who had said that? Jamie shakes his head. He can't remember and he doesn't want to think about it. All he can think about is the text from Lucy: not exactly an invitation but an opening gambit in an encounter that will be as complicated as a game of chess. Luckily, he's very good at chess.

How on earth, he asks himself, does this work? How do I integrate a grown-up daughter, her husband and her child, into my life? How is it to be done?

Jamie is fearful and exalted at the same time. He has a child, a daughter: a beautiful, brave young woman. He longs to see her again yet he can imagine all the pitfalls, the wrong moves, the possibility of failure. A mental picture of his old enemy, Nigel, comes back to arouse his antagonism and jealousy: this man for whom

320

he was abandoned, who was a father to Lucy for more than twenty-five years. Anger pulses in him, he feels the tension in his body rise inexorably, and braces himself more firmly on his stick. A gull swoops low, screaming overhead, and instinctively he ducks and almost loses his balance. At once the awareness of his disability swamps him; makes him unable to face the prospect of having to explain it all to Lucy; to Daniel. How are they going to view him?

His fists clench, he looks down at his feet and, at that moment of vulnerability, of self-pity, he hears the familiar thrumming of aircraft engines. Quickly he raises his head. His eyes scan the horizon, looking for what he knows is there. The engine note is unmistakable but against the gloomy sky it is difficult to see his target. He stands up, his eyes sweeping from sea to sky, starting to his right and scanning left. A flash of white and red anti-collision lights and he has them; two of them. His aircraft, the Hercules, at low level, is almost head on to his position, seeming stationary in the sky as they both close in. He has a momentary sensation of childish glee, that same sensation that led him into the air force all those years ago; that overwhelming need to be there, that desire to fly, to be in one of those machines. They are closer now and he can see the four turbo props on each aircraft. The lead ship begins to climb for the coastal crossing, gaining height to avoid the gulls that always gather at cliff edges. But Jamie is puzzled. Only two ships? Where is the third? And then he has it, line astern from the leader, even lower to the sea, and coming directly towards him. The first aircraft coasts in above him and, to his left, the second aircraft, drifting back from echelon to line astern, passes further away. But the third seems to aim straight at him so that, momentarily, he fancies that he can see into the cockpit before the pilot pulls back hard on the stick and the aircraft climbs rapidly to roar over his head.

Even as he turns to track it, the reminder of that controlled, precise atmosphere, the difference between the purposefulness of his past life and the aimlessness of his present one, overwhelms him with bitter regret. And worse, he has not paid attention to his limitations, and he realizes that he is dizzy; severely dizzy. He reaches out for the shooting stick but his hands cannot find the handle. Involuntarily he stumbles and steps backwards. He is acutely aware of the closeness of the cliff's edge, of the sound of the sea on the rocks below. He wants to fall to the safety of the ground but he is struggling to orientate himself, struggling to discern which way is safety and which way oblivion. The earth seems to heave and spin, as if it were trying to throw him from the cliff and, as he drops to all fours, he feels the turf under his left hand give way and he is sure that he is falling. He doesn't hear the flurry of barking or the pounding of paws, he just feels his arm seized, his coat pulled firmly to the right, and he topples in that direction on to solid ground. The tugging is insistent and he half crawls, half scrambles in the direction in which he is being pulled until his arm is released and the dog, flesh and blood and bone and fur, is beside him, butting him with his head and whining joyously.

"Brioc," he says. He wraps his arms around the dog, burying his face in the warm coat. And then Hugo is there, and Mort, and he is surrounded by them, being helped away from the edge of the cliff to safety.

"Good grief, Jamie," Hugo is saying. "What the hell were you doing?"

Jamie lies back on the ground, letting the spinning slowly reduce, feeling the solidity of the earth stabilizing him, beginning to restore his equilibrium.

"Lost my balance, got too close to the edge. Did you see them?"

"See them? Bloody hooligans. What were they doing here?"

Jamie grins. "Low-level training. Might be going into St Mawgan. I came down here once. Thought I'd have a look at the old place from the air." He laughs. "Perhaps the lazy sods were following my route — it's probably still on the database. Gave me quite a turn, I can tell you."

Gingerly he sits up, using Brioc for support. He roughs the dog's coat.

"Thanks, old boy," he murmurs and then looks at Hugo. "What were you lot doing up here?"

"Saw your note," Hugo answers. "Skiving off as usual instead of getting supper ready." But his look is anxious. "Do you think you can make it back?"

Jamie nods and holds up his hand in an unspoken request. Hugo steps in and grips Jamie's arm, helping him as he stands up cautiously. Hugo hands him the shooting stick, putting his arm around his cousin's waist.

"I'm OK," Jamie says, almost defensively.

"Sure you are," agrees Hugo, but still he keeps hold of Jamie's arm, steering him away from the edge of the cliff. "Let's go home."

Hugo follows Jamie down the cliff path, shaken by the sight of his cousin out of control, so near the edge of the cliff. Oddly he feels angry, as a parent might when a child avoids danger after some foolish prank.

Ned is in the drawing-room when they arrive back.

"Go and play to him," says Hugo, "while I feed the dogs. He's still recovering from that injection. It seems to have been a particularly unpleasant filling."

He watches Jamie climb the stairs, clinging to the banister, then turns back into the kitchen. He's still mad with Jamie, mad at him for taking such a risk just to watch an aircraft. As he apportions food into the dogs' bowls and freshens their water, he still can't get the scene at the edge of the cliff out of his mind; the way Jamie was staggering, toppling to the ground. Hugo knows that it had been a very close-run thing.

"Thank God for Brioc," he murmurs, and leans to put an extra spoonful of food into the dogs' bowls.

He leaves the dogs to their suppers and goes upstairs and into the drawing-room. Ned glances up at him as he comes in and then nods towards Jamie at the piano.

"What's he playing?" he asks.

Hugo looks at his cousin; Jamie grins at him. It's a grin that contains both contrition and humour, and Hugo breathes in deeply through his nose and then reluctantly begins to smile.

324

"It's an Elton John number," he tells Ned. "It's called 'Sorry Seems To Be The Hardest Word'."

CHAPTER
THIRTY

The day of the party dawns warm and still. Mist, grey and luminous, lies on the sea, drifts along the river and dims the brightness of the sun. All morning, Dossie and Adam work together, prepping supper, choosing wine, taking cakes from the freezer. Adam has arranged that he will fetch Janna and Sister Emily, although Clem and Tilly and Jakey will be coming from Chi-Meur.

"It would be a squash for them in Clem's little car," Adam says. "It's OK. I don't mind."

But Dossie knows that he wants to do this: to bring Janna and Sister Emily to The Court. She wonders if it's making him feel that this party is truly a joint affair, not just for her friends, and she agrees that it's a good idea.

They carry extra tables and chairs into the garden as the sun begins to draw up the mist, and Adam finds two old umbrellas and their metal stands in the barn. These can be dusted down and erected so that they will provide shade on the terrace.

He unpacks the extra plates and cups that Dossie keeps for her parties, though there's plenty of pretty china on the dresser.

"Just in case," he says. "Best to be prepared." He grins at her. "This is fun."

She grins back at him. She loves to do this; to be getting ready for a big party that lasts on into the evening. She remembers that the last big occasion at The Court was for Pa's birthday — and that Adam made some excuse and didn't come. She tries not to think about it but wishes that Mo and Pa could see this difference in Adam; could be here to celebrate with them. She knows, though, sometimes it needs change, however final and sad, to bring about a new direction.

"Jakey can make himself useful," Adam is saying. "He's old enough to be sensible and if he thinks he's responsible for certain things he won't get bored. It's a pity everyone's so much older than he is. We should have suggested that he could bring a friend."

"Jakey's used to it," she answered. "He lives alongside a convent, remember. He's very good with older people. But I agree. We'll keep him occupied."

They have a scratch lunch of soup and rolls and then go upstairs to shower and change. It's hot now and the big umbrellas cast welcome shadows across the terrace. They make a last check round and then Adam drives away to fetch Janna and Sister Emily. Dossie is suddenly and unaccountably nervous, wondering how it will be with all these very special people together, what it will be like to be with Jamie here amongst her family and closest friends. And then she hears a car engine, Clem and Tilly and Jakey come rolling up the drive, the atmosphere changes, and she feels happy again; confident and excited. The party is about to begin.

The tea party has been a great success. The festivities spilled out of the kitchen and into the garden, whilst the guests mingled, were introduced to each other, and little groups formed and re-formed, and Dossie flits about, now here, now there, making certain that everyone is being looked after. She watches and listens.

Ned sits with Sister Emily. His expression is amused, delighted, as if he has discovered some rare treat, and Dossie hears Sister Emily say: "Oh, but people get some very strange ideas about prayer, don't they? Lists of requests and demands, a litany of names."

She looks bemused by this approach, and Ned asks: "So what are *your* thoughts about prayer, Sister?"

Dossie moves slightly closer to hear the response.

"Oh," says Sister Emily, "I think the short prayers are the best, don't you? Prayers that come directly from the heart."

"Yes," says Ned slowly. "Could you give me an example?"

"Well, yes." She looks surprised that he should need one. "For instance." She looks slowly around the assembled gathering in the garden, her face warming into love and amazement and raises both hands in appreciation. "Wow!" she says. A little pause. "Then, of course, there are those moments of despair, of disaster."

"And then?" he prompts her.

"Well, that's obvious." Her face creases, as if in anguish at the thought of world suffering. "I just cry 'Help!'"

Ned nods. "I think I'm beginning to understand."

"And the last one is easy." She puts her hands together and smiles gratefully. "It's 'Thanks.' Quite simple, you see. You only need those three."

Dossie turns away from the expression on Ned's face, lest she should burst out laughing, and nearly bumps into Adam and Jakey, who are bringing out trays with glasses ready for the Prosecco moment before supper. She beams approvingly at them and hesitates near Hugo's table, where he is seated with Clem and Tilly and Janna. He is discussing the probability of allowing the local TV news team into Chi-Meur, to film what happens there.

"I'm sure I could arrange it," he is saying enthusiastically. "Just think what the publicity could do for you."

She can see that Tilly is alight with the possibilities of getting the Retreat House out to a wider audience, whilst Janna is watching him with an expression that is a mix of admiration and alarm. Clem glances up at Dossie and raises his eyebrows, as if in disbelief and amazement at Hugo's confident enthusiasm, his revolutionary ideas. Clem's approach is much more cautious.

She beams at him, bends so that only he shall hear, and murmurs: "God moves in a mysterious way His wonders to perform," and Clem puts up a hand to hide his grin.

She goes into the house hoping that Ben and Prune have arrived. They couldn't make it in time for tea but should be here any time now for Prosecco and then supper. Jamie is coming out of the kitchen and her heart does that foolish little jump, but she remembers Hugo's advice and grins at him.

"Hiding?" she asks. "Nobody to play with? Billy No-Mates?"

"No," he says. "I was just making sure that there were enough goodies left for our picnic tomorrow. Be ready, won't you? Ten-ish?"

She stares at him. "Tomorrow? Why? Where are we going?"

And now she sees that he is carrying two glasses of prosecco. He holds one out to her and raises his own.

"To Land's End," he answers.